RIVER OF DREAMS

Jenny Lykins

JOVE BOOKS, NEW YORK

TIME PASSAGES is a registered trademark of Penguin Putnam Inc.

RIVER OF DREAMS

A Jove Book / published by arrangement with
the author

PRINTING HISTORY
Jove edition / July 1999

The Penguin Putnam Inc. World Wide Web site address is
http://www.penguinputnam.com

ISBN: 0-515-12607-1

A JOVE BOOK®
Jove Books are published by The Berkley Publishing Group,
a division of Penguin Putnam Inc.,
375 Hudson Street, New York, New York 10014.
JOVE and the "J" design
are trademarks belonging to Penguin Putnam Inc.

PRINTED IN THE UNITED STATES OF AMERICA

10 9 8 7 6 5 4 3 2 1

For Mom and Dad

Chapter 1

"A SÉANCE? YOU'RE kidding, right?" Brianne Davis eyed her lifelong friend and wondered exactly when he had lost his mind.

"No! I'm serious. Beats the heck out of going to the movies again." David Marks gave her his little-boy, let's-do-it-because-it-sounds-like-fun smile that creased his cheeks with two quarter-moon dimples.

She groaned. She'd never been able to turn down that smile. It had led her into trouble more than once.

"Where are we going to find a séance?" She leaned back against the headrest and looked at David as the scenery sped past in a blur. As he stared straight ahead, his sandy brown hair whipping with the breeze, a sneaking suspicion niggled its way into her mind. "No, don't tell me." She knew before she asked. "You already know a place, don't you?"

He continued to grip the leather-wrapped steering wheel of his sporty red Viper, rolled his eyes heavenward and whistled off-key. She punched him in the arm.

"You turkey! You had this planned all along, didn't you?"

There came that smile again. If she had been any other woman, or he had been any other man, she would have fallen for that smile.

"Okay. I admit it. But it was Heather's idea. You know how she loves that kind of stuff. She and that guy she calls her psychic, Dufus, invited me to come along."

"His name is *Dayus,* and you know it. Some day you're going to call him Dufus to his face."

"Oooo! And that would be a *bad* thing?"

She just laughed and leaned into the leather seat. Heather and Dayus made a good pair. Heather Wilson-Thomas was about as phony as a person could get, and seemed to think her hyphenated name was as impressive as having no last name at all—as Dayus had chosen to do.

One of life's biggest mysteries was why in the world David Marks was engaged to Heather. It was a topic Brianne had learned to steer clear of, though. David had made his decision clear, for whatever testosterone-inspired reason, and his friendship meant more to her than voicing her opinion. She had to give Heather the benefit of the doubt and assume she wasn't really as shallow as a gnat's wading pool.

"So if you were invited, where do I come in?" she asked.

He glanced at her, mock horror in his eyes. "You don't expect me to go do this without someone to crack jokes with, do you?"

"Oh, heaven forbid that you would take anything seriously."

"Hey!" He dipped his eyebrows down until he looked sufficiently hurt. "I take lots of things seriously. Just not stupid stuff."

She had to wonder exactly how Heather fit into the picture if he didn't take the stupid stuff seriously. She rolled her eyes and dropped the subject. Anyone with his job was entitled to be insane in his free time.

"C'mon," he said, that troublemaking grin back in place. "Whaddaya say?"

She let out a huge dramatic sigh and decided she'd make him pay for this, one way or another.

"Okay, then. I give. But where are we going?"

David flicked off the radio and did a U-turn in the middle of the road.

"There's an old spiritualist camp out in the boondocks near White Castle. Heather said to meet them out there. Remember Bob Madden? His mother goes all the time, trying to contact her dead husband."

"You know someone who's going there to contact someone? David Marks, you'd better be on your best behavior!"

He just glanced at her, trying his best to look wounded.

"Promise me!"

He crossed his fingers on both hands and gave her a wide-eyed look of innocence.

"I promise to be on my best behavior."

"You've lost your mind, you know that?"

David nodded seriously.

"Well, as the bumper sticker says, 'Of all the things I've lost in life, I miss my mind the most.'"

Brianne just shook her head and smiled. How could someone so smart be so insane? Her life would be dull as dirt without David to drive her crazy. Dull as the past two years since Shaelyn had . . . disappeared. Since David had been in Russia working as civilian project engineer for that Lockheed/Sputnik satellite venture. Thank God he was home now, even if it was to marry that bubblehead.

They headed for the country and Brianne sat back to enjoy the ride. It'd been ages since she'd gotten this far out of Baton Rouge. Birds squawked in the lacy green branches of the trees, settling down to roost for the night, and the pungent smell of damp earth, humid air, and lush foliage teased her nostrils. The setting sun splashed a watercolor of orange and pink and violet smears across the sky. Brianne watched the colors feather with fading beams of light until David turned down a dirt road and they bumped their way to a huge old plantation house.

Her mouth dropped open at the sight.

"This is it? This is a spiritualist camp? I visualized . . . I don't know . . . a rustic lodge or tents or cabins or . . . anything but this!"

"You ain't seen nothin' yet, woman." David jumped over the door—Brianne was sure he hadn't opened it since buying the car—unfolded a body too tall for a sports car, then bounded to her side. With a flourish, he flung her door open wide and bowed. "Ahfta you, milady."

Brianne tossed her head and gave him a snooty once-over as she stepped out of the car.

"Come along, peasant. Don't dawdle."

They strolled up the walk to the white-columned mansion. The house, well-kept but aged, sat like a little old lady, regal yet ancient, clinging to the days of debutante balls. As Bri marveled at the beautiful old home, a final shaft of golden light from the dying sun arrowed through the alley of trees and lit the many windows with a deep gold blaze. She had the curious sense of being welcomed.

When they reached the huge cypress door David hesitated, though obviously not suffering from the same sense of awe as Brianne.

"Let's see. Was it knock twice, wait a second, then knock three times, or was it knock three times, wait, then knock twice?"

She abused his arm again. He yelped dramatically, rubbed his muscle, then rapped out "Shave and a Haircut" with his knuckles.

The door swung inward. A soft peach-tinted light poured

across the porch and spilled into the yard in the clear violet twilight. Brianne had expected some scarf-bedecked gypsy with foreign coins dangling from her costume and a crystal ball in her hand to wave them in mysteriously, or even a hoopskirted Southern belle with an ivory fan to greet them. She did *not* expect the grandfather type with the cardigan sweater and shock of silver hair.

"Mr. Conroy?" David's right hand shot out and grasped the elderly gentleman's at his nod. "Has Heather and Duf . . . Dayus gotten here yet?"

Mr. Conroy glanced at Brianne and gave her a playful wink. "Why, yes. You must be the Marks boy. Heather told me you'd be coming."

Brianne slid an accusatory glare at David, who blatantly ignored her, pushing her through the front door into the foyer and tossing out a casual introduction.

She stopped and gawked at the interior, spellbound by the opulence. Arched doorways, fifteen inches thick, rose nearly to the eighteen-foot ceilings. Murals of the four seasons covered the walls of the entry hall. A chandelier dripped soft prisms of light, the starry pinpoints reflected in floor to ceiling pier glasses.

"We're using the ballroom tonight," Mr. Conroy told them. "It's this way."

Brianne lagged behind David, trying to take in every detail of the magnificent old house. For all its grandeur, the place seemed so . . . homey. She craned her neck as they passed each doorway, catching glimpses of splendor, snatches of the Old South. She could almost hear the tinkle of a pianoforte, smell the pungent scent of mint juleps and expensive perfumes.

"David," she whispered and tugged on his arm, "I didn't know this place was here. Why isn't it on the home tour?"

David glanced over his shoulder and shrugged. "I think it's still a private residence."

"It is," Mr. Conroy said as he led the way. "My Katherine, God rest her soul, and I raised our four daughters here." He seemed no more impressed with his home than if it'd been a row house in the low rent district.

The ballroom left Brianne speechless.

White. Everything was white: walls, floors, rich brocade draperies puddling on the floor with silk-fringed tiebacks. White Italian marble mantels above the twin fireplaces. The only colors in the room were the bends of light from the crystal chandeliers and the colors in the portraits above the fireplaces. Early 1800s from the look of the subjects' clothing. A woman on the left, a man on the right. They looked as if they were gazing at each other, yet their eyes seemed to follow Brianne around the room. She'd heard of these kinds of paintings.

Weird.

"David Marks! You rascal, you did come! Heather said you would."

A gray-haired grandmother in lilac double-knit slacks and a flowered blouse separated from the small group in the center of the room and wrapped David in an affectionate bear hug. He squeezed her back, lifting her off the floor until she playfully ordered him to set her down.

"You're as big a brat as my Bobby." She whacked him on the arm, but Brianne could tell the woman loved every minute of it. "You need to stop by for a visit, young man. You nearly lived at our house when you and Bobby were in school. Now who's your little friend? Aren't you the prettiest thing? Haven't I seen you on TV?"

Brianne smiled and mumbled yes. Her modeling job paid the bills while she studied to become a midwife. She'd never gotten used to being recognized from the commercials. Mrs. Madden took Brianne's hand and patted it.

"What lovely hair. Tell me. Are those sun streaks natural?"

Brianne had to grin at such straightforwardness. "Oh, yes. They're what naturally happens when you put peroxide on brown hair."

The older lady chuckled and whispered, "Never could get mine to do that." She patted her hand again. "Now come over here and meet the gang." She herded them toward the middle of the room, singing out, "Yoo-hoo," on the way. The group of eight or so turned as one.

"Gang, I want you to meet . . . Oh dear. David, you didn't tell me her name."

"Brianne Davis," Brianne supplied.

Heather separated herself from the others and came to hang on David's arm. She looked her usual perfect self. Perfect cornsilk hair without a hint of mousy brown roots showing, perfect capped teeth, perfect silicone cleavage, perfect acrylic nails—none of which would have bothered Brianne in the least if Heather had had anything at all genuine about her personality. But the Heather introduced to people was more fake than the perfect rosy blush staining her cheeks. The only genuine thing Heather could claim was the clear, violet shade of her eyes—and it infuriated her when people asked if she was wearing contacts.

"I'll take over from here, Mrs. Madden," Heather cooed, dragging David closer to the group. She turned around and gave Brianne a big, perfect smile. "Well, come on, silly. You want to do this, too, don't you?"

Brianne stifled the urge to gag. Instead she just blinked, looked behind her, then pointed to herself with a questioning look on her face.

"You're so funny, Bri," Heather declared to the room.

"Everyone, this is my fiancé, David, and his little friend, Brianne." She hesitated only long enough to give her words subtle meaning. "I didn't realize Brianne was coming." She turned to the group and named them off, one by one. "This is Stuart, Alonzo. You've met William. And this is Martha, Chuck, Deidre, Debbie, and Maria. And, of course, Dayus. We won't bother with last names until you get to know us better."

Brianne was surprised at the differences in the group. Some looked like professionals, a couple looked to be retired. At least two of them were younger than she and David.

Dayus stood out like a sore thumb among the group. His dark brown hair was pulled back into a scraggly ponytail, and his thin, short frame looked even thinner beneath the flowing shirt and slacks he chose to wear. Brianne always thought of him as a Yanni-wannabe, only with a short-man's complex and no personality, other than believing he was God's gift to the world. He was the antithesis of David in every way.

"Shall we get started?" Dayus said in his master-of-the-world voice.

"We're neophytes at this," David offered. "You probably should give us some ground rules."

"Oh, it's not as mysterious as they make it on TV," Heather said as she pulled David to the table, still hanging on his arm. "Just open your mind, try not to break the circle, and concentrate."

"Don't worry," Mrs. Madden piped up. "We haven't lost anyone yet."

"What about when Marcus Letterman fell out of his chair?"

"Oh, you know he'd been tippling that night. He doesn't count."

Brianne and David took seats beside each other while Heather sat on David's other side. The group joked over who else they might have lost, ignoring Dayus's intolerant glare, but the minute they were all seated and joined hands, the mood turned serious and the room fell silent.

Mr. Conroy, who insisted on being called William, lit several tall, white candles on the shiny mahogany table then turned out the lights of the chandelier. He sat down, took the hands of those on either side of him, then stared into the candlelight.

"We are here tonight," Dayus began, "to make contact with the other side. To speak, once more, to those loved ones who have gone before us. We quiet our thoughts and open our minds to receive the spirit of our loved ones."

The room seemed eerily silent. It had to be just her imagination, falling into the "mood" of the evening. In the spirit of the group, she tried to open her mind and experience what it was these people actually felt.

Everyone remained quiet. Brianne tried to look around without moving her head. They all seemed to be staring at the flickering flames dancing on the candles, so she gave it a try. The orange-yellow lights undulated in her vision hypnotically. She could almost hear the hiss of the wicks burning.

"Are there any spirits who can reach us?" Brianne almost jumped at Dayus's voice, but she managed to stifle the movement.

The candlelight flickered. Brianne slid her eyes from side to side. She could see nothing but darkness past the dimly lit faces surrounding the table.

"Are there any spirits who want to tell us something?" Dayus prodded.

The air literally buzzed with silence. Brianne glanced

around the table again, then was horrified when a giggle started working its way up her throat.

Oh, no! Not that! Anything but that!

The harder she tried to suppress it, the more the giggle grew. Could she turn it into a cough? Would she break their concentration and make them all mad at her? The snicker rose in her chest like a bubble rising in a champagne flute.

Oh, no! Oh, no! Think of something sad! Quick! Think sad!

Just as her lungs poised to shove the giggle into the silence of the room, someone gasped.

Amid quickly muffled intakes of breath, all eyes flew to the side of the table where one of the ladies, Martha or Maria, stared over William's head. Brianne followed her gaze and released a little gasp of her own.

The room stood in tomblike silence as the image of a dark-haired, handsome man formed in the air behind William. The apparition remained misty in substance, yet fully formed.

Brianne scanned the room for the flickering light of a projector, but all remained dark except for the candles. The trick couldn't be done with mirrors. The only ones she'd seen were in the foyer.

Once the apparition was clearly defined, he seemed to let his gaze fall upon each person at the table, one at a time. When his eyes turned to Brianne, she squeezed David's fingers and tried to stop her knees from knocking together.

Oh, gosh! This was where the branch of a tree was supposed to scrape against the window. Or a dog howl in the distance, or a trumpet float through the air. She waited but nothing happened. The apparition continued to study her. Chillbumps marched up her arms, across her neck, down her back.

Why the heck hadn't they gone to the movies?

The more she tried to convince herself that the thing was a hoax, the more she realized it was impossible to manage. The spirit seemed illuminated with an inner light. And though he was clearly visible, the light didn't cast itself any further than his body.

Just when she'd gotten her trembling under control, the apparition moved closer, standing behind David.

She feared she might break David's fingers if she squeezed any harder, but for the life of her she couldn't relax her death grip on his hand, even though her fingers had grown numb and her birthstone ring cut into her flesh. David twisted slowly in his seat, leaning as far away as he could from the specter without dragging Brianne with him, shooting a threatening stare at the shape.

The misty vision stared at her with eyes the color of a summer sky. Eyes that seemed to bore right into her soul. As scared as she was, as much as she had to remind herself to breathe, she also felt a strange, inner affinity with this man. A kindred spirit, she thought, then grimaced at her pun.

The kindred spirit looked to be in his midthirties, with wonderful hair that fell in dark careless layers, and a jaw that might have been carved by a sculptor's knife. If the spirit of the man could command such presence, what had the man been like in real life?

The specter's gaze finally left her and moved to David. He looked him up and down, then moved even closer. David glared at the spirit and leaned away, toward the table edge, then let out a low "Ohhhh" as the specter melted into him.

Brianne tried to snatch her hand back, but the iron grip of David's fist held her tight. When the apparition disappeared fully into her friend's body, David sat back in his chair, his back rigid. Then he turned his gaze to Brianne.

"Come to me," he said, his husky voice tortured, pleading, seductive.

Brianne jerked and struggled to free her hand. The voice coming from David's mouth wasn't David's! She yanked on her hand but his fingers remained steadfast.

"Come to me," he begged again.

David couldn't fake that voice even if he'd been professionally trained. "This isn't funny! Somebody help me!"

Everyone around the table sat like statues. Brianne pulled on her hand, but David raised his and caressed her cheek with a feather-soft touch. She stopped struggling and stared into his eyes. Eyes that should have been a warm, sweet brown but were now the clearest sky blue. All thoughts of hoaxes and mirror tricks fled her mind. *No one* could turn his eyes from brown to blue. Not without contacts. Not there in front of everyone.

She'd stopped struggling but still trembled like a newborn kitten. He touched her cheek once more, then drew his finger across her lips.

"Come to me."

At that the spirit rose from David's body, and David slumped slightly. He blinked, then jumped around to stare at the specter.

Brianne hadn't taken her eyes from the misty form. He held her gaze, his look pleading. Agonized. He held out his hand to her, and it was almost as if an invisible thread bound them together. She no longer quivered in fear. She knew him. Somehow she knew him.

Trancelike, she raised her hand and stretched it out to meet his. Would he feel cool, like fog? Would he be warm?

Before she had a chance to find out, he dissolved into the humid evening air, with nothing left to even hint that he'd been there except for her heart thudding like a drum in her chest.

The room remained in stunned silence for a split second, then everyone erupted in shouts and gasps, except Dayus, who continued to sit as still as a statue. Brianne still held David's hand, and the moment her mind started to function again she jumped to her feet and grabbed his face.

He stared at her, his eyebrows at his hairline and his lips all squished from her grip. He stared at her . . . through brown eyes.

"What are you—" He shook off her grip and plowed a hand through his hair. "What are you doing?"

"I'm looking at your eyes! You have brown eyes!"

"You're kidding! I do? So *that's* why it says that on my driver's license."

"But they were blue—"

Before she could finish, the others crowded around, all talking at once and no one getting heard.

"Did you know him?"

"Could you feel him, David?"

"Did it feel weird?"

"Weren't you terrified?"

"Brianne, you've got to come back so we can contact him again!"

David stood up and patted the air with his hands. "Whoa! Whoa, now. One at a time. Alonzo, what did you mean, did I feel him?"

Alonzo blinked and shrugged. "Just that. Could you feel him after he entered your body?"

David went very still. "He didn't enter my body."

Everyone yelled at once.

"Yes, he did!"

"He did!"

"He stepped right into you!"

David turned and glanced at Heather and Dayus, then looked to Brianne for the truth. She couldn't believe he hadn't felt it; couldn't remember it. She nodded.

"You don't remember? You said, 'Ohhh,' like you could feel it."

His face turned the color of milk.

"He was standing behind me, then he acted like he was going to touch me. I backed away, and when I turned around he was looking at you."

Brianne shook her head the whole time he spoke.

"We need to get out of here. This is just too weird for words." She looked at Heather and Dayus. "Are you guys coming? I'm outta here." She grabbed David's hand and pulled, but everyone surrounded them.

"Brianne, you have to come back! This is the most successful we've ever been!" Mrs. Madden piped up.

"Promise you'll come back tomorrow!"

"Yes, please!"

She had to admit that the thought of seeing the spirit again intrigued her. After all, he hadn't harmed her. He hadn't been threatening. He'd been . . . pleading. She didn't think she'd be nearly as frightened if she was prepared for him.

And what had he meant by asking her to come to him? Did he think she was someone else? She couldn't walk away from this without trying again.

"Okay, I'll come back, but David has to come with me."

"Oh, thanks but no thanks," David huffed. "Being possessed isn't my idea of a night on the town. Besides, Heather and I have a date."

"She'll let you out of it, won't you, Heather?"

Everyone argued at once until Brianne held up her hands.

"Come on, David. You're not chicken are you?"

That got his attention.

"Hell, no, I'm not chicken! But what if he climbs in and decides to take up residence? No thanks. I'm not into split personalities." He fished his car keys out of his pocket and marched into the foyer. "Heather, if you and Dayus are coming, come on."

Brianne shrugged and turned to the others.

"All right then. I'll come back by myself. When do you guys want to do it again?"

They all decided to meet again the next night, while the spirits were friendly. When Brianne followed David to the car she had to run to keep up with him. Once they were on the road, with Heather and Dayus in their separate cars following them, he turned to her and nailed her with that glittering brown gaze.

"All right. I want to know what happened. Start to finish. And don't leave anything out."

"We're here tonight to make contact with those on the other side. To speak, once more, with those loved ones who have gone before us. We quiet our thoughts and open our minds . . . "

Brianne blocked out Dayus's voice, concentrating on breathing evenly and slowing her pounding heart. David squeezed her fingers until she glanced up at him and smiled.

She'd known he would come back with her, even if Heather hadn't insisted. Since their earliest days in diapers together Bri had always known which buttons to push to make him accept a challenge, no matter how stupid the idea was. Her little talent had landed them in hot water more times than his boyish grin.

She flexed her fingers so that David eased up on his vise grip a bit. He shrugged and shot her an apologetic smile.

She scanned the faces around the table, just as she had the night before. This time, though, she didn't have to worry about stifling a giggle.

Dayus droned on, cajoling the spirits to show themselves. It seemed they'd been sitting there for hours. Had it only been a few minutes? Would the spirit show up? Had he really shown up the night before, or had they all suffered some kind of mass hysteria?

Dayus's voice took on a kind of desperate, coaxing quality. Several around the table squirmed in their seats. Stuart muffled a cough. The candles burned down until they sat in pools of hot wax.

He wasn't coming. They might as well give up. If he really did appear the night before, it had probably been a fluke.

The air grew very still and all the fidgeting stopped. Heather squeaked. Brianne turned in her chair and looked into a pair of misty blue eyes. Her gaze dropped to David, who stared straight at her and bristled.

"He's behind me, isn't he?"

Brianne looked back up into the piercing gaze and nodded.

"Well, just tell him to stay—"

The man-shaped mist melted into David. Brianne's heart thundered up her throat as she watched her friend's soft, earthy-colored eyes turn the color of the ocean off a Caribbean island.

The death grip on her fingers eased to a gentle holding of her hand. She couldn't have taken her gaze from his if her life depended on it.

"Come to me, Amily."

She jerked again at someone else's husky, soft voice coming out of David's mouth, but the name shook her to the core. It proved to her that the spirit thought she was someone else.

"I'm . . ." She swallowed to moisten her dry throat. "I'm not Amily." She tried to tell him as gently as possible.

"Amily," the voice repeated, a verbal caress, and David's hand traced her jaw.

She glanced around at the others, who all sat there with mouths agape. She gave them a look begging for help.

Dayus snapped out of the stupor first. "*Ahem.* Are there any other spirits with you?"

The blue eyes never wavered. Brianne wondered if he'd even heard the question. She decided to give it a try.

"Who are you?" she whispered.

David—or rather the spirit—smiled with more love and adoration than Brianne had ever seen. She envied this Amily at that moment. He covered her hand with both of his.

"I am Griffin."

The name pierced her heart like an arrow on the fly. It seemed familiar. Loved. Yet she wasn't even sure she'd ever heard that name before.

"Griffin," she repeated in a whisper. He closed his eyes and breathed in, as if hearing her say his name brought him untold joy.

When he opened his eyes again, he searched her face. Did he see now that she wasn't Amily?

He leaned toward her, ever so slowly, and she realized he was going to kiss her! Ohmigosh, he was going to kiss her! Heat flared across her face, blood roared in her ears, keeping time to the tap dance of her heart against her ribcage.

His lips touched hers with all the power of a lightning bolt. He kept the kiss chaste in nature, but there was nothing chaste about the ache that exploded within her or the sudden want that spiraled to the very core of her. She leaned into him and nearly cried when their lips parted.

The kiss seemed to have shaken him, as well. His eyes held the tortures of the damned. How could anyone communicate so much with only a look?

With a bow of his head, he brought the back of her hand to his mouth.

"Come to me, Amily," he begged.

And then he vanished.

"—the hell away from me," David growled. He stopped and looked around at the others in the group. They all stared at him with eyes the size of dinner plates. He turned his gaze back to Brianne and sighed. "Been and gone?"

She simply nodded.

He hung his head while everyone snapped out of their trance at once.

"What did he say his name was?"

"Griffin. He said it was Griffin."

"Does anyone know a Griffin?"

"Did he call her Emily?"

"Amily, with an A. Turn up your hearing aid, Stuart."

"Brianne, do you know him?"

Brianne shook her head, still quaking from the after-shocks of the kiss. *No one* had ever kissed her like that. She looked at David. The few times they'd tried to ruin their friendship by kissing as teenagers, they'd both walked away laughing at how it'd been like kissing a sibling. They'd grown up next door to each other, been best of friends all their lives. The kiss that had come from David's mouth held no resemblance to those kisses.

"Let's get out of here." She grabbed his hand and pulled him to his feet. Before they left, they had to promise to meet back there the next night. Heather insisted they didn't have to come, since she had a Junior League function to go to, but Brianne didn't have the heart to turn the other's down.

"Are you coming, Heather?" David asked as he headed for the door. She and Dayus had their heads together. She glanced up.

"Be right there, sweetie," she called, giving him a smile that showed those even, white teeth to perfection.

Brianne followed David out the door, but before they got in the car, he stopped her with a hand to her arm.

"What is it, Bri? You're white as a sheet."

Brianne turned and looked up into the brown eyes of her friend.

"He kissed me, David. Griffin kissed me."

David jerked his head back as if he'd been slapped, then he cursed, grabbed her by the hand, and marched her to the car. Not until he'd gotten behind the wheel and revved the engine did she dare ask him what was wrong.

He slid his heated gaze to her, like whiskey warmed in front of an open fire. "We may just be friends, Brianne, and I may be engaged to Heather, but I can do my own damn kissing."

Chapter 2

Brianne HAD NEVER been so obsessed with anything in her life. Night after night she and David met the others at the spiritualist camp. Heather came when her schedule allowed, but Dayus was always there. Night after night Griffin came to her through David, always calling her Amily, and always asking her to come to him. He never responded to the questions of the others, and never stayed more than a few minutes.

And he never kissed her again.

She hounded her agent for more modeling jobs and threw herself into her midwife studies. Anything to keep busy during the day. She shot three commercials and did a couple layouts for local stores and their flyers. She assisted in several home births, grateful for the late night calls, since she couldn't sleep anyway. That and her studies kept her busy and kept her mind off the mysterious man who called to her now in every waking moment.

Tonight was the first night in a week that she and David wouldn't be going to another séance. They simply needed a break from the turmoil, and the others hadn't tried too hard to persuade them. She imagined they were anxious to try to call other spirits, and that would be easier without Griffin's appearance.

She'd just finished washing the layers of makeup off her face from her last shoot and was painting her toenails when the doorbell rang.

"Come in," she yelled. "It's unlocked."

David pushed open the door and kicked it shut behind him. He balanced a pizza box and six pack of diet soda in one hand and a couple of videos in the other.

"What have I told you about leaving your door unlocked? One of these days an undesirable is going to walk in on you and make you sorry."

"Like now?" she teased, picking up a pillow from the couch and throwing it at him. "I just unlocked it two minutes ago. My toenails are wet and I didn't want to get up." She wiggled the soft-peach nails at him as proof. "Heather couldn't come?" she asked, managing to actually sound sorry that the bubblehead wasn't with him. What he saw in the little social climber was beyond her. She simply wasn't David's type.

He skootched down beside her on the floor and dropped the pizza and sodas on the coffee table.

"No, she had a fund-raiser to host tonight. Five hundred dollars a plate, with half a dozen politicians and a few minor celebrities. She sends her regrets."

Brianne just nodded. Heather made no pretense of doing the fund-raising for the sake of charity. She was in it to meet the people with clout . . . for David's sake, according to her. The problem was, David didn't need clout. He had his own.

"What movies did you get?" She eyed the blue and white boxes stacked atop the pizza and changed the subject.

He handed them to her. "*Tombstone* and *Star Wars*. Which one do you want to watch first?"

"Didn't they have *Wuthering Heights*?"

He opened a soda and slid a sideways look at her.

"I'm not *that* good a friend."

"Did it ever occur to you men that you could learn a thing or two about romance if you gave it a try?"

"Nope. Do you want a veggie slice or a pepperoni slice?"

She rolled her eyes and let the topic drop. Men. Someday scientists would discover that testosterone causes brain damage.

David chose to watch *Star Wars* first. They polished off the pizza while arguing over Brianne's assessment of it being a space-age western.

Just as she was wondering how Harrison Ford got that rugged little scar on his chin, a sudden shiver struck her.

"Amily."

She started so hard she showered herself with diet Coke.

"Not funny, David. And how did you do the voi . . ."

She looked into David's eyes. Griffin's eyes looked back at her.

She slowly set the drink down and wiped the soda off her jeans, taking the time to collect herself.

"How did you come here? I didn't call you."

"You've no need to summon me, Amily. I have searched for you for generations."

She sighed. As much as she hated to, for fear of never seeing him again, she had to try to convince him of the truth.

"I'm not Amily. I'm Brianne. Brianne Davis."

He didn't seem upset by her words.

"You were Amily when I knew you. When you were my betrothed."

Another shiver struck her. She really did have to be dreaming this.

"When was I your betrothed?"

"We were to be wed in 1832. My first wife, Florence, was your cousin. After her death I no longer denied my feelings for you."

Brianne was speechless. Could she possibly have lived another life before this one? He spoke with such certainty.

"Why haven't you told me this the other times you appeared?"

He grinned and her heart flip-flopped in her chest.

"I wanted you to grow accustomed to me." His gaze raked her face like a dying man looking at Heaven. "And these are words meant for no other ears. Come to me, Amily. We have yet to finish our life together."

"But if I'm living another life, why aren't you?"

The light behind his eyes dimmed for a moment.

"I am," he said. "But he has shut love out. He has shut out the part that lives on forever. We live. We die. Our bodies turn to dust and we fade from the memories of the living. But the love remains."

Brianne tried to absorb his words.

"Who are you? Today, I mean. Who's the man who has shut love out?" She would find this man and teach him to open his heart.

Griffin smiled sadly and traced her jaw with his fingertips.

"I can tell you only when he has let me in, or when you have taught him how to love. If he fails to learn, he will soon lose the spirit within him; the essence of why we exist."

She opened her mouth to ask him more, but he stopped her.

"You, too, trust no one, except for your family and this David. Too many people have hurt you, and now you distance yourself so they cannot cause you pain."

She didn't try to deny his words. He spoke the truth. Men and women alike had always judged her by her looks. The

women took one look at the model's face and trim body and
decided she must be like Heather, too shallow to bother with
forming a friendship. Or they were too jealous. She couldn't
possibly be likable. The men wanted her as a walking trophy
to parade around on their arms. The judgments used to hurt,
because no one ever looked beyond the surface to see the
shy, insecure person who desperately wanted to make
friends. Only Shaelyn and David had ever seen beyond the
façade. That's why, when she'd first met Heather, she'd tried
hard to find that same insecure person in *her*. But one thing
Heather never suffered from was insecurity.

"But how do I—"

"I must go." His warm finger drifted across her lips.
"Think about me, Amily, and come to me."

The blue faded from his eyes, replaced by the familiar,
soft brown. David picked up a piece of pizza and took a sip
of soda.

"Hey! Something's wrong with this video. They cut out a
bunch of scenes."

Should she tell him? He wouldn't be happy to know that
Griffin now "possessed" him whenever he wanted to. But
she couldn't not tell him.

"They didn't cut out any scenes, Davie."

"Sure they did. They cut out that whole scene where
Luke . . ." He stopped and looked hard at Brianne. "Don't
tell me. Not here."

She nodded.

"Damn!" He tossed his pizza back onto the box. "This is
a nightmare! I wish I'd never agreed to that idiotic idea to
go to that séance! Where's a priest?" He jumped to his feet.
"I'll get this sucker exorcised!"

"David, wait! Sit down. I think you'll change your mind
when you hear what I have to say."

• • •

"Just once more. Please?"

Brianne had to talk David into coming over one more time. Since Griffin had appeared in her apartment several nights earlier, she'd spoken with him numerous times and knew most of his and Amily's story. If she could persuade him to tell her who he was in the nineties, she would find him and somehow make him open his heart to her.

"I don't want to, Bri. I feel like this guy's ventriloquist dummy, perched on some ghostly knee with his hand in my back making my mouth move while he talks. No. If I make myself scarce, he won't have an opportunity to use me. Besides, Heather will have a conniption if I break another date over this."

"Please?" she wheedled. "You'll do it for me, won't you? Your oldest friend. The one who didn't tell on you in fifth grade when you put the chewing gum in Mrs. Bowe's chair."

"You know, I think I've more than paid you back for that little incident."

"All right. How about the time you got me drunk on that vintage bottle of wine your dad was saving and I—"

"Paid my dues on that one, too."

She huffed, but she couldn't help but smile. She knew when he was playing hard to get.

"Okay, how about if I don't tell the future Mrs. Marks about your penchant for—"

"All right! I'll be there in fifteen minutes. Blackmailer."

She grinned as she hung up the phone. As much as she hated to, she'd smooth things over with Heather for him. And she hated asking him to get out in the brewing storm, but she was driving herself nearly crazy. She had to get this settled.

True to his word, David arrived in less than a quarter of an hour, dripping wet from the lashing rain that had started. He marched through the door, trying to act mad.

"You know, there are laws against—"

"Yeah, yeah. I owe you one. Sit down and I'll get you a towel. You want a glass of wine?"

"No. This is the last time, Bri. This guy's not taking over my life."

Brianne sank to the couch, afraid for the first time of losing David's friendship.

"Do you really mean that? Will you stay away from me so Griffin won't come to you?"

David softened, sighed, then shook his head. He flopped down next to her and took her hand.

"No. Pain in the ass that you are, I'd miss you like the devil. Now do your little hocus-pocus thing and let's get this over with."

She breathed a sigh of relief, trying not to let it show. He would tease her unmercifully if he knew she'd really been worried.

"I don't do any hocus-pocus. He just appears unannounced."

"Yeah, unannounced and uninvited."

Thunder rumbled as a bolt of lightning lit the room like a strobe light.

"Let me get you a towel. You're dripping all over my couch." She hopped up and returned in seconds with two towels tossed over her shoulder. "Do you want to put your clothes in the dryer? I've got a robe you can wear."

David towel dried his hair, then blotted at his shirt.

"Nah. It'll dry in a few minutes. Besides, I'm not into ruffles." Brianne stuck out her tongue at him while he drummed his fingers on the arm of the couch. "What do you want to do until Mr. Wonderful makes his appearance?"

"I don't know. Wanna play cards?"

David shrugged. "Why not?"

Brianne fished a dog-eared deck out of the drawer in the end table. She shuffled them a few times then dealt out five cards each.

"Jacks or better to open, deuces and one-eyed Jacks are wild," she declared.

"Oh, geez, Bri. You play like a girl."

"Well, duh."

They played while the storm grew outside. Rain splattered on the patio door like thick drops of mud as the wind howled around the corners of the building. Lightning lit the sky brighter than high noon and thunder followed in the long, reverberating rumbles of a timpani drum. The power flickered, then went out.

"Oh, great," David's disembodied voice came to her in the darkness.

"Stay put and I'll get some candles."

She felt her way across the room, only banging her knee once on the corner of the coffee table. The emergency flashlight flickered on and off in the kitchen, guiding her way. In no time she had candles lit and scattered all over the room.

"This is kind of nice," she said as she settled back on the floor next to David.

"Quite," a familiar voice said—Griffin's voice.

She scooped up the flashlight and shined it in his eyes.

Griffin's eyes.

He pushed the light away and smiled at her.

"You still cannot believe, can you?"

She shook her head. "Would you if you were in my place?"

"I fear I would be even harder to convince."

"Griffin, tell me who you are in this time. I can find him. Teach him to love. Our spirits could be together again."

"I can only guide you, Amily. I cannot—"

"I know, I know." She jumped to her feet and marched to

the window. "You can't tell me who you are." She spun to face him. "Well, why the hell not? What purpose does this serve? I was perfectly happy until you showed up. Now I'm this obsessed whacko. I don't eat. I don't sleep." She turned to the window and stared out into the night, her arms wrapped tightly around her waist.

She felt his presence behind her before he took her by the arms and turned her to face him. The blue of his eyes glistened in the bursts of lightning, and then his mouth was on hers, hungry, demanding, desperate.

Her breath left her in a rush as the taste of his tongue pulled a sigh from deep in her throat. Strong, rock-hard arms wrapped around her when she melted against him, then his hands pulled her tighter as the kiss changed to a languid giving that weakened her knees and left her wanting much, much more, touching parts of her no other kiss had ever touched. His hands wandered down her back, cupping her hips, pressing her closer, until her eyes fluttered open to drink in the whiskey brown eyes gazing back at her.

"David!" She shoved him away just as his eyes cleared from the drugging kiss.

He stepped back, his stance belligerent as he raked a handful of hair off his forehead.

"I'm sorry, Bri. I warned him I could do my own damn kissing." He turned away, plowed his hand through his hair again, then swung back to face her. "Bri, we need to talk."

A crack of thunder boomed and lightning struck a tree just off the patio. A neighbor's cat yeowled and clawed at the patio door.

"Muffin! What are you doing out there?" Brianne jumped and ran to the French doors, then stopped and stared at the silhouette of Heather standing in the open front door. "Heather, wait," was all she managed to say before the girl turned and slammed her way out of the apartment.

"Amily!" Griffin's voice came to her then. "Come back here! Get away from—"

A jagged blue-white light tore across the sky, passed between the smoking branches and shot through the glass door.

Pain hit her chest with the kick of a mule, searing through her to her fingertips and toes. The impact hurled her backward in a surreal slow motion, while her body felt as if it were on fire.

"Griffin!" she cried as she slammed against the back of the couch. She slid down the rough surface, her knees buckling under her like a rag doll's. Pitch black closed in around her and the floor came up to meet her. Her face slammed against the rain-wet carpet.

The last thing she heard before she sank into the inky oblivion was Griffin's frantic voice.

"Amily!"

Chapter 3

"AMILY, DARLING, CAN you hear me?" A feminine voice prodded Brianne out of the dark depths to which she'd fallen. A soft hand rubbed her fingers then tapped her cheek.

With more energy than she would have ever dreamed possible, she forced her eyes open and looked around. She closed them, denying what she saw, then opened them again.

An attractive woman with hair the color of dark honey sat on the bed next to her. She wore a high-necked gown straight out of the nineteenth century. Her hair was done in an intricate puzzle of braids and curls. The room was not one she'd ever been in, and most definitely belonged to someone of wealth. Dark green velvet drapes puddled on the floor. The walls were covered in pale green moiré. Even Brianne's inexperienced eye could tell that the pieces of furniture were works of art done by the finest craftsmen: Belter, Mallard, Linke.

Where in the world was she?

"Florence, is she all right? Should I send Gaston to fetch the doctor?"

Griffin! That was Griffin's voice! She struggled to sit up but gentle hands pushed her back down.

"Amily, do not try to rise. You were struck by lightning in the storm. How do you feel, darling?"

Brianne stared at the woman. Griffin stepped to her side. The real Griffin. The flesh and blood version.

Had she died? Was she dreaming? Had he possibly called her back to him, to be together once again?

"Griffin!" she choked out. He leaned over the woman's shoulder.

"Yes, Amily? How do you feel?" When she didn't answer him he turned to the woman beside her. "Florence, Gaston should fetch the doctor."

Florence. Where had she heard that name? A jolt of recognition hit her almost as hard as the lightning bolt. Florence was his first wife!

Why did this feel so real? Was Griffin communicating with her in her sleep, making her dream this was really happening?

Or had she traveled in time, truly?

She accepted the possibility far more quickly than most. Hadn't her best friend, Shaelyn Sumner, sworn that she herself had traveled back in time, and shown her parents and Brianne the record of her marriage in 1830 to Alec Hawthorne? Hadn't she disappeared again in front of witnesses?

If Brianne really had traveled in time, then she had traveled back to when Griffin was married to Amily's cousin!

What year was this? When had Florence died? How in the world would she get back to her own time?

Griffin turned and called for Gaston, but Brianne struggled to her elbows.

"No, wait!" Both sets of eyes turned to her, and she fell

back against the pillows. "I'm fine. I'll be all right. I just got the wind knocked out of me."

Florence felt her forehead.

"Are you certain? You are pale as a ghost."

She couldn't help but smile at that. "I'm sure."

"Then you must stay abed. I shall have Esther bring your supper to you." Florence rose and started toward the door. "Would you stay with her, Griffin? She shouldn't be left alone."

He nodded, and Florence disappeared into the hallway.

Brianne looked at Griffin. He smiled down at her, but not with the longing she had seen in his eyes before. This smile was more the smile of a stranger.

When had he fallen in love with Amily? When did they finally get together? How in the world would she get back to her own time?

"Griffin, where am I?"

He cocked his head toward her.

"I beg your pardon?"

"Where am I? I'm not home."

He pulled a chair to the bedside and perched on the edge of it.

"Amily, you are at Shadow Oaks. Do you not remember coming to live with us when your father died? Do you not remember who you are?"

Shadow Oaks? Wasn't that the plantation home that had burned to the ground in the 1940s? The burnt out ruins on the banks of the Mississippi were a favorite place for teenagers to park.

Strangely enough, Brianne seemed to be catching wisps of memories as Griffin spoke. Almost as if Amily were sharing her memories with her. She saw an elderly gentleman drawing his last breaths. She glimpsed a funeral through a black veil and felt an overwhelming sense of sadness. Amily had truly loved her father. Brianne could feel it. She tried to remove the concern from Griffin's voice.

"Yes. I remember. I'm just a little confused." She peered up at him through her lashes. "What year is this?"

He stared at her for a moment, then his brows dipped to a V and he shook his head.

"It is 1832."

She closed her eyes and lay back. Griffin had told her they were to be married in 1832. But his wife was still alive. That didn't make sense.

A dull throb started at the back of her head and worked its way around to her temples. This was all more than she could deal with. A spirit inhabiting David's body, calling her Amily, asking her to come to him. That was unbelievable enough. But now, struck by lightning, waking in the past, and waking so far into the past that the man of her dreams was still married to his first wife.

Maybe she was dead and this was Hell.

She closed her eyes and asked to be forgiven. Good heavens, she might as well have wished Florence dead!

"Are you sure you are well enough to forego the doctor, Amily? It would take but moments for Gaston to fetch him."

A doctor from 1832. Leeches. No sanitary conditions. Not much more knowledgeable than the average layman of her time. She didn't think so.

"No, Griffin. I have a headache, that's all. Thank you for offering though."

She took his hand and patted, then winced at the pain in her seared fingers. But even at that, a surge of heat shot from his touch and curled into a warm, tingling glow right below her ribs.

Did he feel it, too? Did he savor her touch as he had savored the first time she spoke his name?

He gently squeezed her hand with no more affection than

he should have given any of his wife's relatives, then straightened and pulled on a tapestry cord by the bed.

"Mum Sal will sit with you until Esther brings your supper. If you feel the least disconcerted, you are to send for me so Dr. Myers can be brought around."

A plump, motherly black woman wearing a blue headdress slipped quietly into the room.

"You send for Mum Sal, Mistah Grif?"

"Yes. Please sit with Miss Amily until my wife returns."

He turned back to Brianne. "Rest now. You have suffered quite an ordeal."

As he walked out the door, Brianne wanted to stop him; wanted to beg him to hold her and reassure her that he was flesh and blood. Instead she watched him walk through the door, leaving her feeling more alone than she'd ever felt in her life. It was obvious she meant nothing more to him than his wife's cousin. Which, she reminded herself, was as it should be.

Griffin closed the door behind him before he allowed himself to breathe. He let his head fall back to stare at the ceiling, his heart in his throat, his self-control stretched beyond the limits of his being.

Thank God she wasn't badly hurt. At least physically. Her odd questions had alarmed him, but perhaps she *had* been disoriented from the jolt of the lightning. Truly, he was surprised she had survived.

When he'd looked up to see her standing at the window, reveling in the storm, he'd warned her to move away. Almost simultaneously the lightning pierced the room, flinging her backward, leaving him with a heart that nearly burst from fear of her death. Would she die before he ever had a chance to tell her how he loved her?

The quiet *shuff* of shoes on the carpeted steps alerted him to Florence's return. He wiped all traces of anguish from his face, drew a deep breath and let it out, then strode toward the staircase.

"How is she, darling?" Florence laid a gentle hand on Griffin's arm when she met him at the top of the steps.

"Mum Sal is with her. She appears to suffer no injury, though she is a bit disoriented."

"I am so relieved. She has endured enough this past year. Thank heavens you were here to take charge. I fear I would have been helpless without you."

He knew that Florence would have handled the incident with her usual thorough efficiency. He was glad he had been there, but for his own reasons. God help him, but it gave him the opportunity to scoop Amily into his arms, to hold her for the first time, next to his heart. To try and memorize the feel of her against his chest. He might never have the chance to feel her thus again, for though he'd fallen hopelessly in love with Florence's cousin, he would never betray his wife. She was all that was good and kind and gentle. And she adored him. She was the proper, reserved, perfect wife his parents had arranged for him to marry, but Amily was the adventurous, emotional, sensual woman he should have wed.

"Esther is preparing a broth for her. I'll go and see if she's in want of anything else." Florence leaned up on tiptoe to place a chaste kiss against his jaw, no more and no less passionate than any other kiss she'd given him in ten years of marriage. He tried not to think what Amily's kisses might be like. Just carrying her to her chamber had stirred feelings best left unexplored. To dwell at all on the possibilities might prove embarrassing and unexplainable. That is, if his wife's gaze ever bothered to drift below his waist, which he doubted it ever had.

When Florence opened Amily's door he wasted no time in

making his escape. Had the anguish shown in his eyes? Had his wife sensed how he coveted her cousin? But then, Florence would never give him any indication, even if she had.

Thank God Amily didn't return his affection; had never given him any indication that her feelings for him were anything more than cousinly fondness. And thank God she had never sensed the torturous ache he suffered whenever he was around her, for she most certainly would not ignore such an indiscretion. She would leave his house and never return if she had even a hint of what warred in his mind and his heart every time he looked at her.

Amily loved Griffin with every fiber of her being.

That was the only certainty in Brianne's dazed mind.

As she'd lain there, trying desperately to sort things out, she awakened more and more to the emotions of this woman she'd been in the past. Amily loved Griffin with a fierceness and passion that left her aching, helpless. Ashamed. The guilt Amily suffered over her feelings for her cousin's husband took a heavy emotional toll.

How very strange to be thinking of these things in the present tense, but Brianne could *feel* the longing in Amily every time Griffin's face flitted through her mind. Longing exactly like that of Brianne's.

Amily's feelings didn't surprise her. From just those brief moments Brianne had spent with Griffin's spirit, she'd been drawn to him, felt as if neither were whole without the other. Her intrigue had both frightened and exhilarated her.

She'd spent two days in bed, regaining her strength, "absorbing" bits of Amily's personality, asking herself questions. Would she stay? Would it take another bolt of lightning to get her home? If she stayed in 1832 long enough, would she eventually become Amily and lose that part of her which was Brianne? Would she ever get accustomed to having flashes of memories that weren't hers? The only way Brianne could describe the feeling to herself was that Amily was a part of herself that she was just starting to remember. A part of herself that surfaced when she needed her most.

She shook her head. So many questions and so few answers.

"You don't like this gown, Miss Amily? I'll pick out another." Ruth, Amily's maid, lowered the gown and turned back to the armoire.

"Oh, no. The dress is fine. I wasn't shaking my head at the dress." One more thing to get used to. People everywhere and never being alone. She seemed to have someone within a few steps of her at all times, and the lack of privacy grated on her nerves.

Ruth helped her into the pale yellow muslin gown over layers of corset, chemise, and petticoats. Brianne gave thanks that the fashion sadists had not yet found the eighteen-inch waist stylish. At least the dresses of the 1830s wouldn't be quite the torture chambers worn in the middle of the century.

Ruth settled the dress around Brianne, then helped her into shoes similar to ballet slippers.

Her hands were still sore from where the electricity of the lightning had exited her body. Her shoulder had an angry red burn where it had entered her, and her fingers looked as if she had picked up a hot skillet without using the handle.

But, at least she was alive. She hoped.

The past two days had given her ample time to think about her situation. What had happened to her body in the future? Did her parents and brothers know what happened? If she went back, would she arrive the moment after she left or did time pass at the same rate? Did David know what hap-

pened to her? Did he come out of his trance to find her
gone?

Her mind spun with more questions. When did Florence
die? When did Griffin and Amily fall in love? The few facts
that Griffin had given her in the future were that Florence
had died following a miscarriage, and he and Amily had
died together in a riding accident just days before the wedding. Surely she could prevent their deaths. She simply
wouldn't ride with Griffin. If she refused to get on a horse,
they couldn't possibly die in a riding accident. But then
again, with her midwife training, she might possibly prevent
Florence's death as well.

"Are you quite improved this morning?"

Brianne pulled herself out of her musings and looked up
to see Florence gliding through the door with a fresh bouquet of flowers in a delicate china vase.

"I'm much better, thanks," Brianne assured her. "I know
I'm ready to get out of this room."

Florence tilted her head and blinked away a questioning
look. Brianne had already discovered that Florence would
never be so "rude" as to question her about her strange
speech, but Brianne would have to watch herself, all the
same.

"Wonderful! I had feared you would be too ill for the
ball." She studied Brianne. "There is still time to postpone
it, if you truly aren't recovered."

"Ball?" Brianne caught a glimpse of herself in the mirror
and stopped to stare. Would she ever get accustomed to
looking in the mirror and seeing someone else's face?
Would she be there long enough to *have* to get accustomed
to it? The shock of seeing Amily's face instead of her own
had left her speechless and shaken two days earlier. If she
would have had a chance to think about it, she would have
expected Amily to look somewhat like herself. But instead

of Brianne's pale blue eyes, multicolored hazel looked back
at her. Brianne's thick chestnut hair had blond, salon high-
lights and Amily's was nearly the color of jet. Brianne's
height and thin build reflected her profession as a model, but
Amily stood at least four inches shorter. Petite, but with
curves in all the right places.

"Amily?"

She snapped out of her trance. "Yes?"

"The ball. Should we consider postponement?"

"The ball?"

Florence sighed and gave her an indulgent smile, but a
flicker of concern passed across her features.

"Yes. The Spring ball. This Saturday evening."

Brianne caught nuances of Amily's excitement over the
event. She would get to dance with Griffin. She would get
to touch him. But were those Brianne's thoughts or Amily's?

"No," she said, then shivered. Would she ever get used to
. . . feeling . . . someone else's most intimate thoughts? "No
need to postpone it. I'll be fine."

Suddenly the topic of conversation sank into her distracted mind. A ball? Good heavens, what was she saying?
She wouldn't be fine at all! She didn't know how to dance
their dances. She didn't know the protocol or customs of
people in 1832. She could barely carry on a conversation
without someone trying to slap their hand on her forehead to
check her for fever. How in the world would she deal with a
house full of people without being carted off to the nearest
asylum?

Oh, but she would get to dance with Griffin!

Chapter 4

GRIFFIN RODE ALONG the river on his way home from Baton Rouge. The long way. He let Tempest set the pace while he contemplated what awaited him at Shadow Oaks. A house alive with ball preparations. A faithful wife. And the woman he'd loved almost since the moment she'd walked into his home three months earlier.

How would he endure the evening? He would be expected to dance with his wife's cousin. Indeed, notice would be taken if he did not. The idle busybodies whose favorite pastime was to scrutinize those around them most certainly would detect any hint, any *flicker,* of emotion stronger than innocent fondness. And they would delight in turning that flicker, real or imagined, into fodder for their interminable gossip parties.

The late afternoon sun filtered through the cypress and oaks that lined the river, casting elongated shadows of the hanging moss, reminding him he'd best hasten. He kicked Tempest into a canter and guided him back toward the road.

The house indeed hummed with activity when he dismounted at the front veranda. One of the many servants' children ran up and took the reins, a huge smile splitting the small, black face. Griffin grinned at the child's anticipation.

"Has John shown you how?" he asked while the little boy fidgeted anxiously. When the woolly head nodded yes, Griffin scooped him under the arms and swung him up onto the saddle. "No faster than a walk now," he instructed.

"Yessuh," the little boy said as he proudly guided Tempest toward the stables. His tiny frame looked not much larger than the saddle horn atop the huge horse.

"Griffin, darling! You are finally home. You must hurry and dress, else the guests will arrive before you are ready to receive them."

Florence glided onto the porch, an island of calm and serenity in the vast sea of activity that swelled around her. She brushed a kiss against his cheek, which he returned out of habit.

"I shall be ready for them," he assured her, forcing a lightness in his voice.

As he made his way to his chambers, servants bustled past him, each of them on a last minute errand to add finishing touches to the preparations.

When he entered his room, he found that, as usual, his man Lucas had been one step ahead of him. His formal attire lay neatly on the dark burgundy counterpane, perfect in every detail with not so much as a crease anywhere in evidence. Before he could even remove his jacket, Lucas arrived with a pitcher of steaming water in one hand and Griffin's highly polished boots in the other.

"Miz Florence says I should hurry you along," he said with mock sternness as he poured a basin of water.

Griffin cast a half-smile at his longtime friend and servant.

"Consider me hurried."

After stripping to the waist, he doused himself with the

water, then decided he'd best shave again. The black shadow of his beard had already darkened his jaw.

He had just wiped the last of the shaving soap from his face when Florence swept into the room.

"Will you be much longer, darling? You were so very late in arriving—"

A blush spread across her face when he straightened and picked up the snowy-white shirt from the bed. Even after ten years of marriage, his wife still could not make herself comfortable with the intimate side of their relationship. Yet she endured it in order to become a mother. Unfortunately she had miscarried every pregnancy.

"I shall be standing at attention, waiting to receive, within the quarter hour. Is that agreeable?"

She ducked her head in something of a nod and hastened to the door. "Thank you, Griffin." She wasted no time in escaping the sight of his bared chest. He couldn't help but wonder what Amily would have done if she had been his wife and had come upon him thusly. He knew, *he knew,* that she would have come to him and cared not if their guests had to wait for their hosts.

But he could not allow himself to dwell on such thoughts.

True to his word, he arrived at the front door by the appointed time, just as the first curricle rolled to a stop on the drive.

Florence emerged from the parlor, smoothing her pale hair, looking delicate and feminine in a gown of some light, airy fabric sprigged with delicate porcelain blue flowers. Amily did not appear behind her, nor was there any sign of her on the stairs. It was not like her to be tardy. Could she still be suffering ill effects from the lightning?

"Griffin, dear, you look positively haggard. Are you quite well?"

He pulled his attention back to his neighbor, Georgina Walthrup, and gave her a nod as she and her husband, Edward, entered the foyer.

"Never felt better, Mrs. Walthrup," he assured the woman who mothered everyone. "Stop seeking a reason to pamper me." He kissed her hand, then wrapped her in a hug while she chided him not to muss her hair.

"Edward, how is the new colt?"

Edward slapped Griffin on the shoulder with enthusiasm.

"A champion, my boy! I daresay he'll win all purses when I race him."

A flicker at the corner of his eye drew Griffin's attention to the stairs. He gave a silent prayer of thanks that he had not been speaking when he looked up, for the sight of Amily would have surely robbed him of voice as it robbed him now of breath.

She hesitated at the top of the steps, looking uncharacteristically ill at ease, her cheeks pink with high color. Her hair had been done up in all the twists and braids the women so insisted on. Short, feathery wisps of near-ebony framed her face and begged to be touched. She looked not so different from any other occasion, yet she seemed almost otherworldly this evening, with an inner glow about her.

She took a deep breath, as if seeking courage, then slowly descended the stairs. Her snowy white gown fluttered with her every move, hugging her form, caressing her as Griffin so desired to do.

She looked up then, and her gaze moved unerringly to his. He forced a polite nod while he tried to swallow back the incredible ache rising in his chest.

"Oh, there's our dear girl!" Georgina hurried to Amily's side, fussing over her as if she were her own. Griffin took the opportunity to force breath back into his neglected lungs. This truly would be an interminable evening.

"My dear, you look no worse for wear. Indeed, I believe being struck by lightning has enhanced your beauty," Georgina declared in her lighthearted manner. "But, truly, are you well? Should you be about so soon after such an incident?"

Amily's brow dipped to a questioning V as she studied Georgina's face, then smoothed as if she'd been given the answer to an unasked question.

"I'm fine," she reassured. "My shoulder hurts a little, and my fingers are burned from where the lightning exited, but the cook gave me a salve. They're much better. And the gloves help. They act like a bandage." She wiggled the fingers of her lace-covered hands.

"Well, my dear, you must not allow the gentlemen to tire you this evening. Do not hesitate to turn down a dance."

"Oh, I doubt that will be a problem."

As Griffin wondered at this latest odd statement—Amily never lacked for partners—more people arrived until a steady stream flowed through the door. He couldn't help but notice that she stayed nearby instead of circulating in her usual manner. Was she indeed well enough to attend the night's festivities? Was the glow to her cheeks from a fever rather than health?

As Florence greeted each guest with genuine warmth, Griffin noticed that she, too, cast worried glances in her cousin's direction.

"Darling, would you pay special attention to Amily this evening? I fear she is not as well as she professes."

Griffin raised his head to meet Amily's gaze. Guilt and euphoria tore at each other in his chest and threatened to rip him in two. If his wife only knew what she asked of him.

But he was a man of honor, and he was married to a saint of a woman; a woman any man would gladly have as wife.

He would neither tarnish that honor nor sully Florence's love for him by allowing his thoughts of Amily to go further.

Nor would he sully Amily's good character. She had never once treated him as more than a cousin. Surely his infatuation had come about because of the passion for life she exhibited. He would simply ignore that passion, pay it no heed at all, and soon this undesirable attention he paid her would disappear.

"I would ask that you dance the first dance with her. If she appears ill or fatigued then you must insist she rest throughout the evening."

He turned his gaze back to Florence, swallowed, then forced an obliging smile. "Whatever you say, darling." He was a man of honor. He would ignore this brief attraction.

The half dozen musicians tuned their instruments while the ladies freshened themselves in the dressing room set aside for them. When the last of the arriving throng had filtered through the front door and been greeted, Griffin escorted both Florence and Amily to the ballroom.

He had not chanced to glance at a program to see which dance would be first. There was no need. The waltz always opened a ball. He had a feeling he would not be so fortunate as to find himself in the rare opening quadrille with Amily.

"Amily, dear, say you will open the ball with Griffin so that I may dance the first dance with General Williams. He has come alone, and I do so want him to feel welcome."

Amily's eyes widened and a look of panic flickered across her face.

"You want me to dance? With Griffin? What kind of dance?"

"Why, the waltz." Florence's gaze flicked upward to Griffin's before settling back on her cousin. "Are you not well enough?"

Amily seemed to turn her thoughts inward before shaking her head and focusing on Florence.

"No, I'm fine. I think I can manage a waltz."

Griffin exchanged a look with his wife at such an odd speech. He wasn't sure what concerned him most, Amily's strange behavior, or what sort of torture he would endure with her in his arms. But he could hardly refuse to dance with his wife's cousin.

When he offered his arm, Amily gently slipped her gloved hand into the crook and walked with him onto the polished floor, followed by Florence and General Williams. Just having Amily beside him, the warmth of her palm burning through the sleeve of his coat, tightened Griffin's chest with a heart that pounded too fast. With the downbeat of the music, he slid his right hand to the curve of her waist and swirled her into the waltz.

The ache that had become a constant part of him grew with the feel of her at last in his arms. Even with dozens of onlookers, even with his faithful, loving wife sharing the floor, he wanted to close his eyes and savor the feel of Amily in his arms.

She gripped his hand with all the delicacy of a vise, despite her burned fingers.

Her stiff, unsure steps surprised him, but he lead her, nearly lifted her, so that no one could tell she faltered. After several seconds of losing circulation to his fingers, he tightened the hand at her waist and dipped his head to her ear.

"Are you well?" he whispered. Surely she must still be ill to show such uncharacteristic nervousness. "Shall I return you to your rooms?" He silently prayed she would tell him no.

When she raised her gaze to his, the world settled into perfect balance. The moment their eyes met she gave him a wondrous smile, her body relaxed, her steps became sure.

They glided around the gleaming floor as one, just as her essence glided into his heart and filled every dark, cold, empty corner with the warmth of a thousand suns. The force of the warmth nearly staggered him. He swallowed back the ache rising in his throat.

"I'm fine now," she murmured.

He looked down at her and forced a bland expression onto his face.

"You worried me for a moment." If he pulled her close right then, her head would have fit perfectly against the center of his chest. He resisted the urge with no small effort.

When she smiled, the tiniest hint of a crescent-shaped dimple appeared. He stared at it, entranced.

Brianne couldn't believe she was here, in his arms, dancing. She felt like Cinderella, and any moment now the clock would strike midnight.

She continued to hold his gaze, as if breaking it would cause her to stumble. But the part of her who was Amily had taken over, and her feet mirrored his steps with confidence.

He studied her face with those soul-searching eyes, setting butterflies free in her stomach. When she smiled at him, he looked away, swallowed, then looked back with a little less intensity, a little more cool reserve.

His eyes truly were the blue that surrounds tropical islands. A blue that nearly matches a cloudless sky. His smooth, clean-shaven jaw could have been carved by a master artist, and his dark brown hair, combed in perfect, shiny layers, glistened with gold from the candlelight.

Her neck ached from looking up at his face. She fought the overwhelming notion to nestle her head against his broad expanse of chest.

The music ended all too soon. Though Brianne could have lingered until the last note died, Griffin gently led her off the floor like the dutiful cousin-in-law, almost as if he was glad to be rid of her. Again, she wondered exactly when he had fallen in love with his beloved Amily.

As they swept past the crowd, Brianne caught a glimpse of a short, young woman with light brown hair, watching as if she could read Brianne's innermost thoughts. The name Rebecca popped into her mind, and Brianne could tell Amily didn't care for the woman.

"Are you certain you're well enough to continue?" Griffin patted the hand that hooked his arm. "You seem distracted this evening."

Brianne pulled her attention away from the watching woman.

"No, I'm fine. I wouldn't miss this for the world."

Before Griffin could return her to the edge of the floor, she had another suitor bowing over her hand, begging for a dance.

Catesby, the part of her that was Amily supplied. A young man, blond, handsome, with pale gray eyes that worshipped her, led her back to the center of the floor.

One dance after another, the men virtually lined up to dance with the woman they knew as Amily. Brianne realized with more and more clarity that she and Amily were one, and the part of her that had lived in this century came to the fore whenever Brianne needed her, supplying names, memories of people, dance steps. She learned to relax and allow the information to come to her.

As the hours sped by, Brianne found herself comparing every partner to Griffin. None were as handsome, few were as tall. Certainly none had those haunting eyes that could bore right into a person, or shoulders wide enough to carry the weight of the world.

She barely had a chance to catch her breath all evening. Florence sought her out more than once, checked her for fever, fussed over her until Brianne coerced her last partner into whisking Florence onto the dance floor.

At midnight the ever proper Gaston announced that supper was served. The famished dancers filtered into the dining room, and Brianne followed, escorted by another admirer of Amily's she knew only as Everett, a man with a nervous stammer and sweaty palms. And those palms seemed to wander around in a way that was too familiar even by twentieth-century standards.

Food covered every inch of the twelve-foot dining table. Stuffed quail encircled a platter holding a huge, steaming ham. Platters of crawfish, bowls of steamed shrimp, and several types of poached fish sat next to mounds of rice, candied yams, winter peas, and a huge tureen of turtle soup. Fresh baked breads, muffins, and cornbread scented the air, along with airy meringue pies and thick, heavy pound cakes topped with brown sugar glaze.

Brianne strolled through the line while servants spooned heaping portions of each dish onto passing plates. She managed to lose Everett in the crowd, and once through the line, she ducked onto the veranda to try and catch a few minutes alone.

She spotted a secluded bench in the gardens and made her way there, settled her skirts around her, then balanced her plate on her lap.

The beauty of the night overshadowed her hunger. Moonlight shone off the patch of river visible through the trees, a silvery, shimmery streak against the inky black waters. She picked at the food on her plate, then finally set it aside to lean back and do a little star gazing.

Were there this many stars in her own time? She couldn't remember ever seeing the sky littered with so many silver sparkles, as though someone had tossed glitter across black velvet. The scent of dozens of flowers perfumed the warm, humid spring air. She breathed in, savoring the scents, and wished she had someone to share the moment with.

She wished she had Griffin to share it with.

Almost before the thought was fully born, she tried to call it back. She couldn't let herself even think like that. Griffin was a married man, and Florence was a wonderful woman. Brianne didn't know how or why Fate had played this trick on her, but one thing was certain. She would never do anything to come between a husband and wife.

The sound of lovers strolling through the garden paths brought an ache to her heart, and for the first time since she'd been there, she truly, desperately, wanted to go home. Suddenly these insane past few days no longer felt like a surreal adventure, but an exercise in torture. Why was she here? *If* she were here at all. Why had she seemingly been given the opportunity to possibly right what had gone wrong in the past, save Amily and Griffin's lives, but also have the opportunity to save Florence? With her certificate to become a midwife within her grasp in just a few months, she felt certain she could save Florence from dying following her miscarriage, if not save the pregnancy. Maybe she could convince her to prevent the pregnancy all together. But if she did, Amily and Griffin would never get together.

A dull ache pounded in her temples. The excitement of the evening faded, and Brianne found that all she wanted to do was go to bed and bury her head under the pillows. She collected her plate and untouched cup of punch, then roamed back toward the house. A passing servant took the china as she stepped through the open door.

"Thank you, Minnie," Brianne murmured, then stopped and shook her head. She'd known the girl's name was Minnie. She massaged her temples as the throb worsened. *Amily strikes again.*

"Are you not well?"

She didn't need to look up. Just the sound of his voice caused her insides to do little flips. She dropped her hands and dug up a convincing smile.

"Oh, no. I'm fine. Just a little tired."

Griffin studied her, obviously not convinced. She brightened her smile and put a little bounce into her step. If he or Florence thought she still suffered from the lightning, they'd bundle her up in bed and send for a doctor before her coach had time to turn into a pumpkin. Though the thought of bed didn't sound bad right now, she wanted no part of 1830s medicine.

"Would you care to dance then?" Griffin asked just as the orchestra struck up another waltz.

If she said no, he'd assume she was feeling ill. If she said yes she might go up in flames just from having his arms around her again.

"I'd love to."

Against her better judgment she stepped into his arms—ignoring the urge to lay her head on his chest, to let him make everything all right.

She faced the facts as he guided her around the dance floor. She'd fallen in love with this man. She'd started falling the moment he'd whispered, "Come to me," and hadn't stopped yet. With every new facet of him she discovered, every smile he sent her way, she tumbled deeper into the sweet agony of a love that shouldn't be happening.

He towered over her. Just looking up at him made her giddy. Oh, how she could love this man if only he were free.

He looked down at her and gave her a hesitant grin. He acted as if he might say something, but instead took a breath and looked somewhere over her right shoulder.

Though Griffin's touch was completely proper, his hands sent spikes of heat through her. She reveled in the spiraling heat for just a moment, then fought down all the forbidden sensations and pulled a wall up around her heart.

Get a grip, she told herself, then made a point to look everywhere but at his face. She needed to get out of there. When the music mercifully ended, she flexed her fingers and chanced a quick glance in Griffin's direction.

"You know, I am a little tired now. And I really should put some more medicine on my hands. I think I'll just call it a night."

He looked down at her. "Call it a night?"

She could have kicked herself. He made her too nervous to think.

"Retire for the evening."

He glanced up and searched the crowd. "Florence should see you to your room."

"Griffin, I'm a big girl. I can tuck myself into bed."

The minute the words were out of her mouth, she realized that Amily would never have mentioned the act of going to bed in front of Griffin. The part of her that was Amily sent blood heating her cheeks, and even Griffin seemed discomfited by her remark. With a mumbled, "Good night," she hurried out of the ballroom and up the stairs. She needed to get away from him. She couldn't feign indifference as long as his arms were around her, looking down at her, even if it was with cousinly affection.

Chapter 5

BRIANNE STARED INTO the darkness, rolled over, punched her pillow, settled in again, only to stare some more.

She'd fallen in love with Griffin. The real Griffin. The one married to someone else.

True, she'd fallen in love with his spirit when he'd come to her through David, but that had been different. She'd fallen in love with his soul, and known there was a man out there who needed her, and she'd been prepared to find him. Now that soul was in a married man's body.

She rolled over again and slammed the pillow over her head.

She needed to go home, wake up, get out of this time, however she'd gotten there. What was her family thinking? Did her parents know yet that she'd . . . what? Died? Traveled in time? Was she hooked to a life support system in a hospital somewhere?

David had to be frantic. Had he seen the lightning strike her? She'd heard Griffin's voice before everything went black. Had David found her body when Griffin left him?

She groaned. How was she supposed to get back to her time? The thought of standing in a lightning storm with a metal pole in her hand didn't exactly appeal to her.

She crammed the pillow tighter over her head and prayed. She prayed harder than she'd ever prayed in her life.

And finally, before morning sunlight chased away the shadows of the night, she slept.

Brianne woke to the sound of a rooster crowing. She didn't have to open her eyes to know she was still curled in the feather mattress in her room at Shadow Oaks. She must not have prayed hard enough.

At least the dull ache in her head had stopped. She tossed the covers back and swung her feet to the floor just as Ruth came in with a pitcher of warm water.

Brianne had stopped trying to tell the rail-thin maid that she didn't have to wait on her hand and foot. When she'd tried, Ruth had looked at her as if she were crazy, then went right on about her business.

At least Ruth was a servant and not a slave. Brianne had discovered from conversations at the ball that Griffin didn't own any slaves, much to the displeasure of some of his neighbors.

"You up to going to church today, Miss Amily?" Ruth asked as she studied the gowns in the armoire.

Brianne stopped in mid-slosh of washing her face and wishing for her alpha-hydroxy moisturizer. Church? As in meeting even more people she didn't know?

"Oh, I don't know, Ruth. I think I'll take it easy for another day or two. How about the lavender cotton? It looks cool."

Ruth felt Brianne's forehead, then turned her hands over and checked her nearly healed fingers.

"You sho you feelin' well enough to get outta bed? You ain't never turned down a chance to go callin'."

Brianne patted Ruth's hand.

"I'm fine. I'm just . . . tired . . . because of the ball. Besides, I saw everyone last night."

The maid quirked a brow at her, but she said nothing.

Brianne finished dressing, silently cursing all the layers of clothes, especially the corset. But she could hardly get by with not wearing the darned thing. She didn't want to give Griffin and Florence one more reason to think they should send for the doctor by defying the rigid dress codes.

She found the two of them in the dining room when she went down to breakfast. Griffin sat, stiff and slightly pale while Florence blushed and fidgeted with her napkin.

"What's wrong?" Brianne asked as Gaston seated her. Griffin rose until she was seated, then fell back into his chair and looked toward Florence. Gaston quietly disappeared.

"I've just told Griffin that I am increasing again," Florence stated with a half-hearted smile.

"Increasing?" It took a moment for Brianne to understand. "You're pregnant?"

Florence colored even deeper and crushed the napkin in her hands before nodding. The look on her face begged Brianne to be happy for her.

Well, so much for talking her out of getting pregnant again. And the thought of Griffin making love to someone else tore at Brianne's heart. She tamped down the irrational spear of jealousy and forced her feelings not to show on her face.

She managed a convincing enough smile, but when her gaze darted to Griffin, she had trouble maintaining it. He didn't look at all pleased.

"You should not have danced last night," he said across the table.

Florence mangled the napkin even more. "I wasn't certain until this morning, when I awoke feeling ill. And I only danced twice, just in case. Very easy dances."

Gaston and a kitchen helper arrived and sat a platter of scrambled eggs, a bowl of creamy white grits, plates of sugared biscuits, sausage, and bacon on the table. The air hummed with tension, but the only sound that broke the silence was the clink of silver against china. Not until the servants left did Griffin speak again, his voice somewhat gentler.

"You've lost six babies, Florence. I am concerned only for your health."

Florence turned a pale blue gaze to her husband, so full of love Brianne felt she should turn away.

"I know, darling. This time I will take myself to bed and spend the whole nine months there if it will bring this child safely into the world. I truly did not exert myself last night."

Griffin relented under her worshipful gaze. He took the platter of scrambled eggs from his wife and spooned a mound onto his plate.

"Just don't do anything foolish," he muttered toward his food.

He ate in silence as Florence chatted about the previous evening's success. Brianne only listened with half an ear, nodding occasionally.

Six pregnancies. Brianne hadn't realized there'd been so many. Could she stop the miscarriage or Florence's death after all? She would just have to keep a close eye on everything Florence did and hope everything she'd learned in her midwife training came to her when she needed it.

Griffin rode through the fields, inspecting the crops more from sheer routine than from any real notice he paid them. His mind focused on Florence's news.

With child again. He prayed, for her sake, that she would

carry this baby and deliver the child she so desperately wanted. At least perhaps that way he could give her something of himself.

He thought of Amily's look when Florence had told her. Had her gaze been accusing when she'd looked at him, or was it merely his guilty conscience for continuing to give in to Florence despite the doctor's warnings?

He pulled the brim of his hat down to shield his eyes from the glare of the morning sun. A trickle of sweat skidded down his neck and into the collar of his shirt. Spring had lasted about a week before the vicious heat of the summer threatened. He pulled a handkerchief from his pocket and mopped the back of his neck.

The snowy white kerchief was one of a set that Amily had given him for Christmas. He looked at the elaborately embroidered monogram of GHE done in perfect stitches of ivory silk thread. Even then, just days after she had come to live with them, he'd already had to fight down his growing feelings of fascination for her. Her childlike enthusiasm for the holidays, every free-spirited smile, every feminine giggle, had enchanted him.

The memory of her in his arms at the ball invaded his thoughts and slapped his heart to a faster beat. While the thought of her brought on an all too familiar ache, his mind fought guilt at what just thinking of Amily could do to him.

Damnation! He was a married man with a pregnant wife. A wife who worshipped the very air he breathed. He had slept with Florence, knowing she shouldn't get pregnant again, knowing that while she struggled to convince him she enjoyed the physical act, his thoughts had been on her cousin, certain that Amily would find passion in what Florence found so embarrassing.

But he would never know. Amily was destined to be nothing more than a distant dream to him. A beautiful dream that promised something he could never touch, never hold, never feel.

He closed his eyes and shook his head. This had to stop. He couldn't continue to daydream about an impossible life. Sooner or later she or Florence would sense something. He'd grown up around too many women not to believe in their intuition. He couldn't hurt Florence, and he couldn't make Amily so uncomfortable that she would leave. She had no other family, nowhere else to go.

He kicked Tempest into a trot, then a canter, then leaned over the dark, shiny mane as the horse broke through the field at a full run. Griffin pushed the horse, pushed himself, as the guilt and frustration that had been building for months surfaced. He raced down the parched road, clumps of earth flying as Tempest's hooves bit into the dirt. Sweat dripped from his skin to mingle with the horse's as Tempest charged into the woods of Shadow Oaks. With a flick of the reins, Griffin guided him into a stream. Water erupted around them as they stormed along the shallow creek. Another flick of the wrist sent the horse leaping onto the bank and over a fallen log. Tempest fought the silent commands, but Griffin, angry at himself and needing control, forced his mount to do his bidding. They burst into a meadow filled with wildflowers, then Griffin turned the horse sharply and kneed him back into the trees. Over and over, he ran the horse through the stream, through the woods, into the meadow and back, then finally he turned toward Shadow Oaks and raced down the road, trying to outrun demons he couldn't exorcise.

The house appeared in the distance. The low stone wall bordering the road curved like a huge brown snake around his property. He charged toward it, as he had done a thousand times. He kicked Tempest on, felt the mount's muscles bunch in preparation to jump, and seconds later he sailed over the fence.

Alone.

His feet kicked and his arms windmilled through the air right before he slammed flat on his back onto the hard-packed earth. The breath left his lungs in a painful *whoosh,* and little sparkles of light swam inside his head. The sound of running footsteps sounded more like rapid gunshots to his spinning brain.

"Griffin! Griffin, are you all right?"

The voice seemed familiar. He opened his eyes, looked up at a canopy of live oak leaves with shreds of Spanish moss blowing, and idly wondered why he was lying on his back.

When a face blocked his view, his mind began to clear.

Amily.

"Are you all right? Is your back hurt? Griffin, can you hear me?" She very nearly shouted the last question.

He finally pulled in a breath of sweet air and shook the cobwebs from his mind.

"I'm fine," he reassured her as he worked himself up onto his elbows. Tempest stood where he'd dug in his hooves, placidly munching on a few roadside wildflowers. Just as Griffin wondered aloud if Esther knew any good recipes for horse meat, Tempest whickered and rolled a belligerent eye toward his master.

Griffin glared at the horse, then caught Amily's worried frown creasing her brow. She would probably insist on helping him back to the house, fussing over him, turning the incident into—

"You big, stupid idiot!" She shoved so hard on his shoulder, he toppled off his elbows and smacked his head on the ground again. "What the heck were you thinking? You could have been killed!"

He rubbed the back of his head where a nice size goose egg would no doubt form. This was not the kind of fussing he'd had in mind.

"Why would you charge a fence on a horse that won't jump?" she continued to rant as she rose and dusted off her skirts in disgust, leaving him lying in the dirt.

He got to his feet, trying his best to ignore the spinning landscape and the thunder in his head.

"The blasted horse has jumped that fence with no more than a nudge for five years."

"Well, you were doing a heck of a lot more than nudging! He probably has boot-shaped dents in his flanks." She scrambled over the stone fence and ran her hands along Tempest's side. The infuriating animal stomped passively and nuzzled her with his nose.

"Did he hurt you, big fella? Did the big bully hurt you? I would have thrown him, too."

Rolling his eyes heavenward only made Griffin's head hurt worse. A bully. The very idea. He wished now he'd said he was injured.

She rounded on him and crossed her arms.

"What possessed you to abuse this poor horse?"

"Abuse!" He winced at the sound of his own voice. "I would argue the definition of abuse with you at the moment." The back of his head felt like a well-used smithy's anvil.

"Try having someone saw a bit in your mouth and kick you in the sides to make you run, then tell me which feels more abusive."

He could only stare at her while she turned and nuzzled Tempest's velvety nose. She had changed. Ever since the lightning struck her, she seemed somewhat different. Bolder. Less formal. As if she had no fear as to the consequences of her behavior. He'd heard of others who had come so close to death that it had changed their lives. Unfortunately, the change made her even more attractive.

"What's bothering you, Griffin? You aren't the type to

ride a horse into the ground." She walked over to him and perched on the stone wall.

He started to deny her words, to insist nothing was wrong. But the guilt of Florence's pregnancy got the best of him. He took off his hat, plowed his fingers from forehead to crown, then settled the hat back low over his eyes.

"It's Florence," he finally said, then dropped to the stone fence, keeping several feet between them.

Brianne studied the man sitting on the fence. He drew up one booted foot in front of him and propped a wrist on his knee. She swallowed so hard she almost gulped.

"Florence?" She pulled her mind away from his masculine position, back to his words. "You're not happy about the baby?"

He looked at her from beneath the brim of his planter's hat. Even in the shadow of the brim, the blue of his eyes had an almost incandescent glow. Why was it that a steady male gaze from under any hat brim could make a woman's insides scramble?

"She's lost six babies, Amily. The doctors have said we should stop trying. Her health could be in jeopardy. And what if she loses this child, too? She wants a babe so fiercely, I fear for her sanity. That's the only reason why I've . . . that we haven't stopped . . ."

He whipped his hat off again and his fingers combed the ring from his thick, dark hair. His eyes looked at her with the tortures of the damned—guilt-ridden, worried. He looked like a man in love and fearful for his pregnant wife.

Brianne couldn't help but worry about Florence, especially with what Griffin told her, but Heaven help her, she also couldn't help wondering when Griffin finally fell in love with Amily.

She pushed those thoughts to the back of her mind, ashamed that they had even surfaced.

"Griffin." She scooted closer to him and patted his hand to reassure him, but the moment she touched him an agonizing want curled through her body. She fought it down. "We'll take care of Florence. I was studying to become a midwife before . . . before I came here." Amazingly, from within her subconscious, she realized that Amily, too, had been learning midwifery before her father had taken so ill. What other common threads did their separate lives share? "I've learned a lot about what causes miscarriages and how to help prevent them. And who knows?" she went on, trying to bolster his hope. "If she carries this one to term, the two of you quite possibly could have several more."

He glanced at her with the oddest look, as if he were delving deep into his own soul. Finally, a sad, half-smile curved one corner of his mouth.

"Yes. Several children."

"Griffin!" Florence's cry cut off anything else he might have said. They both turned to see her rushing down the drive. Brianne jumped up and ran to her.

"Florence, slow down! You don't want to do anything to cause—"

"But Mum Sal saw Griffin thrown from his horse! Are you hurt, darling? What in the world caused Tempest to throw you?" Though she slowed at Brianne's insistence, she moved straight to her husband and took his heart-stopping, tanned face in her tiny porcelain hands.

"I'm fine, Flo. Nothing hurt but my dignity." He rose, smiled down at her with that same odd look, then tipped up her chin with his knuckle. "Have a care for yourself. You should not be running in your condition."

Her face positively glowed with her smile.

"Yes, darling."

He took up the trailing reins that threatened to be eaten with the wildflowers, then swung astride the horse's back.

"Will you excuse me, ladies? I believe I've just acquired a new horse's hide to tan." As if Tempest understood, he neighed and tossed his head.

With a no-nonsense grip on the reins, Griffin cantered back toward the road, swung around, and rode straight for the fence again. Florence squeaked, and Brianne couldn't stop a gasp, but this time horse and rider sailed effortlessly to the other side. He turned back to the women, calling over the sound of Tempest's prancing hooves. "Shall I send Cubby back with the pony cart?"

When Florence shook her head and waved him happily away, he turned the horse toward the drive and showed him who was master.

Brianne walked Florence back to the house, trying not to let the sight of Griffin racing across the manicured lawn double her heartbeat. She couldn't help but notice how Florence's gaze kept wandering in the direction Griffin had ridden. A blind man in the dark could see how the woman was besotted with her husband. Guilt nagged at Bri's mind and shame welled up from deep within her. She resolved to let her feelings for Griffin go no further. If she had to run in the opposite direction whenever he came near, she would stop this headlong tumble into love.

Lost in her determined thoughts, Brianne climbed the wide, welcoming steps to the front veranda. Not until she reached the top did she realize she was alone. When she turned, she found Florence frozen at the bottom step, her face drained of color and panic in her eyes.

"Florence, what is it?" Brianne clattered down the steps to her side.

"A pain," Florence gasped as she cradled her flat stomach.

Chapter 6

"Don't move." Brianne turned and yelled toward the house, "Gaston! Gaston, come here!"

The servant appeared in seconds, his dark eyes wide with alarm. With one look at his mistress, he raced down the steps and scooped her into his arms. As he strode through the house, he called to one of the girls cleaning the parlor.

"Della, find Mistah Grif and send Cubby to fetch Doc Myers."

Within minutes they had Florence settled on her bed. Gaston left for the kitchen to have Esther brew some chamomile tea, with a promise to have Ruth bring it up immediately.

"First thing we're going to do is get you out of that corset." Brianne didn't allow Florence a chance to argue. She set about unlacing Florence's bodice, then started in on the corset strings. "You're not to put this torture chamber back on until at least two months after the baby is born, understood?"

Florence looked shocked at the idea of not wearing a corset, but with one look at Brianne's stubborn face, she agreed.

"Why in the world women ever wore these things to begin with is beyond me," Brianne muttered as she loosened the ties and watched Florence grow a good two inches. "And to put them on little girls, just so they'd have tiny waists when they grew up. Talk about child abuse!" Florence watched her, her golden brows slowly drawing together, and Brianne realized she'd been talking out loud. "Can you raise up so I can pull this thing off of you? Then I'll get you a loose robe to wear."

Florence blushed a delicate rose pink and her hands came up to shield her breasts.

"I . . . you can't . . ."

Brianne could never understand such modesty between women. She wiggled her eyebrows and grinned.

"Have you got something under there that I haven't got?"

Florence blushed even deeper, but the corners of her mouth came up in a shy grin. Brianne turned and rummaged in the armoire.

"Tell you what. You slip out of your things while I find a dressing gown. I promise not to look."

Brianne could hear the rustle of fabric behind her while she looked through Florence's clothing. Just as she found an airy, white eyelet robe, the door flew open with a bang, and Griffin burst into the room.

"Della found me in the stables. She said—"

Brianne turned just in time to see Florence gasp and try to cover her bare breasts. Griffin spun on his heel, turning his back to his wife and staring at the ceiling.

"Are you all right, Florence? Della was crying so hard I couldn't understand her. Is it the baby?"

Florence's face had turned the color of a raspberry. She reached for the robe with a pleading, mortified look. Brianne snapped out of her shock and helped her into the delicate wrapper.

"I had a pain, darling," she finally answered him, "but it is passing."

Griffin turned, glancing once to make sure she was covered before completely facing her.

"I've sent for Dr. Myers." He looked to Brianne. "Is there nothing we can do before he gets here?"

Brianne had already thought of that. Considering their reactions to a little bare flesh, she decided to wait until Griffin left to find out if Florence was bleeding.

"I've already gotten her out of that corset, and she's not to put it on again until that baby is at least two months old." She looked to Florence again, who nodded, wide-eyed. "I've also sent Gaston to have Ruth bring up some chamomile tea. Now I want the foot of her bed elevated. Put a couple of bricks beneath these two bed legs so that her head will be lower than the rest of her body."

"What possible good will that do?"

"If she's bleeding, it might help stop it, and if she's not, it might help prevent it."

Griffin glanced at Florence, but she busied herself with finding anywhere else to look besides at her husband.

Ruth arrived with the tea, and Griffin left to find some bricks to put under the bed legs. Brianne poured a cup of the chamomile brew and drizzled in a generous helping of honey.

"We need to see if you're bleeding," she said as she handed the cup to Florence. Not that there was much she could do to stop it, but at least she'd have a better idea of what she was dealing with.

At another bout of flaming cheeks, Brianne wondered how Florence ever managed to get pregnant to begin with, or how Griffin ever managed to get that far with her.

"H-how do you do that?" The cup rattled in the saucer.

Bri couldn't help but take pity on anyone so painfully modest.

"Here." She took the cup and saucer and sat it on the bed-side table. "I'll turn my back and you just check your un-derthings."

She turned around and waited, remembering how Griffin had spun around when he'd seen Florence undressed. He certainly didn't strike Brianne as a prude, so he must have turned away out of respect for Florence's wishes. What in the world went on behind closed doors, if a husband would feel the need to turn away at the sight of a little bare skin? Especially if his wife might be losing his child.

"No."

Bri turned back to Florence. "What?"

"There's no . . . blood."

"Well, that's good news. Now, I need to know how far along you are. When was your last period?"

Florence shook her head in confusion. "My what?"

"Your monthly courses."

"Oh." Another bout of blushing. "I am . . . not certain. I have never been . . . they've never come in a timely man-ner."

Well, that *wasn't* good news. Not knowing how far along she was certainly wasn't going to help matters. And with six previous miscarriages and the abdominal pain she'd just suf-fered, Brianne wasn't prepared to take any chances with her patient.

She fervently wished she'd gotten her midwifery certifi-cation. Just another few months and she may have been bet-ter prepared for this situation.

She settled her back into a mound of pillows, then handed the tea back to Florence.

"Amily?"

"Hmm?" she said as she straightened covers and racked

her brain for how to deal with this situation with nineteenth-century technology.

"When you were helping the midwife in New Orleans, did you ever see someone like me? Someone who had lost several babies?"

Brianne caught flashes of memories, Amily's memories, of a woman in an ornate tester bed, desperate to carry a baby to term after four miscarriages.

"Yes. I remember one woman."

"Did she carry the baby? Was it born healthy?"

Bri closed her eyes and relaxed so the memories would come easier.

"Am . . . my father died and I had to leave to come here before she could have the baby. I don't know if she carried it to term."

Florence's shoulders drooped. "Oh."

"Now, don't worry about what other women have or haven't done. You need to relax and have a positive attitude."

Griffin came back in carrying an armload of bricks, followed by a huge black man Brianne instinctively knew was named Isaac. The man dwarfed the large bedroom as he ducked his head uncomfortably. Griffin laid the bricks on the Persian carpet next to the bed legs, then he and Isaac grasped the footboard.

"Would you put however many you need under each leg when we lift the bed, Amily?"

When she stooped by the bed, both men heaved upward. Brianne stacked two bricks then hurried around and stacked two on the other side.

"All done." She looked up at Griffin, then he and Isaac slowly lowered the footboard onto the bricks. Their arms shook and muscles rippled from the weight of the bed. Brianne's mouth went dry and her heart climbed in her throat as she looked up the length of Griffin's body. Had a more perfect man ever been created? Not until he looked down at her still stooped on the floor did she manage to drag her gaze from taking inventory of his perfections.

"Umm, yes, that should do it." She stood and studied the bricks, then took a deep, calming breath. She smoothed a few nonexistent wrinkles from her skirts while Griffin let a relieved Isaac escape the feminine bedroom.

"How are you feeling, Flo?" Griffin stepped to the bedside and towered over his wife. He looked even more tortured and guilty than before.

"Like an infant myself. And feeling silly for causing so much concern. I should have known better than to run, but I so feared you were injured."

That didn't seem to help his guilty look. Brianne moved to Griffin's side and perched on the edge of the bed.

"Well, you're not going to have a chance to run for a while. I'm going to have the garden parlor set up as a bedroom today, then tomorrow we'll move you down there." She took one of Florence's hands and patted. "I want you to stay in bed for a while, then if everything seems fine, you can get up for short periods. With the bedroom downstairs you won't have to climb stairs and you'll be close to everything that's going on. And," she went on to reassure the overly responsible woman, "I'll take care of your household chores. The less worry you have, the better for the baby."

Florence blinked glistening eyes. "Thank you, Amily. I have never been able to take to my bed when I had problems before. You're a godsend."

A godsend. The words sent a shiver down Brianne's spine.

"Well, then. You rest now while Griffin and I turn the parlor into a bedroom for you." As she turned to leave, Florence took Griffin's hand, kissed his knuckles, then pressed his palm to her cheek. Brianne tried not to think about what it would feel like to be able to do that. She shoved the thought aside and focused on rearranging the parlor.

You're a godsend. The words had rattled around in her brain all day and into the night. A godsend. Was that what she truly was?

What if something had gone wrong in the original history, and instead of Griffin falling in love with Amily after Florence's death, Florence should have survived and bore a child? Was Brianne's part in this life not to fall in love with Griffin, but to save Florence and their baby?

She laid aside the book she had been holding and rubbed her tired, grainy eyes. She hadn't turned a page in the volume of Shakespeare's sonnets since she picked it up. All she could think about was Griffin and Florence and what she was supposed to do.

When he'd come to her through David, Griffin had told her that he and Amily had loved each other, even before Florence had died. But if the man was in love with Amily, she never wanted to meet him across a poker table.

A sudden idea sent a shiver racing through her blood. What if she, Brianne, behaved so differently from Amily that Griffin didn't fall in love with her? Was her very presence changing the way things were supposed to be? Maybe she wasn't meant to be there at all, but was a loose thread in the fabric of time.

She sighed and tried to rub away the dull throb in her temples. All she could do was be herself and do what she could to save Florence, which wasn't much without the help of turn of the millennium medicine. She'd decided against any type of aggressive examination, for fear of aggravating Florence's condition. For the time being she would just keep her calm, on her back, with the foot of the bed elevated.

The tiny porcelain clock on the mantel chimed twice and her exhausted eyes burned in the dim light of the candle. She snuffed the flame, then dragged her weary body to the bed and slipped between the cool cotton sheets. As her mind drifted off to sleep, the memory of Florence brushing a kiss across Griffin's knuckles stole into her restless dreams.

With Florence settled in the garden parlor, Brianne spent the next several days keeping her entertained by playing cards, chatting, or just sitting quietly with her while they both read.

The boredom threatened to kill her.

She kept reminding herself that at least she could get up and do whatever she wanted, unlike Florence. Just that thought kept her glued to the accursed chair whenever she started toying with excuses to escape.

She had finally found an opportunity to question Florence about her other pregnancies. When she discovered that Florence had carried the other babies for a good six months, Brianne realized that this most probably was not the beginning of a miscarriage. Florence had all the symptoms of suffering from an incompetent cervix, and though she would need to go to bed later, she simply wasn't far enough along to lose the baby yet. Since none of her other miscarriages had happened this early, Brianne suspected the pain she'd suffered had simply been from running, in a corset, no less. The doctor, however, had recommended bed rest, and Brianne thought it best just to go along with him rather than try to convince Florence otherwise.

Fortunately, on the third day, visitors started to arrive, and then there seemed to be a steady stream of them. Apparently Amily knew them all, but more than once Brianne had to do some quick tap dancing until that inner voice supplied a name and snatches of other information.

Not so fortunately, one of the many visitors was the

squinty-eyed woman from the ball. Rebecca. She had been one of the first to visit, and one to visit most often. The woman would have been attractive if not for the pinched look on her face and the perpetual squinting of her eyes. Brianne had a feeling the expression was more from nosiness than from poor vision. Brianne wouldn't have been able to stand the busybody, even if her Amily side had liked her. The woman sat by Florence's bed with what she no doubt thought was a sympathetic face, but Brianne could almost hear the woman's thoughts: *Poor desperate Florence. You must have done something to deserve this. I'm so glad it's you and not me.*

Florence, ever gracious, tolerated her much better than Brianne would have under the same circumstances. When the woman's gossip grew too tedious, Florence would mumble something about being fatigued and then thank Rebecca for coming. Once, as Rebecca was leaving, Brianne caught her actually running her white-gloved fingers across the top of a picture frame in the foyer.

"We have servants to do that," Brianne had said, and Rebecca had spun around as if shot. Her glare could have disintegrated Brianne into a puff of smoke. Their animosity seemed to grow in leaps and bounds with every visit thereafter.

"No one should look that serious. What has you so vexed?" Florence laid aside her needlepoint and took a sip of herbal tea.

Brianne allowed a little sneer to convey her feelings. "Rebecca Busybody Masters." She laid the leather-bound book she'd been staring at on the rosewood table. "She walks around here inspecting things like a drill sergeant. One of these days I'm going to—"

"She's just jealous that Bradley Randolph is smitten with you. She's had her cap set for him for years. As it is now, she's probably on the shelf for good."

Bradley Randolph. Brianne couldn't recall dancing with anyone by that name at the ball. A ghost of a memory surfaced, and then she knew he was tall, muscular, with soft brown eyes and a handsome face. Amily liked him, but she'd done nothing to encourage him.

"He wasn't at the ball," Brianne prodded as she poured herself some tea.

"I suppose his trip to Richmond took longer than he expected. I know he looked forward to being there. I suspect he planned to ask for your hand that night."

Brianne nearly choked on her drink.

"He what?"

Florence gave her a knowing smile. "Now do not protest you didn't suspect. The poor man would have proposed months ago if not for respect for Uncle James's death." Florence leaned forward like a teenage girl with a secret. "Do you plan to accept when he offers?"

"Accept?" The word came out as a squeak. "I . . . well . . . I . . . I hardly know him."

"Why, Amily Tannen, we all grew up together. How much better must you know someone?"

Oops. She should have waited until Amily supplied that little tidbit of trivia.

"Well, I don't know. I . . ." Brianne's mind so totally rejected the idea, she couldn't even come up with a decent answer. "I don't love him."

Florence leaned back into the pillows, a dreamy smile lighting her face.

"Yes, that is the most important thing. You must have love."

Brianne swallowed back the ache rising in her throat. She

wouldn't think about Griffin. She refused to think about Griffin.

"Darling!" Florence's smile nearly blinded Brianne before she slid her gaze to the man standing in the doorway.

Almost as if her thoughts had summoned him, he'd appeared. *He's just another man,* she told herself. Just any other man . . . who could turn her knees to butter with a mere flick of those soul-searching eyes.

"Ladies." Griffin greeted them, then wandered into the room and brushed a kiss across the cheek Florence presented. "How are you feeling?"

"I feel wonderful. I have a most conscientious doctor," she said with a wink at Brianne.

He turned and gave her a cousinly smile. "Yes, we're fortunate to have you here, Amily. You have been a godsend."

There was that word again. If they only knew how she might be screwing up their lives.

She forced her lips into a smile and stood. "Well, I'll let the two of you visit. I have a million things to do." She took a step backward and nearly fell over the chair. Griffin's hands shot out and caught her at the waist to right her.

The moment he touched her, his hands sent a jolt straight to her heart, like someone had slapped some of those electric paddles from a hospital crash cart against her chest.

She couldn't take this. She couldn't live in this house with this man and not be in love with him. She stepped away from his hands, shook out her skirts, then cut a wide berth around the chair.

"Thank you. Now I'll just . . . I'll just leave you two alone."

She left them staring after her, but she didn't care. She walked calmly from the room, then mounted the stairs and walked to her bedroom. Not until she closed the door, not until she turned and felt its cool wood against her forehead, did she let the tears stinging her eyes spill onto her cheeks.

Chapter 7

GRIFFIN STARED AT Florence as she ate her breakfast from the wicker bed tray. A hot tingle spread across his neck while his heart thudded against his ribs.

"She seems reluctant to ask you for anything, darling, and she must go into town for shopping. There are some things the servants simply cannot buy. Besides," she reached out and took his hand, smiling up at him in that way that always twisted the guilt in the pit of his stomach, "she deserves a day in town. She has worked so hard taking over my duties. She refuses to let me do more than embroider or read. And I vow, I'm feeling more hopeful every day because of it."

How in bloody hell would he ever survive a day alone with Amily? Passing her in the hallway could be torture enough. But an entire day? As her escort?

A tiny part of him thrilled at the idea, which affirmed even more that to do this would be a mistake.

"I simply haven't the time, Flo. I have . . . several errands to run in town, which should take most of the day. I'll instruct Gaston to take her and—"

"Griffin." Florence laid her fork aside and looked up at him with dread. "I am not blind. Nor am I stupid. It is very plain how you feel about my cousin."

The muscles in his neck suddenly ached with the gulp he fought to stifle. Heat blasted from beneath his collar, but he refused to run his finger around the starched rim. He forced his face to remain passive.

"How I feel?"

"Yes!" his soft-spoken wife almost yelled, then stopped and collected herself. "Don't bother denying it. I've known for weeks now."

Weeks! And he'd thought he'd conquered his feelings, at least outwardly. He sank into the chair beside the bed, unconsciously raking his fingers from temple to crown, then squeezing the handful of hair.

"Florence, I don't know what you're thinking, but you've obviously misunderstood my reaction to Amily."

"I think not, Griffin. You really aren't a very good actor. And I know you too well for you to hide your feelings from me."

He struggled not to let the shock show. Or the dread. He never meant for this to happen. He never meant to hurt Florence. No matter how much she insisted, he would never admit the truth to her. She could never be certain if he didn't admit it, and maybe she wouldn't be hurt quite so much.

"And what's more," she continued, "Amily feels the same way about you."

His head jerked up, a denial on his lips, but Florence stopped him.

"I cannot fathom why you dislike her. She is sweet-tempered, honorable, well-favored. But the two of you make a habit of avoiding each other, then barely speak when you do meet. Perhaps you simply need to spend some time together, to see what fine people you really are. That's why I want you to take her to town. So you can get to know each other."

Griffin stared, his heart thundering with relief. She didn't know. Thank God, she didn't know. But Heaven help him, now she wanted to literally throw them together. How in the world could he get out of this? How could he keep his distance from Amily, yet convince Florence that he didn't dislike her. *Dislike*. The word would be amusing if it weren't so terribly untrue.

"Really, Flo. You have misread my reactions. I like Amily very much." *Too much.* "Perhaps I have been a bit distracted of late . . ."

"So you will take her to town today?"

He mentally dropped his head to his chest. She would not give up. His sweet, complacent, biddable wife had a thread of iron in her when it came to getting what she wanted; that same thread that kept her striving for a baby after six miscarriages. If he denied her this, she would wonder at his reasons.

"Of course, I will, if it means that much to you, though I'm fond enough of Amily without taking her for an excursion." He stood and walked to the window. Gardeners planted, trimmed, and pruned the foliage while one of the peacocks strutted with tail fanned for his drab little peahen.

Griffin tried desperately to ignore the little voice inside him cheering in jubilation that he had his wife's insistence to spend the day with the woman he loved. The sparks of joy were beneath him, and beneath his respect for Florence.

"Well, then." He shoved away from where he'd leaned on the window frame. "It's off to town, then. Can I bring you something?"

"Oh, yes." She set aside the bed tray and scooted off the bed. "I need some skeins of silk embroidery thread." She rummaged in the vanity, then swirled around with a colorful scrap of fabric. "All these colors, if you can manage. Especially this shade of pink, and this shade of yellow."

He tucked the scrap into his waistcoat pocket, then leaned to brush a kiss across the cheek his wife offered. She smiled up at him, her worries gone, obviously confident that her husband and her cousin would return from town the best of friends.

Somehow he managed not to groan.

Why didn't someone just shoot him and put him out of his misery?

The carriage bounced again, jostling Amily's thighs against his, stirring up her elusive scent, causing all manner of undesirable effects on him. His hand came up and unconsciously rubbed the back of his damp neck. Damn the unseasonable heat.

The seat springs squeaked in time with Scupper's trotting hooves. Griffin held the reins and gave more concentration to driving than need be. He'd left the coachman, Daniel, behind, choosing to drive them himself. He had to have something to occupy his mind besides Amily's magnetic pull. Perhaps he should have chosen a carriage larger than the cramped chaise, but he couldn't have explained the need for extra room, and no doubt Florence would have seen the gesture as an attempt to put distance between himself and her cousin.

He glanced at that cousin only inches away. She looked as miserable as he felt.

Her expression jarred him to the core. Had he been so intent on remaining aloof that he had made her feel unwelcome? Did she truly dislike him, as Florence had said? Her next words certainly didn't settle his thoughts.

"I have a feeling you were as coerced as I was to take this

little day trip." She turned to him, a forced smile if ever he'd seen one fixed on her lips.

"Coerced?" He kept his face pleasantly blank.

"Yes. I'd much rather admit it and get it out of the way than spend the day pretending Florence didn't have a little talk with both of us."

So much for playing dumb. He wouldn't insult her by denying the facts now.

"Coerced might not be the most accurate word," he admitted. "But she seems to be laboring under the misconception that we dislike each other." He looked straight ahead, down the road between Scupper's bouncing ears. "I have been so busy these last months, I must apologize if I've made you feel unwelcome. It was never my intention to lead anyone to believe—"

"Oh, no. You've never made me feel unwelcome. I guess we just . . . haven't taken the time to get to know each other."

Though her words sounded true enough, her voice lacked the conviction of belief. Perhaps he had indeed made her uncomfortable in his home.

"Well, then we shall have to convince Florence that we are the best of friends." *And put you at ease at Shadow Oaks.* "I'm ashamed that she even felt the need to speak to me."

"Oh, well," Amily picked at the skirts of her gown, "she was none too easy on me, either. She swore I didn't like you. Can you imagine that?" Her laughter sounded just a bit hollow to Griffin's ears.

"Yes. Imagine that." He rippled the reins across Scupper's shiny chestnut back, not at all sure now whether Amily disliked him or not. But there was one thing of which he was certain. He would convince them both that he was extremely fond of Amily Tannen, in a cousinly way, and he would do it today, so that he never had to "prove" himself again. Keeping his body in a perpetual state of hot, tingling, aching agony, wanting to touch her, look at her, taste her, was not something he wanted to suffer through again. Oh, no. He was not a man who went looking for torture.

Traffic on the road increased as they drew nearer to town. Clouds of dust from carriage wheels and horses' hooves hung in the still, humid air. Amily mopped at her face and neck with a lacy handkerchief that had wilted several miles back. When the White Dove Inn came into view, Griffin's stomach reminded him he'd skipped breakfast to speak with Florence.

"The inn is up ahead. Would you like to eat, or would you rather do the marketing first?"

Amily ran the snowy handkerchief down the length of her neck, turned to him, then blew an errant curl out of her eyes.

"I would kill for some iced tea . . . er . . . something cold . . . anything wet. Just get me out of this heat." Her cheeks glowed above her long-suffering smile. He watched a glistening drop of perspiration trickle from the hair at her temple before she caught it at her jaw with the scrap of limp linen. What he wouldn't give to trace that same moist path with his . . .

He drew in a deep breath to pull his thoughts back to neutral ground, then reined Scupper to a stop beside the carriage block. So much for cousinly thoughts.

The meal, though agonizing, proved more enjoyable than he would ever have dreamed.

Amily seemed to finally relax with him. He watched her eyes sparkle as she listened to him talk. Her giggles gilded the air when he told about the pine cone battles he and his brother, Paul, had waged. She laughed so hard that she snorted when he told about the licking they'd gotten after seeing who could get the biggest scoop of butter to stick on the dining room ceiling.

She shook her head as her laughter died. "Geez, it must be the testosterone. How could you not know you'd get in trouble for that? Or was the challenge worth the spanking?"

He grinned and shrugged. "I was only six at the time. Paul was eight. That age never knows better. And what's testosterone?"

Her glass of chilled wine hesitated halfway to her lips. Her smile froze as she took a sip, then set the stemware back on the snowy tablecloth.

"Oh, I think I read an article about it. Some . . . theory that it's something in men that makes them . . . masculine."

He wondered what kind of articles they were printing in those ladies' journals.

"Then Paul and I must have been filled with it, for we most certainly were all boys. And there's still a faint path to the wood shed to prove it."

Her smile warmed and she relaxed again. Whatever had spooked her must have gone away.

"Where's Paul now?" she asked, and again he had to wonder if the lightning had affected her memory.

"He's at the family home down river."

"Oh. Right," she said, nodding as if this were new information. He made a vow to himself to watch her more closely.

"Are you revived enough to do the shopping?" he asked as he rose and pulled out her chair.

She downed the last of her wine, then arched a brow at him.

"Point me toward the market. With a glass of wine on my brain, I'm mellow enough to tackle anything."

He held back his smile. The woman surprised him nearly every time she opened her mouth.

The marketplace teemed with people, and the heat shimmered in the still air. Every now and then a cloud would pass over the sun and lend a few moments of relief, but Griffin hardly noticed. All he could see was Amily. He watched her walk amongst the shops and stalls, completely enthralled, as if she'd never been to market before. The more he watched her, the more of an enigma she became.

And the more he ached to touch her.

They spent the afternoon going from shop to shop. Amily consulted a list Florence had made, muttering to herself on occasion.

"Oxalic acid and crocus martis. Sounds like a Kevorkian cocktail."

"I beg your pardon?"

Her head shot up and she gave him a wide-eyed smile.

"Oh, I was just wondering what oxalic acid and crocus martis is, and what it's used for."

"I believe Gaston mixes a copper polish with it."

"Hmmm." She walked on, perusing the list. She stopped and squinted at the paper. "Spermaceti?" She glanced up at him, then back at the list. "Nah." She shook her head, as if settling something in her mind. "Okay, I give. What the heck is spermaceti, and why would Florence want it?"

He studied her, certain she must be teasing. How could she not know? The substance was a household staple.

"She uses it to make lotions and creams. It's an oil from the sperm whale."

"Ohhh," she said, nodding with a look of relief.

He watched her, the half dozen questions on his tongue forgotten when she raised her head and sniffed.

"What smells so good?" she asked, then inhaled again, her nose searching the air for the scent.

Griffin drew in a deep breath, then turned her toward a

bakery and aimed her face toward the door. "Pecan tarts? Lemon pie? Cinnamon rolls?"

"Mmmm! I want one of each." She crossed the street and all but pressed her face against the glass. "Can we?"

Within minutes they strolled along the banquette again, Amily balancing a golden pecan tart in one hand and a fat, steaming cinnamon roll in the other. Griffin carried a box containing a lemon meringue pie.

She took a bite of the tart, then closed her eyes in heavenly euphoria as she slowly chewed and hummed another "Mmmm."

Next came a bite of the cinnamon roll. Griffin nearly groaned aloud as he watched her sink her teeth into the pastry, then close her eyes again in sensual bliss. She licked her lips, the sight of which sent little aching arrows to places best not dwelled upon.

"Mmm. Taste this." She turned to him, holding the dessert to his lips. Had his hands not been full of packages, he would have taken the pastry from her, but as it was, he simply opened his mouth and allowed her to feed him.

The sweet bread, delicious, warm, and moist, all but stuck in his throat when Amily reached up and brushed a crumb from his lips before taking another bite from where he'd just bitten. The gestures, so tiny, yet so intimate, knocked the wind from him more effectively than a drunken sailor in a bar brawl.

"Here. Try this one and tell me which is best." She offered the tart, waiting patiently for him to swallow the other bite, which took no small effort. She fed him, there on the streets of Baton Rouge, and grinned up at him, mischievous, sparkling, outrageously alive. The world and everyone around them vanished.

As the sweet filling melted across his tongue, as he watched her lick the tips of her fingers, as she looked up at him with that breathtaking smile, he came to a stunning revelation.

When he looked into her eyes, he saw everything he'd ever wanted in his life.

And it scared him to death.

"Both," he blurted. "I like them both. I don't like one better than the other."

She raised a brow at him, then took another bite.

"You're right. It's hard to choose. Isn't it nice we don't have to?"

He juggled the packages in his arms and struggled to regain his composure. He had to accept what his heart had been telling him for weeks. Not only did he love her, but there would be no getting over her. No avoiding her until the infatuation died. No waking up one day and discovering he no longer cared.

"Hello?" Amily's hand waved in a blur in front of his nose. He blinked and focused on the face that would haunt him for the rest of his life. "Those short naps are great, aren't they?" She offered another bite of pastry, but he quickly shook his head. "Oh, look. There's an apothecary." She popped the last bite of cinnamon roll into her mouth, then dusted off her hands as she headed for the door. "Let me run in here and get those last few things, and then I'll be done with the shopping."

He stood there, laden with parcels, quite possibly looking like the village idiot as he tried to force his brain, or was it his heart, to back up and still believe he could control this love raging inside him. He hadn't even moved when she returned, carrying her own armload of packages.

"All done. How about you? Do you have any shopping to do?"

"No." He shook his head and shifted the packages. Even her strange way of speaking stirred him to distraction.

Thunder rumbled in the distance. He managed to pull his gaze from her and look up at the sky. Huge black clouds rolled in from the Gulf, obliterating all patches of blue to the south.

"We're going to get caught in that if we don't leave now." He nodded toward the sky. Amily followed his gaze.

"I'm ready when you are."

They carried the packages to the chaise parked just around the corner. Scupper snorted and stomped as they loaded the boot with their purchases. Griffin considered forgetting he was a gentleman for once and just letting Amily climb into the carriage by herself, but his breeding won out in the end. When he handed her into the leather-tufted seat, he tried to keep his mind blank to the effect just that mere, impersonal touch had on him.

He climbed into the seat next to her, still ignoring the heat left by her hand, then suddenly, out of the blue, he remembered Florence's embroidery thread.

"Damnation!"

Amily jerked and Scupper shied in his braces. Two fashionably dressed ladies crossing the street turned and glared.

"What?" Amily stared at him, her hands to her heart.

He leapt from the carriage and strode toward the nearest likely looking store.

"I forgot something," he called with disgust, then shoved his way into the mercantile.

He didn't bother to pull the swatch of fabric from his pocket. He simply bought every single color of the dozens of embroidery thread they had.

Damn himself and his schoolboy fantasies. If he'd had more self-control, if he'd forced himself to remain indifferent, he would have remembered to do this small favor for his wife, instead of being struck with the thought on his way out of town.

The mustachioed clerk wrapped the skeins of thread in brown paper while Griffin slammed a sufficient amount of money on the counter. He snatched the package from the little clerk, then marched toward the door.

"Mr. Elliott, sir! Your change!"

Griffin waved away the man's concern, flung himself through the door, then leapt into the carriage and slapped the reins across Scupper's back.

Amily stared at him. He could see her out of the corner of his eye. But he concentrated on maneuvering through the traffic and getting on the road to Shadow Oaks. The road to safety.

"Is it something I said?" she asked as they finally reached the outskirts of town.

Her voice sounded so small, so apologetic, he cursed himself for the blackguard he was.

"No." He dropped his head and took a deep breath before trying for a reassuring look. "It wasn't you. It is just . . ." What could he say? He had no explanation for his behavior. None that he could give her, anyway.

He let the words hang there, and she did not pursue them. They rode in silence for several miles, the rumble of thunder coming closer on their heels. Griffin clucked Scupper to a faster pace. If he had not had to go back to the mercantile, they might have made it to the Randolph plantation and waited out the storm. He doubted now if they would make it before the rain started.

The first drops fell, fat and thick, and then the heavens opened up, drenching them in a matter of seconds. He reined Scupper to a stop, then reached to pull the carriage top up. Just one more thing he would have thought of earlier if his mind had been clear.

"There's an oilcloth beneath the seat," he yelled above the

slap of rain against the leather of the carriage. "Put it over you while I set the top up."

"Oh, no. This feels too good."

He stopped his slippery struggles, and against his better judgment looked back at Amily.

She sat there, her face turned to the rain, smiling as the water poured over her, smoothing the curls from her hair, pooling in her lap. A tiny pulse throbbed in the graceful curve of her neck. She sighed.

"For the first time in weeks, I'm actually cool." She opened her eyes and rolled her head toward him with an enthusiastic grin. "Let's go for a walk."

"A walk?" Surely he hadn't heard right.

"Yeah! What's the matter? Afraid you'll get wet? Come on."

She gathered a handful of dripping skirts and jumped from the chaise. Scupper turned his head and looked at her, his ears pinned back, his eyes half closed against the downpour. Griffin knew exactly how he felt.

"Come on," she called. She strolled toward a nearby pecan orchard, her face still heavenward. He watched as she threw her arms wide and spun in a circle.

He shouldn't do this. He should stay in the carriage, demand she get back in. But then he might be dooming himself to another of these excursions to make it up to her. He paid absolutely no attention to the little voice cheering over the fact that either way, he would spend time with her.

That little voice had nothing to do with his decision to climb out of the carriage and walk with her.

By the time he reached her, she'd gathered her skirts to keep them from dragging in the mud, displaying not only a healthy glimpse of ankle, but an expanse of silk-covered calves as well. She looked up and smiled at him, blinking against the downpour.

She frolicked like a child while the rain battered at them. The thunder and lightning had stopped. There was only the loud, steady hiss of water pelting leaves, grass, mud, rocks . . . a beautiful woman. How could she do something so childish, yet be so sensual?

"Come on! Enjoy it!" She grabbed his arm and pulled him toward a huge puddle. Before he could react, she jumped right in the middle of it, exploding water in all directions.

"You're insane!" He laughed in spite of himself. Her response was to jump again. He dodged the liquid barrage, but she followed him around, her skirts clinging above her knees now as she stomped with every step.

"You little imp!" He rounded on her and stomped back, doubling any damage her puny little feet could do. She squealed and danced away, as if she could possibly get wetter.

"En guarde!" she called, sending another burst of water his way.

They chased each other, dueling in the puddles, laughing together, the world forgotten, until the downpour dwindled to a steady, gentle rain.

They called a truce, still laughing, their breaths short from their battles.

"Oh, my, that was fun." She grinned up at him, then stopped and flicked a glob of mud from his coat sleeve. He returned the favor by removing one from her shoulder. "I guess we should get your poor horse out of the rain. He doesn't look too happy with us."

Scupper still stood with ears back, managing to convey exactly how he felt about all this nonsense. Griffin shrugged and smiled down at her.

"I wager he can be bribed with an extra bucket of oats."

Brianne swiped at a sodden tendril clinging to her face.

After her second try, Griffin reached up to help her with the stubborn strand.

Her skin felt like warm, wet velvet as his fingertips skimmed across her cheek. She lifted her warm, multicolored gaze to his, and his fingers stilled. That look, that unexpected, heart-stopping, agony-filled look slammed into him with the force of a bullet. She dropped her gaze and leaned her head into his hand, ever so slightly, and then he knew without a doubt.

He knew, and the knowledge nearly brought him to his knees.

She loved him, too.

Blood thrummed in his ears and he thought his heart would explode in his chest.

She loved him, too.

He took her face in both hands, forced her to look at him. When she did, his breath froze in his lungs.

Her eyes pierced him with such fierce passion it startled him. She loved him, had loved him all along, and had become an even better actor than he.

His hands hesitated only a moment before he yanked her to him, wrapped her in his arms and pressed her tight against his chest, basking in his newfound knowledge. She melted against him, slid her hands beneath his coat and held on for dear life. He rubbed his lips against her wet hair, buried his fingers in the tangles, as she rained quick, desperate kisses upon his chest, sending his heartbeat into an erratic dance beneath her lips and driving all coherent thought from his mind.

Then finally she looked up.

He cupped her face in the palms of his hands and searched the depths of her eyes while raindrops, warmed by her skin, trickled over his fingers.

He loomed over her, those sensuous lips only inches away, calling to him like a siren of the seas. The distance narrowed, ever so slowly, until their breaths mingled as one and he absorbed her into his soul. With eyes locked, he could all but taste the coming kiss.

They both jumped apart as if lightning had struck them.

What in hell was he doing?

Amily stood there, her back nearly to him, refusing to look at him, wringing her hands and staring at the ground.

He pushed his dripping hair off his forehead, waited for her to look at him, agonized for endless seconds. He prayed for God to give him the strength to simply stand still, to do nothing. If he went to her, he would be lost. He would never have the will to turn back.

The rain splattered around them and he raked his hair back again. What could he say? What could he do?

She'd kept her gaze from his, but then she suddenly turned and faced him, her eyes filled with such misery it ripped at his heart. Misery, but no accusation, no condemnation. And then he knew she didn't blame him for how he felt.

"Amily," he whispered. Her brows came together as she visibly wrestled with the pain. "This didn't happen." He swallowed back the thick knot of emotion threatening to choke him. "It's the only way. The only way."

Her chest heaved with a sob, and then she nodded. Her eyes glistened, but not from the rain.

"I know." Her voice, so thick with tears, raked at his conscience. He wanted to comfort her, pull her into his arms and make everything all right. But he dared not even touch her.

He stood there, his hands clinched at his sides, while she gathered her composure without his help. At long last she drew a deep breath and looked him in the eyes. For a moment he thought she would falter, but she fixed a determined look on her face and nodded toward the carriage.

"We should go now," she said, her voice quivering on the last word.

She walked ahead of him, her back stiff, the playful bounce gone from her step. When they reached the chaise he started to help her in, but she gave her head a quick, violent shake.

"Please," was all she said, and he understood.

Just as Griffin climbed into the seat, a closed carriage rounded the curve. The old black driver pulled his horses to a stop and shouted through the rain, "You in trouble, Mistah Elliott?"

Rebecca Masters peered out from within the warm, dry confines, her gaze taking in every minute detail, no doubt to be shared later over tea with anyone willing to listen.

"No, Frederick. We just got caught in the storm, and I stopped to put the top up."

"Hello, Griffin, Amily," Rebecca called, her tone the slightest bit smug. "You must ride in here, where it's dry. You can tether your horse to the back."

"No," Amily hissed under her breath.

"Thank you, Rebecca, but the damage is done. We will be fine." He unfolded the leather top and fastened it into place. "We appreciate the offer, though."

The woman's gaze bounced back and forth between Griffin and Amily, much too perceptive for Griffin's comfort.

"Suit yourself," she said, then tapped on the ceiling. Frederick tipped his hat, sending a tiny waterfall from the brim, then clucked the horses into a trot.

Amily remained rigid, her gown clinging to her, her arms wrapped around her midsection, as if holding in the pain. The rain picked up just as Scupper lurched into a trot. As they rode toward Shadow Oaks, Griffin knew exactly how a condemned man felt on his journey to Hell.

Chapter 8

BRIANNE SHIVERED IN the rain, thankful for the cold that seeped into her mind and body and kept her numb. She fought to blur the memory of Griffin's arms around her and the rock solid comfort of his chest, the warmth of his breath across her face, with their lips so close she could almost taste his kiss. Her most vivid imagination had never even come close to how his arms would actually feel around her: fiery, content, dangerous, safe. Heavenly.

Both parts of her soul—Amily as well as Brianne—had forgotten about Florence, reveled in his touch, ached for his kiss. Ached for him to do more than kiss her. She had been lost in wonder at the knowledge that he loved her, too. Lost, until, at the same moment, they had remembered themselves.

Pulling away from him had been like pulling away from a life support system. Her very spirit seemed to drain from her body.

She had been in a state of tortured ecstasy all day. Being with him had been heavenly. Acting as if he meant nothing to her had been hell. She'd tried to be friendly, even teasing, so that Griffin, as well as Florence, would be convinced she liked him just fine; liked him well enough to never have to prove it again.

Though that would have been preferable to what faced them now.

Now, every time she sat across the table from him, every time she passed him in the house, every time they had to share a carriage or a church pew or be in the same room together, she would know what it felt like to hold him, to run her hands along the contours of his back, to have him crush her to him and cradle her head gently in the palms of his hands.

She could never look at him again and tell herself she didn't care. She would know he loved her and that she loved him.

And all of this, he would know as well.

After an eternity, the chaise turned up the oak-lined drive, with the trees silhouettes against the growing dark. Neither Brianne nor Griffin had spoken. Brianne hadn't even dared a glance at him, for fear her resolve would fail her if she so much as looked at him. If she could just get into the house, maybe she'd be safe.

"Amily, I think we should talk about this."

She closed her eyes and clenched her teeth against even the precious sound of his voice.

"There's nothing to talk about," she finally managed. "It didn't happen. It couldn't have, because then our lives would be impossible." She finally turned and looked at him, then wished with all her heart she hadn't.

Through those blue, heart-stopping eyes, he hid nothing from her. She saw in them the depth of his love, and she saw his pain and guilt, as well.

"If things were different . . ."

"I know," she said. "And that's enough. That has to be enough."

A muscle in his cheek worked for several long, tense seconds before he swung his gaze forward. She studied his profile in the dark gloom, memorized the clean lines of his jaw, the straight nose, the masculine lips that made a woman think about long, languid kisses. She etched every detail into her memory, because she didn't know when she'd ever have the courage to really look at him again.

Cubby scampered out of the darkness through the rain to meet them, taking Scupper by the bridle and holding him while Griffin leapt from the carriage. Brianne snatched up her skirts and scrambled down before Griffin had a chance to offer help. She would never survive his touch right now.

Gaston appeared at the door with towels and two snifters of brandy on a silver tray.

"Purely medicinal, Mistah Grif," he said, then offered them each a glass.

Brianne swallowed the liqueur in one gulp, and would have swallowed more, given the chance. Numbing her mind one way or another sounded pretty darned appealing right then.

"Thank you, Gaston," she said as she handed back her glass.

"Yes, thank you," Griffin said. "Ever anticipating my needs. Cubby," he called to the boy leading the carriage away, "give Scupper an extra bucket of oats."

"Yessuh," Cubby called back as he disappeared around the corner of the house. Brianne closed her eyes against the pain just that small reminder of the day caused.

"Miz Florence say she want to see you when you gets home." Gaston closed the door and took the towel Griffin had used on his hair. "I'll tell her y'all's gettin' dry clothes on."

The last thing Brianne wanted to do was be grilled on the "success" of their outing. She handed Gaston her towel, gathered up her heavy, still-dripping skirts, then headed for the stairs without once looking at Griffin.

"Is Florence feeling ill, Gaston?"

"No, ma'am. She's feelin' right good."

"Then tell her I'm exhausted," she said as she dragged herself up the steps. "I will see her in the morning."

Griffin pushed open the door to his wife's parlor bedroom, a smile fixed on his face, his thoughts held in rigid control. She sat up in the rosewood half-tester amongst a half dozen satin pillows, a brilliant smile lighting her eyes at the sight of him, giving her the look of a golden-haired angel.

"I'm so glad you're back." She stretched upward to meet his kiss. "I worried when the storm started. Did you take some of Esther's tonic to ward off a chill?"

Griffin bent over her and brushed his lips against her cheek. "Not even to ward off a water moccasin bite." The cook's elixir had a reputation for its nastiness, with conjecture that she mixed raw sewage with grain alcohol for its particularly memorable flavor. He wouldn't take it to ward off snakebite, but if it would banish thoughts of Amily he would down an entire bottle.

Florence grinned, then leaned forward with a look of anticipation. "Well?"

He knew what she waited for, and he'd spent the past hour in his room deciding what to tell her.

"Florence." He pulled a chair to the bed, sank into it, then took his wife's hand. "I . . . I am not exactly certain how to phrase this." She tilted her head, a faint line etched in her brow. He stopped her question with an upraised hand. "Sometimes two people, against all their best intentions . . ." He almost reconsidered when she gave her head a tiny shake of denial. Almost. "Sometimes, even though they try, they are not compatible."

"But, Griffin, darling—"

"Amily and I are not compatible, Flo, and all your wishing to the contrary will not change that." The lie tasted as bitter on his tongue as Esther's tonic.

"But how can you not simply adore her? She is everything sweet and good and—"

"Yes, she is a good person, and I am indebted to her for all she has done for you." He thought his heart would explode in his chest. "I do not dislike her. I simply do not enjoy her company for extended periods of time. It is a matter of personalities." If lies were fatal, his body would be dust.

"But—"

"Please, Flo. I tried. She will always be welcome in our home. As I said, I do not dislike her. But please do not ask me to endure daylong outings with her again."

He would have preferred a slap in the face to Florence's look of disappointment.

"Very well," she finally murmured, her voice small, dejected.

He kept his mind blank to how her voice made him feel; blank to the guilt gnawing away inside him; blank to the intense, exquisite explosion of passion Amily had set off, and which still rippled through his blood. He took a deep, settling breath.

"Here." He handed her the brown, string-wrapped parcel he had been dangling from his fingers. "I almost forgot."

She opened the damp, fat package, then laughed at the rainbow of colors that spilled out.

"My heavens, did you buy out the store? Surely all these colors aren't in that fabric swatch."

"I just"—*was lusting after your cousin*—"thought you could use them all eventually."

"Thank you, darling. You are ever thoughtful." She took his hand and pulled him forward to place a kiss on his cheek. She smiled up at him. "I am so very blessed."

Her sweet words of praise wrapped around his throat and squeezed. He lifted her hand and kissed her knuckles, then backed toward the door.

"As am I, Flo." He forced the words past his constricted throat. "If you'll excuse me, perhaps I will take a dose of Esther's tonic after all, for prevention." He nearly bumped into Della bringing in a pot of hot chocolate. He used the opportunity to escape, then stormed back out into the rain, to cool his blood, to wash away his guilt, to try to find a way to once again breathe with a clear conscience.

Brianne sat on the veranda, across the small wicker table from Florence, pretending to enjoy the cool aftermath of the previous day's storm. Shafts of morning sunlight filtered through the dozens of live oaks while the scent of sweet olive from the gardens perfumed the breeze around them. Camellias dripped petals in shades of pink and white, showering the ground with a new layer every time a bird took flight from the branches.

If only her thoughts were as peaceful as the setting.

Surprisingly, Florence had not played Twenty Questions about the trip to town with Griffin. She had merely expressed her dismay at their getting caught in the rain, then chatted about inconsequential things. She seemed a bit distracted, but not enough for Brianne to believe that Florence had somehow picked up on the sexual energy humming between Griffin and herself.

They had all but ignored each other when he'd marched across the veranda on his way to meet with the overseer. But every nerve in Brianne's—Amily's—body had reached out for him.

No, Florence was not acting like a woman who sensed her husband and her cousin were in love with each other.

"Are you feeling all right?" Brianne finally asked after a long, uncomfortable silence between them. "You don't seem yourself."

Florence glanced up, continuing to stir the tea she'd been stirring for a good two minutes.

"Oh, my, I'm fine. I am convinced that the pain I suffered that day was nothing more than a stitch from running."

Brianne had believed that all along. But putting her patient to bed had given Flo some peace of mind, and Brianne would have had the bedroom moved downstairs in a month or so, anyway, as a precaution.

"You seem awfully preoccupied. Are you sure there's nothing wrong?"

Florence finally took a sip of her tea, then set the cup back on the saucer.

"I suppose I am a little put out with myself. I should never have forced you and Griffin to go into town together."

A hot wave of shock and guilt swept over Brianne. Had Florence sensed something between them after all? How well could she read Griffin?

"You didn't really force us," Brianne insisted. "But I really do think you've misread the situation. Griffin and I like each other just fine."

"Yes." Florence went back to stirring her tea. "Griffin said as much last night. I feel like such a ninny."

So, Griffin had told Florence *something* last night. Whatever it was, he must have convinced her. Florence looked up, her soft eyes smiling, apologetic, rather than accusing. Brianne had never felt so rotten in her life.

The sound of a carriage rolling down the drive drew their attention. Brianne moaned out loud at the sight of Rebecca Masters squinting out at them from within the vehicle.

The rigid woman stepped from the carriage with the help of her driver, Frederick, then swept up the wide steps to Shadow Oaks as if she owned the place.

"Florence, dear, you're looking well." She turned and let her gaze flick toward Brianne. "Hello, Amily."

Without waiting for an invitation, Rebecca perched on one of the wicker chairs and made herself at home. Brianne couldn't stay around the woman long without fear of losing her breakfast. She scraped her chair back and rose.

"If you'll excuse me, I'll leave you two to visit. Mum Sal is dipping candles and I told her I'd help." She gave Florence a quick kiss on the cheek. "You know how finicky she is with her candles."

"Oh, yes." Florence looked as if she'd like to go with her. "I'm surprised she lets anyone help."

Brianne wasted no time in escaping the veranda and the heavy rose scent Rebecca wore. Once out of sight, she walked past the overseer's office and the smokehouse before finding Mum Sal in the workshed. The relatively cool air outside had not found its way into the building, where fires kept the tallow and beeswax hot. Mum Sal and her daughter, Tandy, dipped dozens of wicks into different candle molds, making sure to keep the beeswax separate from the tallow.

"There yo is, chile," Mum Sal rasped with her gravelly voice. She worked away, seemingly oblivious to the heat. "Tandy, fetch Miz Amily that row of beeswax we done started. You mind doin' the beeswax, Miz Amily?"

"No, that's fine." Brianne shook her head, already feeling the dampness of perspiration from the hot room.

She took the rod that had a dozen wax-coated wicks dangling from it, then, keeping the rod horizontal, lowered the wicks into the molds of hot wax. She watched Mum Sal and Tandy work, and grasped nuances from Amily on how to dip the tapers. Before long she had a rhythm going as though she'd made candles all her life.

Taking over for Florence had given Brianne a whole new respect for the plantation mistress. Granted, she had spent hours on end with Florence, but she'd also had to oversee and help with the washing, the menu planning with Esther, mixing the brass polish according to Florence's recipe, as well as mixing the lotions from the ingredients she'd bought in town. Monday she'd been called to the servants' quarters to "doctor" one of the children who'd turned out to have chicken pox. Now, of course, there was a veritable outbreak among the little ones, and Brianne had set up a nursery to keep them cool and out of the sunlight. She'd helped make soap—not one of her favorite jobs—and been on call to unlock the larder or the tea caddie whenever something was needed out of either.

With a house the size of Shadow Oaks, the maintenance and upkeep was a never-ending job, especially without air conditioning to filter out the humidity. Florence had Brianne checking all sixteen rooms for signs of mold and mildew, insects, and any other problems the humidity might cause. She'd done more physical and mental labor in the past two days than she'd done in years combined in the future. And she only did a fraction of what Florence was accustomed to doing every day.

No wonder Florence had never been able to completely put herself to bed with the other pregnancies. So much for the myth of the pampered plantation wife.

A steady trickle of sweat developed at Brianne's temples, and her gown clung to her like wet tissue paper as she finished another batch of candles. She hung up the rod, then dragged the back of her arm across her forehead to rake a damp curl out of her eyes. What she wouldn't give for a cool shower and a year's supply of Arrid Extra-Dry.

"Chile, you needs to get you some fresh air. You looks like a body done throwed a bucket o' water at you."

Brianne smiled as she blinked away a stinging drop of sweat.

"I just want to finish. We're almost through."

Mum Sal waddled over and shooed her toward the door.

"Me and Tandy can finish. Won't take us no time. 'Sides, a lady ain't got no business sweatin' like a field hand. You go on now and freshen up."

Brianne started to protest, but then she thought perhaps Mum Sal and Tandy weren't entirely comfortable around her. They hadn't exactly chattered away since she'd started helping.

"Well, if you're sure."

The big, lovable servant took the new rod from Brianne.

"Won't take us no time t'all."

Brianne thanked them both and stepped through the open door with a backward glance of gratitude.

The cool air washed over her in a refreshing, cleansing wave. She took a deep breath and strolled toward the house, but the sight of Rebecca Masters's carriage still sitting in front of the stables had her turning toward the gardens.

For the first time since waking in 1832, she knew the welcome feeling of solitude. She enjoyed the aloneness as she meandered along the paths that wound through profusions of camellias, tea olives, azaleas, forsythias, crepe myrtle, their scents a delicious potpourri that swirled in the air. A fountain trickled in the center of a ring of azaleas, and a white lattice gazebo lent a shady haven to sit and enjoy the view. Brianne sank onto one of its benches and lifted her face to the breeze.

Within a manicured hedge on the other side of the gazebo lay a reflecting pond, its dark, glassy surface mirroring the blue sky and an occasional white fluffy cloud, as well as a matching gazebo across the pond.

The white-columned house and a stretch of the river was visible from where she sat, and as she looked at it, she truly felt, for the first time, as if she were dreaming—an impossible bystander, witness to a bygone life. Though the future would bring wonderful things, the thought of the loss of this home in the mid–twentieth century brought tears to her eyes. All the time she'd gone to the ruins as a child and a teenager, she'd never given a thought to the true home and lives of the people it sheltered. Had the family who had been living there when it burned been descendants of Griffin and Florence? But how could they have been, if Florence had died, and then Griffin and Amily had died shortly before their marriage?

Brianne rose and wandered on through the garden, putting those thoughts behind her, working her way back toward the house. Perhaps she should rescue Florence from her nightmare visitor.

Just as she drew near the overseer's office, Griffin stepped through the door with a determined stride, his planter's hat pulled low over his eyes. He marched down the steps and onto the path, looking up just in time to avoid colliding with Brianne.

"Oh, I beg your . . ." He grabbed her arms to steady her, then pulled them back as though he had touched fire. "Amily." His voice caressed her. A momentary flicker of want flashed in his eyes before he masked it.

Brianne wanted to turn and run, and she might have if Jake Dunstan, the overseer, hadn't stepped out of his office.

She nodded to Jake. Griffin turned and glanced at the man, tipped the brim of his hat, then somehow, without touching her, guided Brianne on down the path toward the house. He clamped his hands behind his back, his gaze locked on the tiny pebbles and shells that cut a walkway through the gardens, no doubt trying to look normal for Jake's benefit.

"Enjoying the morning?" he asked. Twenty-four hours earlier, the quiet question would have seemed natural, but now it sounded hollow, forced.

"Yes," she managed past the constriction in her throat. And then, "I made candles." The inane comment hung there between them, words for the sake of filling in the uncomfortable silence.

They walked on, his boots making louder crunches on the path than her slippered feet. How companionable the sound might have been if . . .

"What about Florence?" Without knowing she was going to, Brianne blurted the question that had been nagging at her since yesterday. She wished she could call it back when Griffin stopped and looked down at her.

"What about her?"

No sense in turning back now.

"Do you love her?"

He took a deep breath and scanned the sky for a moment.

"Of course, I love her. As a friend." He looked down at Brianne, his eyes begging for understanding. "I would never do anything to hurt her."

Brianne understood completely.

"Neither would I," she said, relieved by his honor, yet selfishly despairing at what might never be. "I would never want to see her hurt."

A colorful little finch flitted from branch to branch above them, carefree and happy. When Brianne continued strolling, Griffin fell in beside her.

"Amily, I'm sorry. I never meant for you to know. I never meant to do anything to make you ill at ease here."

She bit the inside of her cheek to stem the stinging in her eyes.

"It's nobody's fault, Griffin. You certainly can't blame yourself." She looked up at him, relished the way her heart sped up, the way butterflies took flight beneath her ribs. "Sooner or later, we both would have sensed it. We may have denied it, but we would have known."

Florence fought to keep her face impassive while Rebecca Masters warmed to her subject. Another sharp twinge flared in her side, then gradually subsided.

"Mind you now, Florence, dear, I am not one to carry tales, but you mark my words. You'll do well to have a care where your cousin and your husband are concerned. It would not be the first time a husband was led astray under his own roof, and I daresay it shan't be the last. Heavens, I saw them with my own eyes, wet as drowned kittens and not looking at all like they minded. Why, they declined a nice, dry ride in my carriage. Now, I ask you, what two right-minded people would decline such a ride?"

"Two people who were already wet and considerately chose not to ruin your upholstery?" Florence offered. "Two people who did not have far left to travel?" *Two people who did not want to spend even a quarter hour in an enclosed carriage with you?* "Really, Rebecca, I resent your coming here and making such slanderous statements about Griffin and Amily. Their characters are beyond reproach. I have absolute faith and trust in them, and I would ask you to refrain from making further such comments about my family, to me or to anyone."

"Well!" Rebecca snapped her bamboo fan shut and rose from her chair as if she were the queen of England. "I had only your best interests at heart, but if you choose to be blind to the possible circumstances, then you may rest assured that I shall never bring up the topic again."

"A gesture," Florence said, "that I will greatly appreciate."

"Well, I never!" Rebecca flounced to the edge of the veranda. "Frederick, bring the carriage around!"

Florence sighed. "I appreciate your visit, as well as your concern, but your worries are unfounded. I am sorry if my fatigue made me cross."

Rebecca *hrmph*ed but settled a somewhat placated expression upon her face.

"I'd best be on my way, at any rate. I would not want to wear out my welcome."

She waited, obviously expecting Florence to assure her of that impossibility, but purgatory would see snow fall before Florence would utter such a statement.

With a deep intake of breath, Rebecca lifted her chin, spun on her heel, then marched to the carriage at the steps. She waited, her nose in the air, until Frederick climbed down and helped her into the conveyance.

Not until they rolled down the drive did Florence even begin to unclench her fists buried in the folds of her skirts. If that nosy, interfering woman only knew how close she was to the truth, all their lives would suffer.

Chapter 9

AMILY ROUNDED THE corner of the veranda just as Rebecca's carriage disappeared down the road. Florence could tell from the trace of agony in her eyes that her cousin had just left Griffin. No doubt he wore that same haunted expression as well.

Oddly, Florence felt no jealousy from the knowledge that her husband and cousin cared deeply for each other.

She loved her husband, but with the love of a contented friend, not as the passionate lover he should have had. She had never been able to overcome the guilt that plagued her for not feeling that fiery want.

Theirs had been a marriage to join two families, two businesses, two properties, as were so many other marriages in the South. The dynasty of the plantation family was all-important, and she and Griffin had been raised from childhood with the knowledge that they were expected to marry. She often wondered, if she had wed someone less familiar, would she have felt that mysterious passion she'd heard others whisper about? Would she have been as embarrassed with the physical aspects of marriage?

She had tried to make up for the absence of that passion in other ways. She took every opportunity to show her admiration for him as a man. She ran his home with total efficiency. She tried desperately to have his child, as much for an heir for him as for the babe she so longed for.

"Oh, dear. Did I miss saying goodbye to Rebecca? What a shame." Amily sank to the chair Rebecca had vacated, her teasing sarcasm wiping the last of the suffering from her eyes.

Florence smiled, amazed that she had been so naïve, so blind, until last night.

She had truly believed Griffin and Amily were not fond of each other. But she knew Griffin almost as well as she knew herself, and the moment he'd walked into her room the night before, she'd known something was wrong. His protestations that he cared well enough for her cousin would have been convincing to a person less perceptive. But Florence, though biddable as she was raised to be, was nobody's fool. She knew immediately that something had happened between Griffin and Amily. Not until this morning, while sharing breakfast with her cousin, was Florence certain that the two had fallen in love with each other, and had fallen against their will.

Looking back, she knew how they must have fought their feelings. Neither had given a hint. No wonder they had each rejected the idea of a daylong outing. Florence's good intentions had forced them into a situation that, she now had no doubt, must have been torture for them both.

How very calm she was, sitting here, contemplating how her husband and cousin were in love. Was she an aberration of nature, not to be eaten alive with jealousy?

Perhaps such calm surrounded her because she knew, as

well as she knew they were in love, that neither would ever betray her. All the Rebeccas in the world, and their gossipy little minds, would not convince her otherwise. They would not betray her, even if that very action would make all their lives simpler: She would no longer have had to feel guilt at not being the woman Griffin should have married. But she couldn't ask them to ignore their morals simply so she could avoid sleeping with her husband.

"Hello? Earth to Florence."

She blinked and drew her attention away from such scandalous thoughts and back to Amily. What had she said? *Earth to Florence?* Whatever did that mean? Just one more odd bit of behavior Florence had noticed in Amily since the lightning had struck her. Odd speech, a casual attitude, a seemingly innocent disregard for many of the conventions. Amily had always been so full of life that she had exhausted Florence, but now she was even more vibrant—the sort of woman Griffin should have married. Just as Florence should have married a quiet, reserved man who preferred riding in a dry carriage rather than in the rain.

"Is something wrong? Are you feeling bad?" Amily's voice cut into her thoughts again.

"Oh, no." She brought her gaze up to meet Amily's worried frown. "Merely woolgathering." She shifted in her seat to relieve the slight pinch in her side. When the pain didn't subside, she massaged the area with her fingertips.

"Something *is* wrong!" Amily jumped from her seat and knelt by her side.

"No. Truly, it is nothing. Just a little pinch down low every now and then. I will be fine."

"How long has it been hurting?"

"It just now started. No doubt a bit of indigestion brought on by having to listen to Rebecca. The woman's disposition is enough to spoil food."

Amily sank back on her heels. "I can't argue with you there." Her eyes narrowed as she studied the area Florence rubbed. "Is that the same side that hurt before."

"Yes, but I'm certain the other was merely a stitch from running. Truly, this is nothing. It's not at all similar to the problems I've had with the other babies."

Amily remained thoughtful, so when the twinge subsided, Florence tried to reassure her again.

"If it will soothe your worries, I shall take to my bed again. I had hoped to relieve you of some of the work."

"You'll do no such thing." Amily settled herself back into the chair. "I'm doing just fine, and the house will survive until we get this baby into the world. I don't think you need to go back to bed, but I do want you to take it easy. And I want to know about any more twinges."

"Yes, Doctor," Florence teased. She poured them each a cup of tea, then studied Amily while they chatted. Distraction shadowed her cousin's eyes. Florence couldn't help wondering which held Amily's thoughts most: concern for the baby, or guilt over Griffin.

Three days passed. Three hellish days of Brianne worrying about Florence, feeling guilty about Griffin, trying to avoid him without raising questions. She suffered through meals with him, dying to look at him, forcing herself not to. At least Florence must have been satisfied that they didn't hate each other, since she hadn't brought the subject up again. Brianne could only assume that she and Griffin were hiding their feelings well. A surprising feat, considering how the turmoil swirled in her chest every waking moment. She found no relief in sleep, either. Her nights were filled with dreams of Griffin, of a perfect life, of his smiling eyes melting her heart, of his soft, sure caress. She would wake, expecting to roll over and find him next to her, then she would suffer the emptiness of realizing it was just a dream.

She sat up and fluffed her pillow, unable to sleep this night. Part of her worried about the twinges Florence continued to experience. Were they becoming more frequent? Stronger? Would Florence tell her if they were, or would she suffer in silence, not wanting to worry anyone? She could only pray they weren't the beginnings of something far worse. Part of her refused sleep, simply because she didn't want to wake, yet again, with empty arms and an empty heart.

The ormolu clock on the mantel softly chimed three o'clock. When a welcome gust of breeze swept through the open window, Brianne tossed aside the pillow and headed for the veranda.

She'd gotten into the habit of sleeping in a cotton chemise rather than Amily's prim and proper nightgowns. The chemise was much cooler; more like the T-shirts she had worn in the future.

She stepped through the window that opened floor to ceiling, then lifted her face to the cool night air. The heavenly, river-scented breeze enveloped her, and she sank into a wicker chair and stared out at the sky glittering with silver-white stars. She sat there, trying to focus on the peaceful sight of moonlight shining through the branches of the live oaks.

She didn't know how long she'd sat there before she realized she wasn't alone—when his hands came to rest on her shoulders. Her heart drummed, then rose in her throat when his fingers gently massaged her skin. Tears stung her eyes and she fought the urge to grasp his hands, to turn and fly into his arms. Instead, she sat there, swallowing back the ache, trying to breathe evenly.

"I had to touch you." His voice came to her, low, tortured. "I will do no more than this, but I had to touch you."

Her breath left her lungs, shallow, trembling, as a single hot tear spilled over her lashes. It took every ounce of willpower she would ever know to keep from rising from that chair and making her dreams come true. Instead, she settled for rubbing her cheek against the back of his hand, brushing her lips once across his knuckles. Anything more and she would be doomed.

True to his word, he took his touch no further. He stood behind her, his warmth and the scent that was his alone curling around her. A tiny part of her begged for him to do more.

Suddenly, tinglingly, she was aware of the expanse of legs showing from beneath her skimpy chemise, the thin straps at her shoulders held up by a ribbon.

She could feel his racing pulse through his fingertips, feel the rigid resolve in his hands to move no further.

"I . . . I should have on a robe," she stammered.

He said nothing. Brianne pictured him standing there, his eyes closed, fighting the natural urges battering at him. She knew then what had to be done.

"We can't keep doing this, Griffin. Sooner or later we'll give in." His fingers stopped moving against her shoulders. "God help me, it's all I can do not to give in now. We're only human. We'll never forgive ourselves if we hurt Florence." She took his hand, cupped his palm to her cheek, then pulled him around to face her. He stood there, his feet bare, his trousers hugging his waist, the muscles in his bare chest outlined by shadows from the moon.

"As soon as Florence has the baby, I'm leaving."

Griffin jerked his hand away, plowed his fingers through his hair.

"You have nowhere to go," he argued. "No other relatives."

"I'll . . . I'll be a midwife."

He dropped to one knee and took her hand in his. "I will conquer this, Amily. I will never touch you again. I cannot drive you from your home because I have no rein on my emotions. I . . . I will do whatever it takes to stop—"

"Griffin." She put her finger to his lips and kept it there until he quieted. "You know in your heart that neither of us can stop this. Look at us." She gestured to her chemise and his bare chest. "I knew you might find me like this, but I didn't care. You had a chance to put on a shirt before you came up behind me, but you didn't. We're *begging* for it to happen, Griffin, subconsciously, consciously. You know as well as I that we couldn't deny each other forever."

"You don't know that. We'll keep our distance."

As Brianne held his gaze with hers, she loosened a ribbon and shrugged the chemise off one shoulder. His eyes followed her movement, searing a path to her shoulder and down. He lifted his hand, mesmerized.

"See?" she whispered.

He snapped his gaze back to hers, then stood and turned away, leaning his weight on the iron railing. An owl hooted in the distance.

"You're right," he finally said, his voice rough, choked.

She went to him then, unable to deny herself one last touch. She slid her arms around his waist and laid her head against his bare, warm back. He stiffened, then leaned into her, pulling her hands to his chest before turning to face her. With a painfully gentle touch, he lifted her chin, cupped the back of her head in his hand.

"Miz Amily!"

They jumped apart as Mum Sal pounded on Brianne's bedroom door.

"Wake up, Miz Amily. Miz Florence is bad."

Brianne ran to open the door, snatching up a wrapper on her way.

"What's wrong?"

Mum Sal turned and hurried down the hall.

"She hurtin' bad. Sharp pains in her side. Oh, lawdy, don't let this poor girl lose another chile."

Griffin burst through his door, yanking on a shirt just as Brianne started down the stairs. They raced in silence to the parlor bedroom.

Florence lay on the bed, her face as colorless as the sheets. Pain and fear etched deep lines at her mouth.

"Where does it hurt? Show me exactly where it hurts." Brianne felt Florence's forehead, wanting to curse when Florence touched her right side . . . the same side as all the other pains. Her forehead felt warm enough for a low-grade fever.

"Okay, Flo, listen to me. Are the pains sharp or are they dull and constant?"

"Sha—" Florence gasped and curled forward, holding her side, her breath caught in her throat. She squeezed her eyes shut as she fought off the pain, the tendons in her neck standing out like tightly drawn cords. She panted quick, shallow breaths, then turned her face to the pillow and whimpered.

Brianne wanted to scream. It couldn't be. Please, God, don't let it be.

"Griffin." She found him standing at the foot of the bed, his face blanched, his knuckles white from gripping the post. "Get Dr. Myers. Fast!"

He took one last look at Florence, then ran.

"Mum Sal, I need to check her for bleeding. Help me get her nightgown up. Gently."

Florence clenched the pillow for several more seconds,

then slowly lay back, her face white, damp curls clinging to her skin. She'd fainted.

They lifted her voluminous bedclothes and immediately saw patches of dark red. Mum Sal's mournful gaze came up to meet Brianne's.

"No," Brianne told herself, then gently took Florence's wrist and found her pulse. Just as she feared. The pulse was fast and weak.

"Damn."

Brianne pushed her hair out of her face, then stood by helplessly as Florence roused and battled through the pain.

"Mum Sal, how far is the doctor?" Maybe if he got there in time, he could operate. Hell, did they even do surgery back then? Would he even know what was happening to Florence? Could Brianne convince him?

"He just live down the road. Mistah Grif'll ride hell-bent and be back here in no time. He done it too many times before." Mum Sal turned her gaze back to Florence, tears rolling down her wrinkled cheeks.

"Am-Amily." Florence gasped. "What is happening? It wasn't like this the other times."

Brianne licked her dry lips and searched her mind for something to say.

"I'm not sure. I need to check your abdomen, Florence. I'll try not to hurt you. Do you think I could touch your stomach?"

Florence let her head fall back against the pillow and visibly braced herself.

"Go ahead," she rasped.

Brianne lifted the gown even higher and folded it over Florence's chest. She knew without touching her that the news was bad. Flo's abdomen, which shouldn't have started to show yet, was distended and hard beneath Brianne's fingers.

Brianne blinked back tears and gently pulled Florence's gown down.

"Do we have any laudanum in the house?" she asked Mum Sal, barely managing to get the words past the lump in her throat.

The old woman nodded. "In the larder. You gots the keys."

Brianne rubbed the muscles at the back of her neck.

"Send someone to get it. The keys are on the vanity table in my room."

When Mum Sal left, Brianne took Florence's hand. "Florence?" she whispered. Florence turned her head and opened her eyes a slit, obviously struggling to remain conscious. Not a good sign. "We've sent for the doctor, and Mum Sal is getting some laudanum. Maybe it will help."

"This . . . is different," Florence managed with a thready voice. "Not . . . labor."

Brianne clenched her teeth and narrowed her eyes against the tears.

"No. It's not labor."

Florence squeezed her hand. "What?"

Brianne looked heavenward, wanting to scream that this wasn't fair. She couldn't tell Florence—this woman she had come to love as much as Amily loved her—that she would die.

Mum Sal returned with the laudanum before Brianne had to lie. Brianne measured some into a glass and then mixed it with water. The baby was past harming with the drug, and so was Florence.

Brianne held Florence's head while she tilted the glass to her lips.

"Drink it all. I know it's nasty, but it will help the pain."

Florence sipped at the milky liquid, then looked up as

Brianne lowered her head back to the pillow. "Shoulder . . . hurts."

A wave of defeat crashed over Brianne at those two words.

"Your right shoulder?"

Florence nodded. Brianne prayed for Griffin to get back with the doctor.

"What's wrong with her, Miz Amily? She ain't never been like this before. She carried the other babies longer. She ain't never looked so bad."

Brianne held Florence's hand as the laudanum relaxed her into sleep.

"This one's not like the others, Mum Sal." She swallowed back tears. "I might have stopped the others."

Footsteps pounded down the hallway moments before Griffin burst through the door. His gaze went immediately to the pale face on the bed.

"He wasn't there. I've sent men out to look for him." Griffin took one halting step into the room. "How is she?"

Brianne smoothed Florence's limp hand against the sheet, then rose and guided Griffin into the hall. Not until she closed the door behind her and moved into the library did she speak.

"She had an ectopic pregnancy, Griffin. She—"

"A what?" He backed away from her, as if he could back away from the bad news.

"Ectopic. That means the baby wasn't in her uterus . . . her womb. It was in the tube leading to the womb."

Griffin looked past her, toward the bedroom.

"She's lost the baby? But she'll be fine."

Brianne grabbed his arm and made him look at her.

"Listen to what I have to say, Griffin. You have to stay calm, for her sake." She waited until he focused on her, until she knew he would hear everything. "The baby is gone. And the tube it was in has ruptured. She's bleeding inside. There's nothing I can do to stop it. I'm not even sure the doctor could have stopped it." Griffin stared at her and shook his head, denying what she said.

"She's going to be fine. Just like all the other times. She simply needs her rest—"

"This isn't like the other times." She held his gaze, willing him not to make her say this more than once. "She's going to die, Griffin."

He jerked away from her, shaking his head, then shouldered past her and strode to the bedroom. She caught up with him just as he sank to his knees by the bed.

"Florence. Oh, Florence," he groaned. He took her hand in his, smoothed a stray tendril from her forehead. "I've done this to you, Flo. I should never have done this to you." His voice caught and he lowered his cheek to her hand.

Her eyes fluttered open and she rolled her head around to look at her husband.

"Not . . . your fault," she managed. He looked up at her. "Do not . . . blame . . . yourself."

"If I had listened to the doctors. If only I hadn't—"

"No," she whispered. "You were . . . good . . . to me. A good . . . husband."

Her eyes closed and Griffin swung around to Brianne.

"Is she . . ."

Brianne moved to Florence's side and felt for a pulse. She found one, though weak and rapid.

"Not yet," she answered through her tears.

They sat vigil for what seemed like hours. Brianne finally persuaded Griffin to rise from his knees and sit in a chair, but he refused to release Florence's hand. Just as dawn turned the live oaks outside the window into inky black silhouettes, the doctor arrived. Brianne met him in the hall and told him of Florence's condition, leaving out as much as she could to avoid questions about her knowledge. After his examination, the doctor turned to Griffin and placed his hand on his shoulder.

"I am sorry, son, Miss Amily is correct. I have seen this before."

Brianne knew the only reason Griffin didn't bellow his rage at the doctor was for Florence's sake. He visibly fought to stay calm.

"Are there no doctors who specialize in women's problems? We will call one of them in. We will—"

"Griffin." Florence had rallied, opening her eyes, appearing stronger. "I see them, Griffin. They've come to meet me."

Griffin glanced at Brianne and then the doctor.

"Who do you see, darling?"

"Our babies, Griffin. I see all of our little ones. Even this one." Her hand moved to cover her stomach. "He is waiting for me. He and his brothers and sisters. He has three brothers, Griffin. You would have had four sons."

Griffin rubbed his eyes and drew in a deep breath.

"Flo, don't—"

"They are all beautiful. All seven of them. We made babies with beautiful souls, Griffin. I finally have my babies with me."

He stared at the ceiling, blinking hard, shaking his head.

Florence turned and looked at him then, her eyes focused, her gaze lucid. She reached for Brianne's hand and placed it in Griffin's.

"Take care of each other," she said, the sound of peace in her voice. "Love each other. You have my blessing." She held their hands together, a serene, loving smile on her lips, then she squeezed one last time before her hand went limp.

Chapter 10

THE SUN WASHED a cloudless sky to powder blue. Birds chirped in the trees, a butterfly alighted on a blue hydrangea bush, insects droned. Just the sort of day Florence would have loved.

Griffin stood at his wife's graveside, numb, guilt-ridden, filled with self-loathing.

He would never forgive himself for not being the husband she'd needed. She had asked for so little, given him everything, yet he had repaid her by falling in love with her cousin.

And, God help him, he still loved Amily more than life itself. And he was driving her away from him with every passing day.

Had Florence known of his and Amily's love? Had her last words been to protect and ensure a home for her cousin, or to truly bless their union? It would be just like her to forgive him for all that he had not been, all that he'd given to someone else, and then to give her blessing as well. He did not deserve one woman so wonderful, let alone two.

The guilt ate at him like a rat gnawing its way through wood. He couldn't sleep. He couldn't eat. He most certainly couldn't spend even a moment in Amily's presence. And that guilt ate at him, too. He saw the hurt in her eyes. He knew she was suffering as much as he, grieving for a loved one, guilt-stricken at loving him.

He tortured himself with the memory that, while his wife lay bleeding to death because he'd gotten her with child, he'd held another woman in his arms, aching to make love to her, preparing to kiss her. Granted, it was meant to be a goodbye kiss, but he feared that once he'd tasted Amily, he would have been doomed to seek more, would have craved her as an opium eater craves his drug. And he would have done that under his wife's roof.

He knelt beside the fresh mound of dirt, then gently placed the armful of flowers atop the stark, brown earth.

"I'm sorry, Flo. I'm so sorry."

His eyes burned with tears he hadn't shed since he was a boy. He pressed the heels of his hands to his eyes, breathing deeply, willing himself to get control.

Their lives together played in his mind: how they'd frolicked as children, ignored each other as they had gotten older, found renewed interest as a young man and woman. They had married without questioning why. It simply was expected. Griffin had been content enough, if not altogether happy. Florence had always seemed happy with her lot, except when he took her to his bed. The more he'd tried to please her, to give her pleasure, the more embarrassed she had become. He'd consoled himself with the knowledge that other men's wives reacted the same. Other men's wives except Alec's.

He'd even suffered guilt at how he had grown to envy his best friend. The idiot had married a woman he'd never met, thought she was someone else entirely, then fell madly, hopelessly in love with his own wife. Griffin had never thought that kind of love possible, until he went to Maine, to console Alec over the loss of his wife, prepared for a funeral, and ended up best man again at their wedding. He had stood there and wished himself that happy. He had betrayed Florence by wishing for a woman who could make him as happy as Alec. God had seen fit to send him that woman, then insured that he could never have her without the face of his wife haunting him forever.

A hand alighted on his shoulder, as hesitant and gentle as a butterfly, bringing him back to the present.

He hadn't heard her approach, but he would never fail to know her touch, or the scent that drifted on the breeze. He wanted to hold her, let her slide her arms around him and comfort him. He needed her comfort, and yet it was the last thing he would allow.

Her hand dropped away when he rose. He turned and looked at her, he allowed himself that much. She stood there, her red-rimmed eyes pleading with him, a bouquet of flowers clutched to her breast. He raised his hand to wipe away her tears but stopped himself before he touched her. He couldn't touch her. Not yet.

"Griffin," she said, her voice torn, ragged.

"I can't." He turned away, forcing himself to leave her standing there, for both their sakes.

Saints, but he needed to get away, to escape the memories, the guilt. He longed to feel the swell of a ship's deck beneath his feet, feel the sea air sweep across his face. He hadn't been on one of his ships in months. When the slave trafficking had slowed down off the Louisiana coast, he had taken a break from intercepting slavers and freeing the poor devils imprisoned on them.

Just the thought of the sea lifted him, drew his spirits out of the miasma of despair in which he'd been suffocating.

He would go. He would take the *Sea Gypsy,* since he'd sent the *Rising Star* to Alec, with a message of Florence's death. If he did nothing more than sail in circles for a week, the trip would give him time to think, to decide what to do about Amily.

With the thought of her, he turned and glanced behind him. The only sign that she'd even been there was the added splash of color from the flowers she'd left behind. The sight left him feeling guiltier than ever.

Griffin paced the length of the Persian rug while Amily sat on the edge of the parlor chair. She stared up at him with an impassive face, only a tiny hint of wariness and dread flickered in her eyes. And why shouldn't it? He'd sought her out—something he'd never done except on that horrible night of Florence's death—and now he couldn't seem to say the words he needed to tell her he was leaving.

"What is it, Griffin?" she asked, her voice dull, tired, lifeless. And he knew he was responsible for that tone.

"I am taking the *Sea Gypsy* out on a run. I've sent Lucas to ready the crew. I will be leaving tonight." She simply stared at him. "I . . . I thought you should know."

The only movement on her face was the slight lift of one perfectly arched brow.

"The *Sea Gypsy.* On a run. How long will you be gone?" She asked the question with no more emotion than if they'd been talking about a stroll in the gardens. But then what the hell did he want? For her to cry and swoon and beg for him to stay? He shoved his fingers through a handful of hair.

"A few weeks. Maybe more. It's hard to say."

She continued to stare, the wariness and dread gone, any trace of her feelings wiped clean from her face. Finally, an eternity later, she stood and shook out the black taffeta of her skirts.

"Well, then. Have a nice trip. I guess I'll see you when you get back." With those words, she turned and strolled out of the room.

He stared at her back until she disappeared up the stairs. He'd expected tears, pleading, entreaties for him to stay. He never expected to be bid farewell as though he were trotting off to market. He stood there, fighting the urge to go yank some emotion out of her, battling down the disappointment that she hadn't begged him to stay.

"Your trunk is on the carriage, Mistah Grif, and Dan'l gots it waitin' out front."

Griffin pulled his gaze from the empty stairway to Gaston. The raging, wounded animal in him wanted to storm up those stairs and demand she care that he was leaving. To bellow at her that he was doing this for the good of both of them. The civilized man stiffened his spine and clenched his teeth.

He snatched up his hat and the small valise of money, then marched to the porch. Without a moment's hesitation, he leapt into the carriage and nodded for Daniel to get the carriage moving.

A thousand times in the short ride down the drive, he wanted to turn and look back at the house. Not until they rolled through the stone fence and turned onto the road did he look back.

And no on was there to wave goodbye.

He stood at the ship's wheel, squinting his eyes against the glare of the sun, the crack of the sails snapping in the brisk wind. He steered the bow into waves made choppy from a storm further at sea.

Three weeks into his voyage, and still he found no peace. He'd set sail with the tide the day he left Shadow Oaks, and since then he'd made the *Sea Gypsy* worthy of her name, wandering aimlessly, steering her toward every storm and hazardous water. The crew had wisely kept their opinions to themselves after the first mate, Mr. Starkey, had made the mistake of questioning Griffin's plans. Griffin had rounded on him, yanked him up by his shirtfront, then threatened to bust him down to cabin boy is he couldn't follow simple orders.

John Starkey had been with Griffin for years. He knew him well enough to know something was drastically wrong. Griffin had apologized later, and John had offered his condolences on Florence's death. Griffin allowed his first mate to believe that was all that tortured his mind. Since then the men had kept their distance, tossing him an occasional pitying look as they carried out orders to sail nowhere.

The wind picked up, the sails cracked like gunshots, and he turned his face into the spume of the waves breaking against the ship. Black clouds scraped across the sky a good five nautical miles to the south, dragging with it a curtain of rain visible even from that distance. He yearned to sail into it and let the turmoil of the sea match his own.

"Ship off the starboard bow!" Mr. Madison in the crow's nest pointed toward a small dark fleck that had emerged from the gray wall of rain. Griffin turned the wheel over to Mr. Starkey and raised the spy glass to his eye.

A cargo ship. And a familiar one at that. Blood raced through his veins, pounded in his ears as a battle cry sounded in his head. He slid the telescope shut and took back the wheel.

"Mr. Starkey, are all identifiable markings on the *Gypsy* covered?"

"Aye, sir."

"Order the men to don their masks and prepare to take the ship."

When the first mate bellowed the orders, the men

cheered, then whipped out black scarves that covered their faces, with large holes cut for their eyes. They scrambled to load cannons, check firearms, and strap on swords. Griffin handed the wheel to Starkey again, then pulled his own mask from the waistband of his trousers and settled it over his head. The wind molded the fabric to his face, but he had long ago become accustomed to breathing through the stifling silk. Better that than be recognized as the captain who liberated random slavers of their human cargo.

"Turn about, Mr. Starkey, and hoist all sails. We'll come up behind her. As low as she's riding in the water, she'll never outrun us."

The ship leaned into the turn. Pulleys squeaked as the men hauled the sheets to hoist the sails. When the added canvas caught the wind the ship lurched, then sped across the water, cutting through waves like a knife through butter and narrowing the distance between the *Sea Gypsy* and what Griffin recognized as the slaver, the *Norcross*.

"Order the men to prepare to scatter the shots around her. I don't want her to sink."

Griffin knew exactly when the *Norcross* realized she was being chased. All sails rose and he could see the crew scrambling like ants over a picnic plate. He took the wheel again and stayed behind her, bearing down on her like a shark after its dinner.

"Fire at my command."

The *Gypsy* skimmed across the water after the lumbering cargo ship. It took less than a quarter hour to draw within cannon range. Griffin turned the wheel and swung the ship around to expose one side of guns.

"Fire!" he bellowed.

Sixteen cannons exploded simultaneously, the roar almost deafening. The shots sailed across the sky, then dropped like giant black hailstones into the roiling water around the slaver. A man would have to be a fool not to recognize the near misses as a warning.

The men reloaded and waited for the next order. Griffin whipped the wheel back around, then set his course back straight toward his still fleeing prey.

When they drew nearer, Griffin watched as four puffs of smoke preceded the sound of return cannon fire. He had no fear of being hit, unless the *Norcross* had replaced its antique artillery, and he knew her captain was too greedy to spend his money on guns.

Sure enough, the cannonballs fell far short of their target.

"Take the wheel, Mr. Starkey, and pull up even with her port bow, but stay out of their range." Griffin stepped to the edge of the helm. "Mr. McVay, one shot to take off her figurehead."

"Aye, sir!" the young marksman shouted back.

Griffin waited until Mr. Starkey placed the ship in range.

"Mr. McVay, wait for my order. Everyone else, fire!"

Fifteen cannons exploded as one. The ship shivered from their force and the deck lurched under their feet. The cannonballs pierced the waters around the slaver. Before the final shot fell, Griffin turned to McVay.

"Fire at will, Mr. McVay."

The young sailor touched the fuse off and sent a lone cannonball arcing across the sky. The black ball sailed serenely through the air, then crashed into the figurehead, shattering the shapely carved woman's body into kindling.

"The next shot will be to the center of your deck," Griffin bellowed across the churning expanse of sea.

One by one the sails of the slaver dropped until it wallowed dead in the water.

"I want to see all weapons on the deck and all hands at the helm."

A raggedy band of men left their posts at the cannon or

climbed out of the rigging, then laid down guns, swords, and knives, and made their way to the helm.

Griffin gave the order to circle the ship, and when he convinced himself that no real threat awaited them, he gave the order to pull abreast.

When the ships bobbed side by side in the water, the men threw out grappling hooks and tethered the vessels together, then laid planks across the rails. Griffin leapt to the rail and strode across the first plank. The black mask hid his look of loathing.

"Well, well. Captain Spade. Did you learn nothing when last we met?"

The scroungy, bearded captain simply snarled in reply.

Griffin turned to his men leaping to the deck of the *Norcross.*

"Check the hold," he ordered Starkey. "I've no doubt what we'll find. I can smell his cargo from here."

The captain bristled but kept silent. The man was inherently a coward.

Griffin waited silently until Starkey climbed out of the hold, taking a deep breath of fresh air before reporting.

"At least a hundred and fifty blacks, sir. Some in as bad a shape as they smell."

"Any other cargo?"

"None that I saw."

Griffin turned to the captain and smiled behind the silk of his mask.

"Well, then, men. I've a notion to take the good captain's ship. He'll be hard-pressed to smuggle more of these poor devils until he gets another vessel. Lower the lifeboats."

The captain sputtered and reached for an empty scabbard just as the point of Griffin's sword came up to press against Spade's fat neck. A thin line of blood trickled onto his filthy collar.

"The cargo is mine, and I am bringin' them into the country legally." A tall, hawk-faced man stepped forward and glared at Griffin with defiance. "I demand you release this crew and allow us to return to our voyage."

Griffin cocked his head and looked at the man dressed in the height of fashion.

"And who do I have the questionable pleasure of addressing?"

"Carlton Tilburn, of the South Carolina Tilburns."

Tilburn. The name rang a bell, then Griffin remembered Alec telling him about a run-in he'd had with a slave catcher by that name.

"Any relation to Franklin Tilburn?" he asked.

The man lifted his chin and nodded as if Griffin should be impressed. A gleam of hope lit his eyes.

"My brother."

Why did that not surprise him?

"Ah, yes. The fine Tilburn brothers. Quite a reputation. One smuggles the slaves in and the other chases them down like dogs."

Anger replaced hope. "I am not smuggling."

"Perhaps you hadn't heard, but the importation of slaves into this country to sell was made a crime after the turn of the century. You are indeed smuggling."

"I have no intention of selling these slaves."

Griffin propped a booted foot on the rail and idly swung the point of his sword to Tilburn's cheek.

"Well, then, you must be a very wealthy man, to buy a hundred and fifty human beings at once without plans of turning an immediate profit. Not to mention," he added as he raised his head and scanned the horizon, "you seem to be a bit off course for South Carolina."

The man's hands clenched at his sides. Griffin turned, hiding his growing rage behind a façade of nonchalance.

This man's arrogance, added to the unrest of Griffin's own soul, left Griffin with a barely restrained urge to throttle him.

"Are the lifeboats lowered?" he asked the first mate, his voice tranquil compared to the tempest roiling in his gut.

John turned and saluted with his sword. "Aye, sir. All but one." His eyes widened. "Captain!"

Griffin spun around just as Tilburn lunged at him with a long-bladed knife. He grabbed the man's arm and slammed his hand against the rail. The knife clattered to the deck with the sound of cracking bone.

Tilburn screamed and grabbed his arm, looking up at Griffin with enough hate to burn a hole through him.

"You will pay for this," he screeched. "I will hunt you down to the ends of the earth until I—"

Griffin's hand shot out and grabbed the man by the throat, his fingers digging into the soft tissue below the jaw. Tilburn gurgled and rose up on his toes. Griffin's only sign of anger was the slight tremor of rage in his hand. He forced his voice to remain calm, conversational.

"I truly dislike being threatened." He squeezed harder and Tilburn rose higher. The scum stared at him through bulging eyes filled with hate as Griffin pushed him back against the rail. "Do not ever threaten me again." With one final squeeze, he gave a mighty shove, sending Tilburn over the rail and plummeting into the water.

An unholy feeling of satisfaction stirred in him, and the first sense of peace settled in his mind.

"First mate," he called, turning on his heel and clattering down the steps, "set these men adrift, along with their captain. We shall send this cargo back in the ship they arrived in."

A roar of protest rose among the captive sailors and their leader until Griffin's men drew their swords and advanced.

One by one, the slavers climbed down the rope ladder into
the waiting lifeboats. Someone fished a moaning Tilburn out
of the water and dragged him into a boat.

Griffin ordered all but a skeleton crew from the *Gypsy* to
remain on the *Norcross* and set sail for Nova Scotia, where
the kidnapped Africans would be given a choice of staying
or returning to their native continent. He allowed the few
married sailors to choose whether they would stay on the
Gypsy or sail north.

Once the men had transferred ships, Griffin, still aboard
the *Norcross,* turned his attention to the mass of humanity in
the hold.

"Are Ginta and Dawba explaining to the blacks that
they've been rescued, Mr. Starkey?" The two former slaves
had themselves been rescued on one of Griffin and Alec's
successful ventures. They had chosen to stay and sail with
Griffin, proving invaluable when it came to communicating
with the captives, most of whom spoke no English.

"Aye, Captain. They should be bringing them up on deck
soon."

The smell, as always, nearly gagged Griffin when the
poor wretches staggered out of the hold. Months of not even
the most primitive convenience had most of them sick and
all of them covered with filth. The sight of mothers with babies in their arms had Griffin fighting the overwhelming
urge to go back and finish the job with Tilburn and Spade.
The next time he very well might.

"Ready to cast off, sir." Starkey came up beside him.

A high-pitched wail rose up from within the growing
throng of blacks. Dawba worked his way through the crowd,
parting them until Griffin could see a woman on her knees,
clutching her swollen belly. He swallowed hard at the sight.
Would he be awash with guilt every time he saw a woman
with child? Could he add insult to injury by marrying

Amily? And would he ever be able to make love to her without fear of her suffering the same fate as Florence?

He had no answers for any of those questions, but he had discovered one thing. He could no longer run from his demons. They would follow him to the ends of the earth until he turned and faced them down.

"Is she in need of the ship's doctor, Dawba?" he called from his place by the rail.

"No, Captain Elliott. The women will help her. She is but having her child."

But having her child . . . Never again would Griffin take such words for granted.

He leapt to the remaining plank joining the two ships, leaving John Starkey to captain the *Norcross*. "Cast off, Mr. Starkey. I leave all decisions in your hands." He marched across the bobbing wood, then climbed to the helm as his crew removed the grappling hooks. "Mr. Madison, set a course for home."

It was time to face his demons.

Chapter 11

BRIANNE KNELT ON the floor of the makeshift hospital, her mind as numb as her body as she sponged down one more of the countless victims of the flu epidemic that had started right after Griffin's departure. She had lost count of how many had fallen ill, but each one she lost was burned in her mind. Seventeen deaths so far to the flu. The *flu*, for God's sake.

She dipped the rag in the bowl of tepid water, no longer thinking about what to do, merely moving like a robot from person to person. At least no one fought her any more about her method of treatment. She had gone behind Dr. Myers and taken blankets off those with high fevers, opened the windows that had been closed against the "bad" air, washed the fevered victims down in cool water. He had argued with her and left in a huff. He'd been found several days later in a closed room, under a mountain of blankets, one of the first victims to die of the virus.

Brianne sighed and struggled to keep her burning eyes open. When was the last time she'd slept?

She raked a forearm across her brow to catch a trickle of sweat. The weather hadn't helped with the epidemic. One day the heat would be stifling, the next so cold they had to build fires in the fireplaces.

Ruth, one of the few servants who had weathered the flu and regained her strength, brought a fresh bowl of water and started in on the patient.

"Mr. Bradley Randolph is at the big house, Miz Amily. He say Mr. Masters done ask him to fetch you. Miz Rebecca and her momma gots the influenza and he need yo help. He say we gots more survivors than anyone else, and he don't know what to do."

Brianne could have cried. The last thing she needed was to climb into a carriage with a man smitten with Amily and trot off to care for a whining Rebecca Masters. She had at least a hundred workers sick with various stages of the virus. She could hardly leave them to nurse two people. But she'd met Mr. and Mrs. Masters, and liked them, regardless of what she thought of their daughter.

"I'll be back in a minute. See if you can get some broth in this one. He hasn't eaten in days."

The world spun for a minute when she rose to her feet. She grabbed the back of a chair until the dizziness passed, then scrubbed her hands with lye soap before heading for the house.

Bradley Randolph paced the length of the parlor, then rushed to Brianne as soon as she stepped through the door. The part of her that was Amily recognized the tall, good-looking blond.

"Miss Amily, I know this is a monstrous burden, but I must beg for your help. Virginia and Rebecca Masters are terribly ill. I just returned from Richmond, and Joshua flagged me down as I passed his house. He begs you come and show him how to care for them. I promise to have you back to Shadow Oaks before nightfall."

Brianne remembered the kind man and his wife. She could well imagine Joshua Masters confronting an army of businessmen, but he wouldn't have a clue when it came to sick women. She couldn't tell him no. She sighed.

"Just let me get my . . ." She tried to focus, to pull her thoughts through the thick mud that had replaced her brain. After several blank seconds she just waved her hand and shook her head. "Never mind. Let's go."

Bradley led her to the carriage and helped her in, then climbed into the driver's seat and slapped the reins. She leaned back into the velvet-tufted seat and forced her body to relax for the first time in . . . she couldn't remember how long.

How long *had* it been? The first case of the virus had erupted two days after Griffin had left. And he had left, or rather run away, almost four weeks ago. Four weeks. It felt more like four years.

The carriage hit a rut in the road and Brianne scrunched deeper in the seat to keep from being jostled. She leaned her head back into the soft upholstery and felt herself drifting blissfully off to sleep.

Griffin rode hard up the river road, anxious to get home and have this confrontation behind him. As he'd sailed for home, he'd searched his soul to decide what course to take.

He loved Amily more than life itself, but he had so many fears. Would his guilt come between them? Would she suffer the same fate as Florence? He would rather die than have either of those happen. He would rather let her go and live without her.

Sometime during the night, in the final hours of his voyage, he'd decided. It would save them both grief if they parted. He would furnish Amily with a house wherever she chose. He would honor Flo's memory. He would never put Amily's life in jeopardy by getting her with child.

The decision tortured him, but time would dull the pain. He knew in his heart he could do no less.

The house came into view as he rounded the bend in the road. The live oaks painted long, peaceful shadows that stretched down the drive. Damn, how he'd missed Shadow Oaks. He'd never in his life looked so forward to coming home.

And why would that be? he asked himself. He shoved the answer into the farthest reaches of his mind before it could tempt him. He'd made his decision and he was resolved to follow it through.

He galloped up the drive, slowing at the sight of the lawn in need of a scythe's cutting. It wasn't like Jake Dunstan to neglect the lawns.

He cantered on, noticing for the first time the lack of activity. Not a single soul moved about outside. The closer he got, the more alarmed he became. When he dismounted with no sign of a stable boy to take his horse, or Gaston to open the front door, he threw the reins over a bush and took the porch steps two at a time.

When he burst through the front door, the lack of household noises chilled his blood. A fine layer of dust covered every surface. Cold ashes still lay in the fireplaces. Cut flowers had withered and turned brown in their vases.

"Amily!" he shouted, hearing the panic in his voice and not caring. "Gaston! Mum Sal!" He ran through the downstairs, flinging open doors, bellowing for anyone to answer him. Finally he heard the slow shuffle of footsteps on the back porch, then Gaston appeared through the butler's pantry.

"Mistah Grif."

The man had aged ten years. His face held a gray pallor, his normally square shoulders slumped, and he looked barely strong enough to stand.

"Gaston!" Griffin rushed to him and helped him into one of the dining room chairs. "What has happened? Where is everyone?"

"We all got the influenza, Mistah Grif. Ain't but a handful of people what ain't got it."

The blood froze in Griffin's veins. Influenza. It could be as deadly as yellow fever.

"Where's Amily? Is she ill?"

Gaston shook his head and blinked as though he could barely keep his eyes open.

"She been tending all the sick ones. The doc died of it near on three weeks ago, and she been doctorin' ever since. She probably out in the workshed. She done turned it into a hospital."

Three weeks! Griffin paced, scrubbing his hand over the stubble on his face. What had he left her here to face?

He headed for the door, then remembered Gaston and turned back.

"Are you all right, Gaston? Do you need anything?"

The older man shook his head. "Nossuh. I be fine. You go on and find Miz Amily."

Griffin spun around and marched across the porch and down the steps. By the time he reached the workshed he was at a dead run.

"Amily!" He burst through the door, then stopped short at the sight of dozens of his people laid out in cots or on the floor, every available space taken except for a narrow path that wound through them. Amily was nowhere in sight.

"Della." He recognized one of the three black women tending the ill. "Where is Miss Amily?"

Della stopped feeding broth to one of the field hands and turned to Griffin.

"I don't know, Mistah Grif. I ain't seen her for hours."

Dread filled every inch of him. "I'll be back," he muttered, then turned and ran for the house. Where could she be for hours? Had she fallen ill somewhere and couldn't call for help? He dashed up the porch steps, then ran through the house. He raced up the stairs to her bedroom and burst through the door.

Nothing.

Where the hell could she be? He worked his way back through the house, checking every single room, calling her name, panicking more with each passing minute. Gaston shuffled into the entry as Griffin raced from the library.

"Ruth maybe know where she is, Mistah Grif. She in the kitchen fixin' more broth."

Griffin started for the separate kitchen in the back, then heard a carriage on the drive.

"I'll see to this, Gaston. You sit down and rest." He took a moment to help the shaky servant into the nearest chair, then went to the front door.

Amily stood on the drive as Bradley Randolph slapped the reins and rolled his carriage down the drive.

"Let me know if you need anything," she called after him. He waved and slapped the horses into a run. Amily wearily gathered a handful of stained, wrinkled skirts and started up the steps.

"Where the hell have you been?" Griffin shouted at her, the sight of her in the company of a known admirer honing a sharp edge to his voice. "And with *him*?"

She stopped on the third step and looked up the length of him. Her eyes, bloodshot and shadowed with circles, narrowed as she climbed the rest of the steps and stood before him. Her pale face held two bright pink spots on her cheeks.

"Ex*cuse* me?" She dropped the limp, dirty skirts and glared at him.

"Where have you been? Have you any idea how worried I was when I came home to find everyone ill and you nowhere to be—"

"Where have *I* been? Where have *I* been? You have the nerve to march in here after four weeks of being God knows where and ask me where *I've* been? You run away from home and leave me here to face four weeks of a flu epidemic and you have the nerve to ask *me* where *I've* been? Damn you!" She shoved both hands on his chest so hard he staggered backward. "Do you think I grieved for her any less? Do you think I feel any less guilty because I fell in love with her husband? I miss her so much it physically hurts, almost as much as the guilt that eats me alive. You're the one who ran away, and you have the nerve to yell at me because I wasn't waiting at the door for your beck and call?"

"That is not why—"

She spun around, lifting her hands and face to the cloudless blue sky.

"I give up! I don't know what You want. I tried to adapt. I tried to figure it out." She marched back down the steps and into the middle of the drive. "Here I am. Hit me with Your lightning. I want to go home! Do you hear me? I want to go home!"

Griffin stood, speechless at this rampage. He had little time to think on it, though, for just as she lowered her tearstained face to gaze at him helplessly, her body went limp and she crumpled into a heap on the crushed shell drive.

Chapter 12

DAVID SMILED DOWN at her with those warm brown eyes of his, grinning that grin that always got them in trouble.

"Hey, Bri, wanna go to a séance?"

Brianne elbowed her way to a sitting position. Why was she on the ground? Where were they?

"C'mon. It'll be fun," he promised.

"David, where are we? What have you gotten me into now?"

"Let's go to a séance, Bri. Maybe we can contact Griffin. You'd like that, wouldn't you? Let's conjure up somebody man enough for you." David still smiled, but his eyes were filled with hurt.

She shook her head. "David, I . . . I didn't know you cared. Honest. When we kissed . . . if only the lightning . . ." When she looked up, David's face had turned into Griffin's.

"Where have you been?" he shouted. "I've looked everywhere for you! You should have been waiting here for me. Florence would have waited. Why couldn't you be Florence? Why did I have to fall in love with you?"

Brianne shook her head at Griffin's accusations when a shiver racked her body. She was cold. How could she be so cold? The sun beat down on them, there in the middle of nowhere. When she looked around, trying to find something familiar, her apartment surrounded her. She almost wept at seeing all her homey things: her stereo, her microwave, her books, her treadmill. Even her bottle of Caribbean Peach nail polish. Little luxuries that were now priceless treasures to her.

"Griffin." She turned to tell him this was her home, but he was gone. She shivered with cold again, and lightning flashed at the window in the cloudless blue sky.

She was freezing. Her teeth chattered, and she tried to get up to find a blanket, but no matter how hard she tried she couldn't seem to rise, almost as though she were glued to the floor.

"David, help me!" she called. "I'm so cold. Griffin, David, somebody help!"

Griffin paced the floor, wanting to scream at his helplessness. Amily lay on the bed, pale and limp, and he had no idea what to do for her. He'd aged ten years when she collapsed to the ground, and he aged another year with each helpless moment that passed.

She moaned and rolled over, curling into a tight little ball. He snatched another quilt from the linen chest and tucked it around her. Her shivers continued so hard the bed shook. He looked at her, remembered his resolve to distance himself, then resumed his pacing.

What should he do? The doctor was dead. What servants who weren't sick were needed to care for those who were. He had no idea if any of his neighbors were well, and even if they were, he refused to leave Amily long enough to fetch them.

Amily whimpered like a child and her teeth chattered in the stillness of the room. He couldn't let her suffer. But he didn't dare touch her. He tucked the covers tighter but she only shivered harder.

"Oh, hell," he sighed in resignation. He yanked off his boots and slid under the layers of quilt to pull her fevered body against the length of him. He wrapped his arms around her, nestled her head on his shoulder, and rested his cheek against her hair. Her shivers continued, then slowly lessened until she stilled and relaxed against him.

He closed his eyes and swallowed. Having her in his arms, no matter what the reason, lifted his heart and lent it wings. As he'd feared, he gave up any thoughts of living without her. He'd as easily live without air.

While he lay there holding her, almost thankful for the opportunity, he realized he would never have been able to forget her. He might have been stubborn enough to send her away, stupid enough to marry someone else, but he would have been miserable, and she would have lived in his heart to his dying day.

He hadn't meant to fall in love with her, but when he did, he'd tried to keep his distance. He'd remained faithful to Florence, and Amily had done the same. No, neither of them had asked to fall in love with the other. It had just happened.

The guilt that·had tormented him for months started to ebb, and a sense of peace crept in to take its place. He pulled her closer, held her tighter. He had almost given her up. The very thought chilled his blood. And the thought that he had yelled at her when she was sick, after weeks of caring for his people, left him loathing himself.

When she recovered, he would spend the rest of his life making it up to her. He never once considered the possibility that she might not recover.

• • •

Every molecule in Brianne's body ached. The slightest movement took monumental effort. Opening her eyes required more energy than she could gather, and even the uncontrollable shivering from the chills drained her of what little strength she could summon. She welcomed the black velvet void, for within the depths of sleep she could forget the pain, forget Griffin and his desertion, and forget his hateful tone when he had come home to find her gone.

"Amily, wake up," Griffin whispered as he gently shook her. "You have to try to eat something."

She felt herself rising from the warm, comfortable void, and she fought to sink back into its depths. She hadn't the strength to fully waken, to suffer the haze of aching muscles and joints. She had no desire for food. She wished he would leave her alone. Why wasn't Florence taking care of her?

The fuzzy, unwanted memory worked its way into her consciousness: Florence was dead.

Brianne turned her head away from something prodding at her lips and tried to turn her mind away from the death of the woman she'd learned to love and think of as her cousin.

Florence had died regardless of Brianne's attempts to save her. Indeed, the moment Florence had conceived, her death sentence had been issued. The only way Brianne might have saved her was if she had been a doctor, and even then Florence most probably would have died. Was the past written in stone, unchangeable?

She tried to shove those thoughts from her mind, but the implications haunted her.

If she couldn't save Florence, would she be able to save herself and Griffin? Would they die even if they never got on the back of a horse again? Could she prevent their deaths if she went away? If they died, would her spirit go back into her other body, or would she end up in another time? Would Griffin?

She rolled over, trying to roll away from the disturbing thoughts. She searched for the thick haze, wanting to cloud her thoughts, but they continued to tumble through her mind like the crystal clear waters in a mountain stream.

Why was she there? To fall in love with Griffin? She'd done that. To save Florence's life? Impossible. To save Amily's and Griffin's? Only time would tell. Time, and a wisdom she wasn't sure she possessed.

Griffin tried to spoon a few more sips of broth between Amily's parched lips, but he feared little of the nourishment got to her. After one last try, he rose to set the tray on the table by the door.

Worry ate at him like a disease. She hadn't fully regained consciousness since she'd fainted on the drive three days earlier, and he had no one to ask for help. He'd never felt so helpless, so humble in his life.

He would gladly give his own life rather than let her die. Florence's death had been bad enough, but he couldn't bear to even contemplate . . . no, he couldn't even think the words.

"Griffin," Amily moaned in a thready, whispery voice. He spun, at her side in an instant, but she merely rambled, still feverish, speaking nonsense he couldn't understand.

"Amily, sweetheart, can you hear me?" He stroked her gaunt cheek with his fingertips, but she showed no sign of waking.

Damnation! He cursed himself for his helplessness. Cursed himself two hundred fold for leaving her here to face this ordeal. Yet she had worked herself to exhaustion and managed to save most of the victims she'd treated. Surely if she could save a plantation full of people, he could save one small woman . . . the woman that meant more to him than his own life.

• • •

The muffled sound of pacing pulled Brianne from the fingers of unconsciousness that had such a grasp on her. Seven steps in one direction, seven steps back, a long pause, and then it started all over again.

Why wouldn't he leave her alone? She didn't want to wake up. She just wanted to drift back to sleep and forget the world existed, forget that even her skin hurt. She wanted to go back to sleep and wake up in her own bed, with her moisturizing bath gel waiting in the shower; her Mr. Coffee already dripping with her morning caffeine; a makeup drawer full of fake beauty; and a medicine cabinet full of bottles and bubble packs of things to make her feel better. And if she was really truthful, she wanted to wake up to find her mother bringing her a glass of ice cold 7UP to settle her stomach.

She looked up to see her mother standing over her, brushing the hair off her forehead, pulling the covers up to her chin. Brianne almost cried at the sight of her, a woman who still looked so young people mistook them for sisters.

"Do you need anything, sweetheart? Can I get you anything?"

Brianne couldn't stop the unbidden tears that welled in her eyes. She'd missed being home more than she'd realized.

"I need some aspirin, Mom. And I feel so grungy. Could you help me change into something clean?"

She closed her eyes then and drifted, waiting for her mom to make everything all right, smiling at the fact that, at the ripe old age of thirty-three, she still wanted her mother when she was sick.

Just knowing that Mom was there, taking care of everything, eased Brianne back into the welcome sleep where she could escape the misery of her body. At some point she felt

the warmth of a damp washcloth down her arms and then
across her face, but she couldn't will her eyes to open. She
settled back into her nice, numb cocoon of black velvet to
wait for the aspirin that would ease the aches.

Griffin stopped his pacing when Amily's eyes fluttered open
and looked straight at him. He brushed a tangled strand of
sable hair from her brow, alarmed anew at the fevered skin
beneath his touch.

"Do you need anything, sweetheart? Can I get you anything?"

His heart lurched at her struggle to smile and the tears that
welled in her eyes, but hope surged through him with her
first lucid gaze in days.

"I need some aspirin, Mom. And I feel so grungy. Could
you help me change into something clean?"

Her words hit him full in the chest, a fistful of shock that
turned to the same gnawing worry that had taken up residence in the pit of his stomach.

She thought he was her mother. And what was aspirin?
What was grungy? He could guess at the latter and cursed
himself for a fool. Of course she wouldn't feel clean. On that
first day, in mindless desperation, he had removed her outer
garments and most of her underthings, but he had left her
cotton chemise and drawers, horrified at how thin she'd
grown in his absence. He'd managed to wrestle her into a
modest nightgown, but since then he'd merely bathed her
fevered brow with a cool cloth.

He left her only long enough to race outside to the
kitchen. A still ashen-faced Gaston and a recovering Esther
worked together to keep a steady supply of broth for all the
influenza sufferers. At least he knew the others were being
well taken care of.

He left them to their work and grabbed a bowl, filling it from the kettle of water on the hearth.

"Mistah Grif!" Gaston called as Griffin made a dash for the door. "She ain't worse, is she?"

The burning ball of fear flared in the center of Griffin's chest. He wouldn't even consider the possibility.

"I don't know, Gaston. Pray for her. Please, pray for her."

He ran then, back into the house and up the stairs, nearly giddy with relief when he reached her side to find her breathing evenly and sleeping without those racking shivers.

He dipped a clean cloth in the warm water, wrung it out, then turned to stare at her, not at all sure where to start, or even where to stop. The day he'd stripped her of her clothing, he had been frantic with worry, oblivious to everything but her welfare. Now he was about to perform something more intimate than he had ever shared with his wife.

"Damn it, you spineless ninny," he berated himself. "Just pick a place and start."

He took a deep breath, blew it out, then peeled the mountain of covers back only far enough to bare an arm. He swiped at it a couple of times, wondered if he should use soap, then decided he'd best keep matters simple. He settled for swishing the soap in the warm water, clouding it enough to satisfy himself. When he finished with the first arm, he carefully covered her, then pulled the covers back to reveal the other arm. He worked away, washing, dipping, wringing, and never once did Amily stir. He washed her face, thinking maybe he should have done that first. He uncovered one leg, amazed at the heat rising in his face when he worked her nightgown and the leg of her drawers up her thigh. Saint's blood, one would think he'd never before touched a woman. He ignored his burning face and bathed that leg, then started to work on the other. Once finished he stood back and stared at her for a moment, scrubbed his hand down his face to rasp at his unshaven jaw, and faced the fact that there was more skin to wash beneath her nightgown.

"Oh, Alec, you seasick bastard," he spoke to his old friend thousands of miles away. "What a field day you would have with this one. I daresay you would never let me live it down."

Alec, he knew, in the same situation, would have no qualms of whipping every last stitch from Amily's body and slathering every last inch of her skin. If the man could sail a ship regardless of getting seasick from just looking at a ship from the dock, he would certainly not allow the ill, unconscious woman he loved to suffer from the grime of a fever.

Saint's blood, he must be punch-drunk to be talking aloud to his friend all the way in Maine, but at least the ridiculous conversation gave him the resolve to do what needed to be done.

With a deep breath of determination, and a denial that his face flamed even hotter than before, he folded back the covers and set to work removing nightgown, chemise, and drawers from the limp, ravaged body of his beloved. That done, he applied the warm, wet cloth, somehow washing her with his gaze firmly fixed on the ceiling. Before long though, he found himself staring at her, blinking back a burning in his eyes at the sight of a painfully thin body and ribs he could count. He wasn't staring at the naked body of the woman he loved. He stared at the price she'd paid while he had left her to run from his demons. How in the world would he ever make this up to her?

Miserable, humbled beyond belief, he bathed her, begging forgiveness with every touch, then settled a fresh night rail on her limp body and brushed a kiss across her lips.

"Forgive me, Amily. Dear God, please let her forgive me."

• • •

"Brianne, we need to talk." David grabbed her then, and his mouth came down on hers as lover to lover rather than best friend to best friend. She expected the kiss to bring them to giggles, as years earlier the other one had, when they'd been curious about the mystery of it all. But this kiss shot straight to everything that made her a woman, curling in a hot, sensuous spiral, leaving her dizzy with want. Her bones turned to liquid and their bodies all but fused. A tiny sigh escaped her throat as the want and surprise in her raged like the storm outside.

Lightning flashed, and the living room door slammed back against the wall. When David raised his head, they turned as one to see Heather standing in the doorway.

"I'll be right there, darling," David said as he stepped back. He looked at Brianne, gave her a peck on the forehead, then turned to his fiancée.

"David!" Brianne called when he draped an arm over Heather's shoulders and walked away. He turned back and stared at her through clear, whiskey brown eyes.

"I'm sorry, Bri. He can find another puppet. I warned him I can do my own kissing."

Numb, speechless, totally confused, Brianne stared at the door he shut behind him. The storm howled outside as jagged streaks of white pierced the Heavens and shot to earth.

David wouldn't do that to her. David wouldn't bring her to her knees with a kiss and then walk away. Not her best friend. No. This wasn't real. Somehow, somewhere in her mind, she knew this wasn't real. None of this was real.

Except that kiss.

The confusion slowly cleared in her mind, and as if rising from the depths of the sea, she felt herself rising out of the dream. With it came her memory, as well as the heat of her fever and the enervating aching of her body.

She was extremely ill, and she was in 1832, in love with someone who might die if she stayed with him. If she died now, before things were settled between them, would that change history for the better?

A part of her spirit refused to let go. If she died, so would Amily. No. She wouldn't allow herself to die. She would survive. She would tell Griffin the truth about herself and what she knew of their future, and then she would decide what to do after that.

The more lucid she became, the more she realized she had to get her fever down. Her mother wouldn't be showing up with that aspirin, and she knew of only one other way to bring down a fever.

With every ounce of her strength she forced her eyes open and tried to focus. Griffin slumped in a chair next to her, his arms cradling his head on the edge of the bed, his breathing slow and even of someone in deep sleep.

It took her two tries to croak out, "Griffin," from her parched throat. He jumped, beside her in a heartbeat, one hand holding hers and another feeling her forehead.

"Yes, Amily. It's Griffin, sweetheart. What can I get you? Here. Take a sip of water."

He grabbed a glass and held it to her lips, his eyes studying her every move. She smiled in spite of herself at the jagged red crease on his stubbled cheek, the same pattern as the counterpane.

The water tasted better than the finest champagne, in spite of tiny rope fibers from the well, but she barely had the strength to swallow. When he took the glass from her lips she had to take a moment to gather the energy to speak.

"I need . . . a cold bath."

He shook his head and patted her hand, and to her amazement, blushed a ruddy red.

"I, uh, I bathed you earlier. You . . . well, you wanted a clean nightgown, so I . . . I took the liberty . . . I hope you realize I didn't . . . you really don't need . . ."

She shook her head. "A *cold* bath. Cold. For my fever."

"Amily, sweetheart, you don't know what you're saying. You're ill. You certainly shouldn't—"

She used her last reserve of energy to grab the front of his shirt and pull.

"Bring the tub. Fill it with cold water."

"But that would be—"

"Do it! Ruth will tell you. Do it!"

She let go of his shirt and fell back. He stared at her for a moment, obviously wondering if she was delirious. Finally he turned and walked to the door.

"I will speak with Ruth. Will you be all right for a moment?"

She had an insane, bitchy urge to tell him she'd managed just fine for four weeks, but she knew he didn't deserve that from her now. She simply nodded.

"Yessuh, Mistah Grif. She done went behind Doc Myers, takin' off blankets and gettin' the fever down by coolin' 'em off. Some of the bad uns she done stuck in a tub o' cold water."

"And none of them grew worse?" Griffin could see the logic in the action, but it went against everything he'd ever heard.

"Nossuh. The fever came down with ever' last one of 'em."

If what Ruth said was true, he might well have prolonged Amily's illness, or even worsened it. Hell, could he do nothing right?

He shook his head and sighed. "Very well. I have tried everything else."

He fetched the bathing tub from a corner of the kitchen and carried it up to Amily's room. She slept peacefully, and for a moment he almost changed his mind, until he felt her brow.

He made a dozen trips to the well, filling the tub two buckets at a time until water lapped close to the edge. Finally finished, he stood by the bed, wondering if he should wake her.

"Amily," he whispered.

Her eyes fluttered open, then closed again.

"You'll have to help me, Griffin. I'm not sure I can get out of bed."

His chest tightened at her admitted weakness. What if he lost her? *Dear God, don't let me lose her.*

He threw back the pile of quilts, painfully conscious now of the heat rising from them, then scooped her into his arms and lifted her with no effort at all. The heat of her skin burned into him.

He strode with her in his arms to the tub, sending up a continuous stream of prayers for her survival.

"Are you ready?" he asked, not certain she was even still awake. She nodded her head against his shoulder.

He knew easing her fevered body into the cold water would be harder on her than just plunging her in all at once. He hesitated for a moment, then sat her in the water, flinching at her sudden gasp, fighting the urge to pull her out and wrap her back in blankets.

She muttered a curse, shocking him to the core that she even knew such language, then her chattering teeth interrupted any further speech.

He couldn't stand it. This couldn't be healthy.

"Amily, this is wrong. This is going to kill you. You will truly catch your death."

He started to lift her out but she shook her head.

"No! I n-need to st-stay in here. L-Let me st-stay."

He rammed his fingers through his hair and squeezed a handful at his crown. The water nearly sloshed over the sides from her shivering. He couldn't stand to see her so cold.

He paced, watching her every move for the slightest sign to pull her out. She eventually leaned back against the tub, sinking further into the water. At one point she sank completely under, resurfacing before he could get to her, but stopping his heart all the same.

A quarter of an hour passed. Her shivering had stopped and her eyes seemed clearer. The terror that ricocheted through him abated, and he thought perhaps he would allow himself to hope the worst was over.

"I think I'm ready to get out now," she finally said. He slumped with relief.

He bent and scooped her up, holding her to him as the water cascaded from her and her dripping night clothes. Her head fell against his shoulder, fitting there perfectly.

"I think I can stand while you get me out of this gown," she murmured.

Saint's blood, he hadn't even thought of that. Seeing her naked while she was unconscious, while he was caring for her was one thing. Undressing her while she stood there, awake and helpless and sick, was something else all together.

"Well . . ." he croaked, stalling for time. He could fetch Ruth to do this. That was it! But then he remembered she had been on her way to to the workshed to feed some of those still sick.

Grif, old man, he could almost hear Alec now, *you have the nerve to call me the Puking Puffin? Dare I riposte with the Reluctant Reverend? Dress the woman, Reverend Elliott, before she catches the ague.*

"Damn you, Alec," he muttered.

"What?"

Saint's blood, had he said that aloud?

"Nothing," he answered. "I was just . . . nothing."

He set her feet gently on the plush rug beside the tub, then swallowed back a moan when he stepped away to get something with which to dry her.

The blasted gown clung to her, transparent and worthless, and she stood there swaying like tall grass in a strong breeze. He snatched the closest pile of fabric, another quilt, since he had neglected to think far enough ahead to bring any towels. He wrapped it around her and rubbed, holding her upright while he worked.

"Griffin."

He stopped his endeavors to look up into Amily's precious face.

"Yes?"

She blinked, and he thought for a moment she had fallen asleep on her feet.

"I'd get dry quicker if the wet gown came off."

Her words echoed in his suddenly empty brain, causing all manner of reactions elsewhere.

"Oh. Yes. Well."

Ah then, perhaps the Procrastinating Parson.

Griffin growled and shoved the voice of Alec Hawthorne to a dark corner of his mind. He dropped the quilt, then without giving himself a chance to think he grabbed the bottom of the sodden gown and peeled it off over her head.

He had the quilt wrapped back around her before the garment hit the floor with a soggy *splat*. She leaned into him, barely standing on her own as he rubbed her dry, then he swept her up and sat her on the bed so he could take a moment to find another gown.

He rummaged through bureau drawers, trying to remember where he'd found the first one. Why the devil did women have to have so many fripperies?

Finally he unearthed a white beruffled thing with lace and bows and dozens of pleats across the bodice. He shook it out and carried it to the bed where Amily still sat, her eyes closed.

He stood there a moment, pondering how best to go about this. His experience lay more in removing these garments, and even then it had been so long he could barely remember his technique.

Amily stopped his deliberations when she shrugged the quilt off her shoulders and opened her eyes to two weary slits.

"Put it over my head and I'll find the sleeves myself."

With a speed that would have had Alec howling, Griffin threw the gown over her head, settled the billowing yards of fabric to cover as much pale skin as possible, then found the neck opening and shoved it over her damp curls. It looked suspiciously as if she had a tiny smile on her lips when she worked her arms into the sleeves, then fell back against the pillows with an exhausted sigh.

Griffin sighed himself, relieved beyond belief that this ordeal was nearly at an end. He swung her legs onto the bed and covered her with one light quilt.

"Griffin?" she murmured as she snuggled deeper into the pillows. "Can I have something to eat?"

He wanted to cheer at this early sign of recovery.

"Yes, sweetheart. I will fetch you some broth."

"And Griffin." He paused and turned at the door. "In a day or two, when I feel up to it, we need to talk."

Chapter 13

GRIFFIN SAT IN the chair he'd occupied for so many days next to Amily's bed, worried anew that her recovery had been nothing more than false hopes.

She stared back at him from the mound of pillows, healthy pink returning to her cheeks, her eyes clear and sober, her entire appearance a contradiction to her words. Could the high fever have caused a problem with her mind?

"Why do you think you are not Amily, sweetheart?"

Rather than looking confused, she blew out a deep, frustrated breath and cocked a look at him as if he were the one having trouble thinking straight.

"We've been through this twice, Griffin. I don't blame you for not believing. Really. But simply asking me over and over again is not going to change my answer. I *am* Amily, but I'm also who Amily's spirit became in the future. My spirit has lived in the future."

"And your name is Brianne." He felt ridiculous even making the statement.

She nodded. "Yes. In the future."

"And my name in the future is . . ."

She stared at him for a moment, like a teacher trying to reach a very dim-witted student.

"I told you, I don't know. You wouldn't tell me."

He nodded, scrubbed his face with his hand, shoved his fingers through his hair and pulled until the roots hurt.

A séance, spirits, the future nearly two centuries away.

He took her hand, refusing to believe that this delirium was permanent. They would work this through together and then laugh about it when it was over.

"Sweetheart, I just want you to rest and recover your strength. You have been to Hell and back with your illness." He paused, wondering if he should go on. "I had planned to wait until you were fully recovered to speak of this but . . ." She looked at him, her hair spilling like silk around her serious face, so sweet, so fragile, so unbelievably precious to him. "Amily, your illness opened my eyes. I loved Florence in my own way, and I will never dishonor her memory. But I came too close to losing you as well, and I do not care to take such a chance again. I love you, sweetheart. From the first moment I saw you, against all my best efforts, I fell in love with you, and I am falling still. When you have regained your strength, I want us to marry." He moved to sit on the edge of the bed, then took both her hands in his. "Will you marry me when you have recovered?" He shook his head and kissed her hands. "Never mind recovering. Will you marry me now?"

He smiled at her, barely able to contain the heart that wanted to float out of his chest. The gossips be damned. He and Amily would weather the flying rumors together.

"I can't."

His heart stopped floating, stopped beating, stopped feeling.

"What?"

Her eyes glistened with misery as she shook her head.

"I can't. When I regain my strength, I'm going back to New Orleans to be a midwife."

"A mid—" His mind screamed denials. This woman loved him. He knew that with the same certainty that he knew he loved her.

He cradled her face in his hands, smoothed a strand of hair behind her ear.

"Amily." He held her gaze even when his voice broke. "Look me in the eye and tell me you don't love me."

She squeezed her eyes shut and tried to turn away, some internal torment carving lines on her brow, but he held her gaze steady. She opened her eyes and looked at him.

"I love you, Griffin. You're the other half of me, and I'll love you until the day I die. But I won't marry you."

His hands dropped away and he jumped to his feet.

"Why? I demand to know why. If this is because Florence—"

She shook her head. "It has nothing to do with Florence. It's because if I stay here—"

The bedchamber door flew open and Rebecca Masters marched in, yanking off her gloves and beaming at the two of them.

"Amily, darling, I wanted to come and see if I could help in your recovery. You were such an angel to come and show Father how to care for us. By the way, Griffin, I knocked and knocked but no one answered the door, so I let myself in. Are your people still sick? I know ours are."

He could kill this woman with his bare hands and smile as he watched her die.

"Yes," he all but barked at her. He turned to Amily and speared her with his gaze. "This conversation is not over." Before he gave in to the urge to wrap his fingers around Rebecca's throat, he turned on his heel and stomped out.

• • •

Brianne stared at Rebecca as the woman felt her for a fever, poured her a glass of water, offered to brush her hair.

"You look dreadful, dear," Rebecca commented as she rummaged for a brush.

"I've been sick." Brianne let the sarcasm hang in the air as she glared at the woman's back. The only thing preventing her from going for Rebecca's throat was Brianne's lack of strength.

Rebecca turned, brush in hand, and grinned.

"You are so funny, Amily. Of course, you've been sick. You know I did not mean—"

Brianne snatched the brush from the meddlesome busybody's hand when she tried to run it through the tangled mass.

"Why are you here, Rebecca?" If she hadn't interrupted, Brianne could have had the torturous confrontation with Griffin over with.

Rebecca managed to actually look wounded.

"I merely came to help. If not for you coming to Father's aid that day, Mother and I might well have died. And you were so ill yourself." She sank to the edge of the chair and traced a fold in her skirts. "I know we have been less than friends in the past, but I regret that now. I felt well enough to venture out today and I wanted to come to your aid as you came to ours."

The woman actually sounded sincere, but Brianne fought back the twinge of remorse niggling at the back of her mind. There had to be a catch. Rebecca Masters just wasn't the type to play nursemaid out of the goodness of her heart.

"I . . . I shouldn't have come." She stood and plucked her gloves and reticule from the rosewood table. "I just thought . . ."

Brianne sighed, wanting to let her go but not having the heart to hurt her feelings.

"No. Don't go. I apologize. I guess I'm just cranky from being sick." She held out the embossed silver brush and shrugged.

Rebecca perked up and took back the brush.

"Well, if you are certain . . ."

Brianne somehow stopped herself from rolling her eyes and managed a half nod.

Rebecca set to work, happily untangling Amily's mass of silky black curls, chattering on about hairstyles, fashions, who had been stricken with the flu and who had escaped it.

Brianne sat there, getting her hair brushed, counting the minutes until her unwanted visitor decided she'd done enough of a good deed, dreading the moment she had to face Griffin again. The longer Rebecca stayed, the more Brianne didn't want her to leave.

Griffin paced, something he'd noticed he had been doing a ridiculous amount of lately. With one ear cocked toward the stairs, he prowled his library, picking up a snuffbox, then slamming it down, picking up a book on geography, then slamming it down, picking up a half-full glass of brandy, tossing it back in one gulp, then slamming it down.

What the devil did she mean, she wouldn't marry him? By damn, he knew the woman loved him. He could see it in her eyes, feel the love emanating from her very body even as she turned him down. What possible, convoluted, female reason could she have for refusing him? He simply would not accept her refusal. He would get to the bottom of this and he would make her see reason . . . if that blasted Rebecca Masters would ever leave.

An eternity, no, *two* eternities passed before he heard the unwelcome chatterbox on the stairs. He defied his breeding as a Southern gentleman and ignored the fact that he should see her off. He would give her no excuse to tarry longer than she already had.

The moment her driver flicked the reins on the carriage, Griffin stormed from the library and took the stairs two at a time. He didn't bother knocking on Amily's door, and when he closed it behind him he flicked the key in the lock.

"Now," he said as he turned and stalked toward the bed, "where were we?"

Amily sat against the mounds of lacy pillows, looking like a fragile, raven-haired angel. The sight made him want her all the more.

"Shall I refresh your memory?" he asked when she failed to answer. "I believe your last words were to the effect of, 'It has nothing to do with Florence. It's because if I stay here . . .' Would you care to finish that thought?"

She stared at him for a moment, a challenge in her eyes, but then she looked down at her lap and shook her head.

"No. What's the use? You won't believe me."

"Amily, you cannot possibly presume to know what I will or will not believe."

She looked up at him. "Do you believe I'm Brianne?"

He stopped his negative retort before he could voice it, knowing his answer might well decide his future.

"I believe you think of yourself as this Brianne."

She nodded, a defeated little nod.

"If you don't believe I *am* Brianne, and I know you have no reason to, then you will never believe why I can't marry you." She stared out the window, blinked a few times, then took a deep breath. "It will be better for everyone if I leave. When I'm well and able to travel, I'll do as I planned and go to New Orleans to be a midwife. Amily . . . rather, *I*, have friends back there. I won't be alone." She looked at him then, a miserable, unconvincing half-smile on her face. "You'll find someone else, Griffin. I'm willing to bet that every woman who has ever laid eyes on you has wanted you. You'll find someone else and you'll forget we ever happened."

He stormed toward the bed, nearly blinded with rage at her words, then grabbed her by the upper arms and yanked her up.

"If you think . . ." he growled, barely restraining a bellow. Then he looked into her eyes at the misery in the depths of her soul. His anger died and he cradled her face in his hands. He held her gaze, willing her to see in his eyes the profound emotion behind his softly spoken words. "If you believe I could ever forget you, ever for one moment not want you, then you do not fathom the depth of my love for you."

She closed her eyes when twin droplets spilled over her lashes. He waited for her to say something, to deny his words, to look at him and tell him he was wrong. Instead she just sat there, those two solitary tears sliding down her cheeks and onto his thumbs.

He jumped up and towered over her.

"Damn it, Amily. Do you not realize I would die for you?"

She jerked her head up and looked at him, more tears now following the first.

"What you don't realize," she said, her voice shaking with a passion that slammed into his heart, "is that if I say I'll marry you, you probably *will* die!"

He blinked, and the sudden silence of the room hummed in his ears. What could he possibly say to that? He dropped into the chair by her bed and just stared at her, shaking his head.

"Why do you think I will die?" he asked, not able to form anything even close to a rational explanation.

She sniffed and swiped at her tears with the back of her hand.

"Because you told me we die. Right before we get married. You said our lives together had been cut short and your spirit had searched for mine ever since."

Saint's blood. Had she dreamed this whole unbelievable story while she lay ill, and now convinced herself it was a reality?

"How do our deaths occur?" he managed to ask without allowing skepticism in his voice.

She shook her head and shrugged. "Some kind of riding accident. I don't know when and I don't know how."

Griffin sat up on the edge of the seat, willing to placate her if it meant a change of heart.

"Well, the answer is obvious then. We shall simply not go carriage riding. It will be difficult, but we can—"

"It wasn't a carriage. You said we were on horseback. I think you said it had something to do with a bridge going out." She rubbed her temples and shook her head. "I can't remember everything you said. Maybe you told me, maybe you didn't. I was too busy trying to find out who you were in the future. To me the past was the past. Dead and buried. I never thought I'd be back here trying to change it."

Griffin shook his head, numb. She truly believed she had lived in the future. She had an entire world in her head that she believed was real. Surely, as she recovered, these delusions would pass. As her body healed, her mind would clear. In the meantime he would tell her what she wanted to hear . . . anything to get her to stay.

"Very well, I will think about what you have told me, and I shall try to keep an open mind. And, if we died riding horses together, then we shall simply never ride together. A simple solution, you must admit."

Somehow he wasn't surprised when she shook her head.

"I don't think it's that simple. I knew Florence would die, but I couldn't stop it. What if we can't change the past?

What if we never ride together and just end up dying some other way?" She shook her head and stared at her lap. "No. The only way that I know I can save you and Amily is to leave. If we aren't together, we can't die together."

He could not believe he was having this conversation. Amily speaking of herself in the third person. Speaking of things she said would happen in the future, yet referring to them in the past tense. Denying the two of them a life together because of an insane idea planted in her head.

He shoved his hair off his forehead and relaxed the muscles knotting in his neck. He would bide his time. She would stay here and recover, and as her body healed, so would her mind.

"We will talk of this later." He rose and looked down at her. "You must be tired, with Rebecca's visit and now this. You rest, and when you feel up to it we will find a solution to this problem."

She just looked at him, neither agreeing nor disagreeing. Her expression said she had already made up her mind. But no matter. He would make her see reason, or he would die trying.

"What do you mean, you are returning to New Orleans?" Rebecca actually looked horrified as she stared across the wicker table at Brianne. She had made herself a daily fixture at Shadow Oaks over the past several days, and though Brianne had yet to figure out Rebecca's change in attitude, at least she now managed to get along with her "new best friend." It had even occurred to Brianne that perhaps Rebecca's change of heart was sincere.

"I'm going to New Orleans to return to my midwifery studies. I can't stay on here and live off Griffin's charity forever. Besides," she threw this in for Rebecca's 1830s mentality, "it wouldn't be proper, me, unmarried, living here with a widower."

"Oh, fiddle." Rebecca waved away any concern. "Most everyone expects Griffin to wed you and give you a home. You know as well as I how common it is for a widower to marry his wife's sister or cousin. And Dr. Myers himself heard Florence give you both her blessing."

Brianne shook her head. Florence's blessing wouldn't save their lives.

"I have my reasons. Trust me when I say it's for the best."

Rebecca frowned and shook her head, a tiny, furious shake, until the curls she'd clustered over one ear bobbed crazily.

"But we have only now become friends. And Griffin cares for you." She stared into the depths of her cup of tea for a moment, then slanted her gaze back to Brianne. "In fact, I daresay he loves you. He has the look of a man in love, just as you have the look of a woman in love."

Brianne stared at her for a long moment, then turned to gaze out at the acres of front lawn dotted with huge live oaks.

Thankfully, before she had to respond to Rebecca's astute observation, a rider on horseback trotted up the crushed shell drive. As he neared, she recognized Bradley Randolph. A little huff sounded from Rebecca's side of the table.

Bradley trotted right up to where they sat on the veranda, then swung from his saddle and leapt to the porch without bothering to take the steps.

"Ladies," he said with a disarming smile, sweeping his hat from his blond hair and bowing with mock formality. He grinned at them then, and Brianne knew without help from Amily that this man had as many female admirers as Griffin Elliott. "It does my heart good to see you both here together, recovered from the epidemic and more lovely than before."

Rebecca straightened in her seat and gave her curls a flirtatious toss.

"Why, thank you, Bradley. It was so kind of you to help Father before even returning home from Richmond. I trust Willow Grove fared well?"

Brianne watched Rebecca all but batting her lashes at Bradley. So that was it. Florence had said Rebecca had her sights set on him. No wonder she wanted Amily to marry Griffin. But why wouldn't she be just as happy to see Amily move to New Orleans and be out of the picture all together?

"Yes, we are far enough removed that the illness reached us late, and we isolated the few cases we had. My overseer had been forewarned and prepared for the worst."

"That's good news," Brianne said. She motioned toward a chair. "Will you have a seat?" she invited, then picked up the little silver bell on the table and rang for Della. She hated using the thing, and had refused until now, but she still barely had the energy to walk from the bedroom to the lower veranda, let alone hike all the way out to the kitchen to ask for a drink for her guest.

As Bradley settled into one of the wicker chairs, Della appeared through the jib window they used as a door.

"Would you like something to drink, Bradley? Tea? Lemonade? Something stronger?" Brianne asked.

Bradley looked straight at Della and gave her one of his teasing winks.

"I have waited all winter for a glass of Esther's lemonade."

Della gave a bashful grin in the glow of Bradley's smile.

"Yessuh," she said, then all but ran to fetch the drink.

Before the sound of her steps faded into the recesses of the house, another set of steps marched purposefully around the corner of the gallery. When Griffin appeared, he hesitated for just the slightest moment, then all but sneered when his gaze fell on Bradley. He continued to the table, yanking on a pair of tan riding gloves.

"Rebecca, how good to see you again." He turned to stare at Bradley. "Randolph."

Bradley lounged back in his seat and looked up at Griffin. "Elliott. Good to see you were spared in the recent epidemic. But then I hear you were at sea most of the time."

Bradley's statement held no censure, sounding merely as an observation in polite conversation. No one but Brianne would have noticed the almost invisible stiffening in Griffin's spine. He just stood there and stared at Bradley with those penetrating eyes before turning them to Brianne.

"Amily, I must ride into town and check on a ship due in. I had planned to invite you along, but since you are entertaining—"

Rebecca turned in her seat and laid her hand on Griffin's arm.

"Why do you not stay and visit? Surely the ship can wait a few minutes, and then Amily may ride with you when Bradley and I leave." She jumped into the seat next to Bradley so that Griffin would have to sit next to Brianne. She'd left him no choice other than to rudely decline.

He stood there a moment, pulling his gloves tighter, the breeze ruffling feathery layers of his shiny dark hair. Damn, but just looking at him sent hot, dizzying surges skittering through Brianne's veins, creating brief second thoughts about leaving. Bradley, as handsome and charming as he was, paled in comparison to Griffin's dark, masculine presence.

Finally he scooted the chair around and dropped into it, sulking slightly and obviously not caring. Rebecca beamed and settled back in her chair, a glint of victory in her eyes. Bradley swept his lazy gaze around the table, lingering on Griffin long enough to issue a friendly challenge.

It didn't take a rocket scientist to figure out Rebecca's motives. With one little gesture, she had put an obstacle in Bradley's way, given Griffin a little shove toward Brianne, and widened her opening to Bradley all at once. But if she thought Brianne was going to take another ride to town with Griffin, she had another think coming.

"You are *not* well enough to leave." Griffin towered over Amily, giving her the glare that had made grown men cower in their boots, but this tiny, fragile woman didn't appear the least bit intimidated. "You were not well enough to make the trip with me to Baton Rouge just two days ago. You therefore cannot be recovered enough to leave for New Orleans tomorrow."

She sighed and cocked her head to one side.

"Griffin, the longer I put this off, the harder it will be. It's going to be bad enough . . ." Her voice broke, the sound a dull knife to Griffin's heart. She stared at her lap for a moment, then lifted her gaze back to his. "Please, for my sake, don't make this more difficult than it already is."

He stared at her for a long while, then slowly leaned over, placing one hand on each arm of the parlor chair, bringing his face to within inches of hers.

"Why should I make this easy on you?" he asked with a whispered calm. "You plan to walk away from here and take my beating heart with you. Do you honestly imagine I am going to make that easy for you?" He leaned closer. "If you leave, you will walk away despite my best efforts to make you stay." He held her gaze, then let his eyes drift down to her lips. "And you will know exactly what you are walking away from."

With his last word his lips claimed hers. She leaned away from him, back into the seat, but he followed her, relentless, his tongue searching, finding hers, his first taste of her ex-

ploding in his mind, in hot rivers of want roiling through his
blood. She resisted for a moment, then rose to meet him,
sliding her arms around his neck, the whimper in her throat
nearly unmanning him. He bore down on her, giving her
every ounce of himself, of his love, and she returned it in
kind. Saint's blood, if he had tasted her kiss earlier, he would
have forgotten every vow he'd ever made to Florence.

He slid his arms under her, his mouth never leaving hers,
then lifted her against him and headed for the entry hall and
stairs. But the woman, though light as a feather, had weakened his knees until he feared he would never make it up
those countless steps. He turned back, sinking instead to the
plush carpet at his feet, settling Amily beside him, wrapping
her in his arms until she lay beneath him, until he was mindless with the passion and love that screamed for release. His
hands slid along the peaks and valleys of her body, then
found a lacing string and set to work.

"No," she murmured against his lips. He ignored her,
deepening his kiss, giving to her everything he had to give,
yanking a knot in the damned string.

"No," she repeated, crying now, shoving at him with her
hands.

Her words, her denial of him, slowly penetrated the
dizzying haze of want, dashing him with ice water when the
meaning finally sank in.

She shoved again and he rolled off of her. His body
burned still, but he would not force himself on her.

"Amily . . ."

She sat up and swiped the tears from her eyes.

"Damn it, Griffin, you can make this unbearable for both
of us. You can seduce me and I will go willingly to your bed,
and I'll spend the night there, but in the morning I will still
get up and walk out of this house. I'm going to New Orleans

tomorrow, no matter what happens between now and then, and I'm going for our own sakes."

He jumped to his feet. "How can you say that?" he bellowed.

"Because I know things you don't!" she bellowed back.

She stood then, her hands on her hips, and glared at him.

He glared back, then got right up in her face. She didn't budge an inch.

"This is not over," he all but whispered, threatening, "unless you can look me in the eye and tell me you do not love me."

She stared at him, defiant, her jaw set. In the depths of her eyes he could see her trying to say the words. Trying, and failing.

He nodded, never releasing her gaze.

"I thought not." He backed away. His hand fell on the knob to the parlor door. He forced himself to stand there, to warn her with one last look that he would not give up so easily.

When he walked out, he slammed the door so hard he rattled the windows.

If one more person tried to convince her not to go, she might very well scream. First the scene with Griffin this morning, from which her body still tingled, then nearly every person on the plantation, from Jake Dunstan to Gaston to Mum Sal, had given their opinion. Even Bradley had had a talk with her, much to Griffin's disgust. Now Rebecca stood there, crying, for Pete's sake, and begging her not to go.

"But I will miss you so! And you have no good reason to go away. Do we not need midwives here? Can you not finish your studies in Baton Rouge?" She sank into the chair opposite Brianne. "Just look at the good you did during the influenza. Indeed, with Dr. Myers gone, we need you here more than ever."

Brianne shook her head, wishing everyone would leave her alone. She was sick to death of this life—or death, whatever it was. She just wanted to get away, to have time to think about all that had happened to her, to find a way to get home. Surely she could get home. Surely she wasn't dead. She couldn't be dead. She hadn't said goodbye to her family. To David.

David. Had he seen her die? Had he watched her life ebb away right after that kiss? That kiss. That kiss.

Damn, she wanted to go home. Home to a fast pace and super highways and telephones and FedEx, microwaves, hot showers, air conditioning, insect repellent, screened windows, and ice cubes any time she wanted them. She wanted a twenty-minute lunch in a nice, cool restaurant instead of two hours around the table in stifling heat. She wanted her jeans and T-shirts, jogging shorts and tank tops. Anything but the puritanical layers of fabric that took thirty minutes to put on and just as long to take off.

She wanted to stop being responsible for events in the past, which she probably had no control over anyway. She just wanted to leave, to try to start a life without Griffin, knowing he was alive because she was gone. The sooner she left, the sooner she could start getting over him, if getting over him were possible.

"I thought we had become friends," Rebecca said, her voice as tiny and humble as Brianne had ever heard. "I will be lost without you." She glanced at her lap. "I don't have many friends, you know."

Brianne sighed, leaning over to put her hand on Rebecca's.

"Just because I'm leaving doesn't mean we can't still be friends. We can write. And you can come to New Orleans to visit me." Good grief, things had certainly changed if she had just invited Rebecca Masters to visit her. "But I am going. My mind is made up. It doesn't matter if anyone else understands. I know what I'm doing, and I know it's for the best." She stiffened her spine, turned off her thoughts, and looked out the window. "I'm leaving tomorrow morning, and nothing is going to stop me."

Chapter 14

THE MORNING BREEZE sent clouds scudding across the pale blue sky like white, fluffy kites without tails. Outside the window, a nest of baby robins chirped for their breakfast, their tiny beaks open, impatiently waiting their turns. Two of the barn cats tumbled and scampered with each other across the dewy lawn.

Griffin growled.

Why the hell couldn't there have been a good, old-fashioned hurricane to start the day? Then Amily might have been dissuaded from leaving, at least temporarily.

He could hear her in her room, making her final preparations for leaving. She hadn't come down to breakfast, avoiding him, no doubt. But he'd be damned if she'd leave without facing him one last time.

He left his room and took up his post in the parlor to wait for her, dismissing the servants, prowling impatiently until he finally heard her on the stairs. Not until she reached the entry did he show himself. He shoved his hands in his pockets, leaned against the doorjamb, and tried his damnedest to look like he didn't care.

"Were you going to leave without saying goodbye?"

"I had hoped to," she admitted. She turned to face him, her eyes watery, red-rimmed, puffy. "I had hoped you wouldn't make this harder than it has to be."

His hands fisted in his pockets and he had to force himself not to wrap her in his arms. He shoved off the doorframe and sauntered to her.

"I am not the one making it hard." He reached up with his thumb and wiped a solitary tear from her cheek. "You don't have to go." It took every last ounce of his will to remain calm.

She stared at the ceiling and blinked, swallowing hard, but saying nothing.

"Will you at least kiss me goodbye, Amily?" He kept his voice almost a whisper.

She shifted her weight, blinked harder, and twin lines appeared between her brows.

"Just one kiss," he promised.

She looked at him then, through hovering tears. With a defeated huff, she put her hands on his shoulders and gave a quick peck to his cheek.

Like lightning, he slid his arms around her waist and brought his mouth down on hers. "I lied," he murmured against her lips, then he pulled her tighter, molding her to him, letting her feel how he wanted her as his tongue searched for hers. She melted against him, opening to his kiss.

"Amily," he rasped as she breathed in his words. "I will get down on my knees, if you wish it. I will do whatever you want. You love me as much as I love you." He took her face in his hands and raised his head only far enough to look into her eyes. "Brianne," he whispered, forcing himself to call her by that name, desperate enough to say whatever she wanted to hear. "Stay with me. Let Amily stay with me."

Instead of her anticipated smile, the glaze of passion left her eyes and she stumbled away from him, pure and total agony etched across her face.

She snatched up a satchel at the sound of the carriage rolling to a stop on the drive.

"I have to go," she said through a sob, refusing to look at him. "The carriage is here."

"The carriage can wait!"

"Griffin." She looked up at him then. "Someday you'll understand. Maybe not in this lifetime, but I swear to you, someday you'll understand."

She grabbed the doorknob, hesitated for one eternal moment, then threw the door wide.

"Er . . . Surprise?"

Alec and Shaelyn Hawthorne stood outside the door, smiling from ear to ear until they got a look at Amily's tearstained face.

"Alec!" Griffin choked, then forced himself to go and greet them, but the two unexpected visitors simply stared at Amily.

"Are you unwell, my dear?" Alec asked as he and Shaelyn stepped into the entry.

Amily stood there, frozen as a statue, pale as a ghost. The satchel dropped to the floor, and then she began to shake.

"Shaelyn," she whispered the name, and then screamed it. "Shaelyn!" She launched into the woman's arms, nearly sending them both to the floor. "Oh, my gosh, Shaelyn! It's you! It's you!" She let go of her bear hug only long enough to search Shaelyn's face, then wrapped her arms back around the shocked woman and kissed her cheeks through a flood of tears. "Shaelyn! Oh, my gosh! Why didn't I think of it? You had to be here! I knew you were here! Why didn't I think of it before? But then, you were in Maine. I mean, I thought you were in Maine. It never occurred to me . . . but you found me! How did you know I was here?"

Shaelyn glanced at Alec, and then they both turned to stare at Griffin. He shook his head, speechless.

"Alec, Shaelyn," Griffin finally managed to utter. "I'd like you to meet Amily Tannen. Amily, this is Alec Hawthorne, and apparently you already know his wife, Shae—"

Amily swung around to stare at Griffin before looking down at herself in surprise, then turned back to Shaelyn.

"Shae, it's Brianne. Brianne! I know you don't recognize me, but I'm Brianne." She grabbed Shaelyn by the forearms. "We sat at your kitchen table and you showed me the proof that you and Alec were married. Did you have a boy or a girl?" Amily hugged her again before Shae could answer, then held the stiff, wide-eyed woman back at arm's length. "You don't believe me! I don't blame you. I'll prove it!" She stared at the ceiling for a moment, looking inward, then turned her gaze back to Shaelyn with a smile. "Our first grade teacher was Miss Ruth. We got our driver's license on the same day. You went to Senior Prom with Bill Terry and I went with Steven Linden. David Marks controls satellites in Russia. Can you believe, the idiot is marrying that bub-blehead, Heather Thomas? Oh, gosh, what else can I tell you?" She slapped her palm against her forehead in thought, then jerked her head up and snapped her fingers. "Remem-ber the time I spent the night at your house and we climbed out your window, took your dad's car, and ended up at the drive-in with John and Eric Townsend? And your mom and dad were waiting in your room when we climbed back in the window. Oh, geez, I thought Mr. Sumner was going to blow a gasket! He grounded us both for a month."

Amily babbled on as Shaelyn stood there and stared at her, her eyes as wide as twenty-dollar gold pieces. Griffin tried several times to stop the insane chatter, but Amily shrugged him off and continued. He looked to Alec for help, but the blasted man simply stood there, his head cocked, a questioning smile on his face. Griffin was very nearly ready to clamp a hand over Amily's mouth to save her from more insanities, when Shaelyn launched herself back at Amily and sobbed, "Brianne!"

The two women clung to each other, laughing, crying, jumping up and down like children. Shaelyn herself jabbered incoherently with, "Why? How? You've got to tell me!"

The entire world had taken leave of its senses, and no one had bothered to tell Griffin. Of course. That must be it.

Alec stood there, calmly watching his wife crying and laughing and bouncing with a woman who had just announced she was someone else, and apparently Shaelyn believed her.

When the two finally calmed enough to take a breath, Amily gasped and Shaelyn spun to follow her gaze.

A woman dressed in the black of a servant stood in the doorway, holding a small child.

"Oooh!" Amily cooed. "Is he yours?"

Shaelyn stepped over and took the little boy from the nursemaid's arms.

"Brianne, meet Christopher Brian. The last time you saw him, he was just a little bulge."

"Oh, he's so precious! Can I hold him?"

"Only if you tell me why you're wearing someone else's body." Shaelyn handed him over and Amily headed for the parlor.

Griffin stood there, confused, feeling as though he'd entered someone else's dream, as the women ignored the men and jumped from Christopher's perfections to comments about long stories and lightning and séances. Amily stopped her ramblings long enough to look up and issue an order.

"Would you have their bags brought in, Griffin? And make sure you put them in the room next to mine."

He couldn't resist raising a brow and challenging her. "I thought you were leaving for New Orleans."

Without missing a beat, the two women looked first at each other and then up at him, and as though they'd rehearsed it for days, said in unison, "Oh, as if!"

Brianne couldn't believe her best girlfriend, the sister she'd never had, sat next to her in 1832. She couldn't wait another second for answers to her questions. The moment the nursemaid took Christopher and left the room, Brianne turned to Shaelyn and grabbed her hands.

"How in the world did you find me, Shae? How did you know I was here?"

Shaelyn shook her head and shrugged, glancing up at Alec, who leaned against the mantel, looking not the least bit disconcerted. Griffin, however, paced the floor, stopping occasionally to pour a fresh drink and glare at them all.

"We didn't know," Shaelyn answered. "We got Griffin's message about Florence's death, and as soon as Alec took care of some business, we came here to be with him."

Good grief. This Alec, Griffin's best friend, was Shaelyn's Alec. If only Griffin had ever used Alec's last name, she might have thought to contact Shaelyn.

Shae squeezed Brianne's hands and let her gaze drift over Amily's body. "The real question is: Why don't you look like yourself? I mean, are you . . . well . . . who the heck are you? Now, I mean."

"I'm Florence's cousin, Amily. At least I was in a previous life. And Griffin and I were in love, but he and Amily died before they were supposed to, so Griffin's spirit came to me at a séance with David and Heather and her psychic. It was Heather's idea, but you know how insane David is. He'll do anything for fun."

Brianne kept sliding wary glances toward the pacing Griffin, afraid to stop for breath, expecting him to explode any minute and send them all off to an asylum. He merely continued to pace, casting them an irritated look of disbelief now and then.

Brianne went on with her story, leaving out nothing but that last kiss with David. Shaelyn would never let her live it down if she knew Brianne and David had shared *that* kind of kiss, and that it had shaken Brianne the way it had.

Finally, apparently, Griffin could take no more of the bizarre conversation.

"Would it be too much to ask," he said, his voice quiet, controlled, his teeth clenched, "for you to explain why the two of you appear to be believing this?"

Alec draped an arm across the Italian marble mantel and shrugged.

"Because we do believe this."

Griffin gave forth with a rude snort. "Oh, yes. How ignorant of me not to have realized. Why did that possibility not occur to me before?"

He stood there, head cocked, and stared at Alec, waiting for a more reasonable answer.

Alec shoved away from the mantel, then slapped a hand down hard on Griffin's shoulder.

"Grif, my boy." He hooked Griffin around the neck with his arm and pulled him close. "Try not to kill the messenger, but what they are telling you is true. Shaelyn is from the future. She was born in the year of our Lord, nineteen hundred and sixty-eight. I have never had the pleasure of meeting Brianne before, but Christopher's middle name is Brian, after her. If my wife says this is Brianne, trust me, Grif, this is Brianne."

Griffin backed away, nodding with a placating look and only a slight roll of his eyes.

"So, whose body is Shaelyn inhabiting? And do not tell me Phillipa Morgan's. Remember, I was there during your misguided attempt to marry your brother's betrothed. I know Phillipa was buried at sea. By the way, how is Charles and his lovely wife?"

Alec took the brandy from Griffin's hand and set the snifter next to the decanter.

"My little brother and Mary are quite happy, thank you. Expecting their second child soon. As for Shaelyn, I think you should have a seat." He gave a constant push to Griffin's chest, backing him up against a chair until Griffin dropped into it.

"Shae is in her own body." Alec turned and looked at the two women for a moment, then walked over and handed the brandy back to Griffin. "Here. You may need this, by the time I get through telling you our little story."

Brianne watched Griffin's face change from impatient annoyance to disbelief to realization that Alec wasn't treating this as a joke.

Alec told his and Shaelyn's story, of how she'd found the betrothal ring in the future and how it had brought her to him. How their marriage had been a result of mistaken identity on both parts. He told Griffin everything, and Brianne learned then, as well, all the details of Shaelyn's disappearance.

"I refused to believe her, too, Grif, even when I thought she was lost to me. But seeing is believing, and I watched her return to me out of nowhere." He poured himself a brandy and went back to leaning against the mantel. "I've no idea why Brianne isn't in her own body, but if Shaelyn is

convinced that this is her friend from the future, then so am
I. It is unbelievable, impossible, preposterous, but nonetheless, it is true." He looked to Brianne and smiled. "Whatever
the reason, I feel certain she is fulfilling her destiny."

Griffin slowly sat his untouched brandy aside, then rose
from the chair and approached Brianne. She looked up at
him as he towered over her, as he stared down at her. He
took her face in his hands and stared into her eyes, into her
heart, into her soul. A dog barked in the distance. A servant
sang softly in the recesses of the house.

She knew the moment he believed, the moment his laser
blue gaze saw Brianne in Amily's eyes. She smiled up at
him, a hesitant, tremulous smile.

He shook his head and backed away, raked one hand
through his hair, turned on his heel, then marched to the
front door and slammed it shut behind him.

Brianne jumped up, but Alec took her hand to stay her.

"Let him have a little time. This is a lot to absorb." He slid
a smiling glance to Shaelyn. "Even now, I find the logical
side of me denying it all." He led her back to her seat as she
fought the urge to follow Griffin anyway. She almost gave
in until Shaelyn took her hand.

"Bri, why don't you tell us again what happened. Take
your time. And then I want to know why you were leaving.
Anybody's fool can see how the two of you are in love."

Griffin leaned against the trunk of a willow tree on the bank
of the river, trying to calm thoughts as turbulent as the waters of the Mississippi. Storming up and down the shore had
eased his frustration, but his mind still screamed denials
even as he accepted the impossible truth.

True. What she'd told him was true. A part of her had
lived in the future.

Even if Alec hadn't been so convincing, Griffin could not deny what he'd seen in Amily's eyes; not so much a physical thing, but more a recognition of souls.

Saint's blood, how could this be? And what of Alec's story of Shaelyn being from the future, that her actual body had traveled in time? He could almost sooner believe Amily's story than Alec's.

He closed his eyes against the ache growing at his temples, then let his head drop back to make solid contact with the trunk of the tree.

He was in love with a woman who . . . No, even now his mind refused to form the words.

The snap of a twig to his left pulled him out of his thoughts. He didn't bother opening his eyes, didn't bother acknowledging whoever dared to intrude on him. He simply stood there, leaning against the tree, a knot on the trunk digging into the back of his head. He recognized her scent, caught on the breeze, even as she stood there, as silent as he.

"Are you going to stare at me?" he asked without opening his eyes. "Or are you going to say what you came here to say?"

When she made no reply, he finally lifted his head and looked at her.

She stood several feet away, just inside the curtain of willow branches, fidgeting with her hands, looking frightened, hesitant, determined.

He propped the sole of one booted foot against the tree and turned his gaze toward the river. If she came here to talk, then she would have to start the conversation. He idly watched a fish plop in the water. The drone of insects blared in his ears.

"Griffin," she said finally, quietly, after what seemed an eternity. "I . . . I did try to tell you. You have to admit that. I did try to tell you."

"Yes, Amily . . ." He stopped and turned to looked at her. "Or is it Brianne? Tell me, which one am I talking to? What should I call you?"

She shook her head, and that little furrow appeared between her brows.

"I'm . . . we're . . ." She looked away, then lifted her gaze back to his. "We're the same person, Griffin. The same soul. Just as you are part of that man in the future who forced you to come looking for me. I know this is a shock. It took me weeks to finally accept that I was in 1832, and I had the advantage of knowing that Shae had time-traveled. Shae . . ." She shook her head. "How in the world did Shaelyn deal with this? I've been so wrapped up in my own problems . . ." She brought her attention back to Griffin, her eyes steady. "I don't expect you to accept this without question. Ask all the questions you want. Take all the time you need, but please, don't shut me out."

His whole body jerked at her words.

"Don't shut you . . ." He shoved away from the tree and stalked toward her. "Don't shut you out?" He could hardly believe his ears. "Were you not in the process of shutting *me* out when you tried to walk out of my door not more than an hour ago?"

Her gaze flickered for only a moment. "I told you why. We die before we get married. If I leave—"

"So what?" He shouted so loud a bird squawked and flew out of the tree. "So what if we die? Did it ever occur to you that we might die anyway? With you in New Orleans and me here? Did it ever occur to you that I would rather spend the rest of my life, no matter how short or long, making love to you every time as if it's the last time we ever make love?" He grabbed her upper arms and gave her a little shake. "Did it ever occur to you that I'd rather die with you here in my arms than live on, with you in New Orleans? Well, did it?" he bellowed when she failed to answer.

She stiffened as if she'd been slapped. "No!" she bellowed back. "It didn't!"

"Well, consider it!" he shouted. "And consider this! We are getting married, and I will hear no more about your leaving!"

"Fine!" she shouted.

"Fine!" he barked back.

"Fine!"

He silenced her with his mouth, hard, demanding, nothing at all like the kiss he'd left her thinking about that morning. This was the kiss of a frustrated man who had waited far too long for the woman he loved. Waited far too long, and nearly lost. He would not lose her now. Fate would never rip her from his arms. Of that, he was certain.

Her arms snaked around his neck and she melted against him with a sigh. That one tiny sound did things to his insides he didn't know were possible. He wished the tree were still behind him, to hold him up as he held her, as his hands pulled her close and roamed over a body he had burned to touch.

Saints, she had been worth the wait. If she could weaken his knees with a kiss, a touch, a sigh, what would she do to him when he finally made her his? He might well die from the experience.

But the death would be exquisite.

He groaned, deep and low, and she hummed another sigh against his lips.

"Griffin," she murmured, "I love you."

He breathed in the words that perfumed the air with the most precious of scents.

"I love you, too, sweetheart. I love you, too."

They clung to each other, their lips never parting, until he thought he heard a giggle.

There it was again.

He raised his head and looked down at the love of his life, and she giggled again.

He blinked.

"My kisses amuse you?"

She smiled up at him, her eyes literally twinkling.

"I was just thinking, that of all the ways I'd envisioned being proposed to, having it shouted at me wasn't one of them."

He couldn't help but grin. "And did you foresee screaming back your answer?"

She snuggled her cheek against his chest, causing all manner of acrobatics in his stomach.

"Can't say that I ever thought about screaming the answer back, but . . . whatever works."

He nuzzled the top of her head with his chin as he held her close.

"Quite," he agreed, barely able to believe he held her in his arms, that they would soon be wed. "Whatever works."

Shaelyn squealed and hugged Brianne. Alec slapped Griffin on the back and told him it was about time.

"When? When is the wedding? Before we leave, of course." Shaelyn turned to Griffin, and Brianne recognized the gleam in her eye of wedding plans being made. She could also see the thought of Florence flit across Griffin's gaze, and she knew exactly what he was feeling.

"Shae, it's only been a couple months since Florence died. We don't want to show her any disrespect. We should probably wait at least—"

"Oh, criminy." Shaelyn rolled her eyes and looked at the ceiling. "Florence knew you both loved her, right?"

Brianne looked at Griffin and they nodded.

"And she loved both of you, right?"

Brianne nodded again. "She loved us both. At the end, I even wondered if she knew how we felt about each other. She put our hands together and told us to take care of each other, and to love each other, and then she gave us her blessing."

"Well, there you have it." Shaelyn shrugged as if it were all decided. "And if I've learned one thing while I've been back here, it's that the practice of waiting a year in mourning before remarrying is simply a myth. Is that not correct, Griffin?" He gave a hestitant, thoughtful nod, then Shaelyn drove her point home. "Especially in a situation like yours. It's a common practice for a widower to marry his wife's relative. If I was on my deathbed, you can bet I wouldn't ask Alec to take care of someone and give them my blessing unless I truly wanted to free them to be together."

Alec sank to the divan beside his wife and smiled at her. Brianne could see in his eyes the depth of his love for her friend. She'd seen that same look in Griffin's eyes when he'd gazed down at her earlier, on the riverbank.

"Grif," Alec said with that we-are-but-helpless-men-in-the-presence-of-women look, "might as well accept your fate. It will be a miracle if you are not a married man by the end of the day."

Shaelyn's eyes widened and she gave her husband a loud kiss on the cheek.

"What a wonderful idea, darling! You're a genius!"

Brianne's stomach did several flips at the very thought. But why not? Why not tonight? She looked up to see the same thought reflected in Griffin's eyes.

The sound of a horse galloping up the drive drew everyone's attention. Griffin pulled back the lace sheers on the window, then headed for the front door. His terse statement, "It's Starkey, Alec," had his best friend close on his heels.

Shaelyn's, "Uh-oh," had Brianne following her behind the men.

"We've word of a slaver coming in, sir, straight from the African coast," the man was saying by the time Brianne got close enough to hear. "I knew you'd want to know, especially with Mr. Hawthorne in port."

"How far out?" Griffin asked.

Brianne looked at Shaelyn for an explanation, but Shae, her face now a sickly shade of gray, stood quietly and listened.

"A week, maybe. Two at the most. The *East Wind* put into port last night. Her men said the *Profiteer* docked in Barbados for supplies and had plans to put in at Cuba before coming on here."

Griffin looked at Brianne for a long, agonizing moment.

"We can let this one pass, Grif," Alec offered quietly. "We don't have to try and take her."

"Er . . . sir . . . ," the man called Starkey said, "the *East Wind*'s first mate swore he'd heard this was the biggest cargo in years."

Griffin continued to stare at Brianne, indecision and misery warring in his gaze.

"What?" Brianne finally asked. "What are you guys talking about?"

Griffin took a deep breath and slid his hand into hers.

"We are talking about slaves, sweetheart. I can either stay here and get married tonight, or Alec and I can try to free a shipload of slaves."

Chapter 15

THE TWO MEN stood on the steps of Shadow Oaks; one a loving husband, one who might have been in a few short hours. Alec grasped Shaelyn and Christopher to his chest with the practiced ease of a man who had said goodbye to his loved ones many times before, even though he hated the prospect of separation. Griffin, on the other hand, looked down at Brianne, his hands hovering for a moment at her upper arms before finally settling there, rubbing up and down while everything he felt, every ounce of reluctance to go, telegraphed to her heart through his soul-searching gaze.

"Every other time I've left on one of these trips," he said as he studied her face, "I was happy to be going. Escaping from a situation I couldn't bear." His hands came up to rub her shoulders. "I . . . I pray you understand I am not running away this time."

His thumbs made gentle circles on her neck, and she willed the tears forming in her throat and behind her eyes to stay put. She wouldn't send him off with the memory of her crying. She closed her eyes and leaned her face into the hand that had worked its way up to cup her cheek.

"Just come back safe," she whispered, then opened her eyes to stare into his, trying to rally a mischievous twinkle, "because I have things planned for you."

He read the unspoken promises in her gaze. She could see them reflected in his own. The sight was like pure salt on her raw, bleeding heart, and if he didn't leave within a matter of moments, she wasn't sure she would have the strength to let him go.

He stared down at her, putting off that last kiss because they both knew it was the point of no return.

"Grif," Alec's voice cut in, the forced humor an obvious ploy to lighten the mood that suffocated them all like the heat of the afternoon sun, "if you are having trouble figuring out how to kiss your charming intended, I will be happy to demonstrate on my own dear wife."

Griffin ignored Alec's good-natured goading, but a wisp of a smile curved one corner of his lips. His eyes narrowed with want, with love, then his head dipped and his mouth slid onto hers as he pulled her into him, fitting their bodies together like the last two pieces of a puzzle. The feel of him sent a hot, liquid need ruffling through her blood to explode into excruciating pinpoints of a want that would have to wait to be satisfied. She gave as good as she got, using her tongue to tell him without words exactly what would be waiting for him when he got home. He held her up when her knees went soft, and she smiled in spite of herself when she felt his own knees giving out.

Finally, only after Alec cleared his throat and Christopher gurgled some nonsense did Griffin slowly, reluctantly end the kiss. He stared down at her and told her how he loved her with nothing more than the look in those intense eyes; told her more eloquently than any words could ever express.

He raised his head and straightened his shoulders, never breaking their gaze.

"I appreciate the offer for the lesson, Hawthorne," he said, still staring at Brianne with that heart-wrenching gaze, "but I can do my own damn kissing."

He spun on his heel and marched down the steps just as every muscle in Brianne's body jerked at his words.

David! Her mind spun with the realization. *Griffin is David!*

Oh, good lord, why had she not seen this before? It all made sense. It all made perfect sense. David was her soul mate in the future. The one man she'd been closest to. The one man she'd ever cared about losing. Their friendship meant everything to her, and that last kiss, that grown-up kiss that had come from David before the lightning struck, had rocked her soul with as much force as Griffin's.

With the *same* force as Griffin's.

Had David realized the truth in that moment? Hadn't he looked at her and said they needed to talk? David never "announced" a need to talk. He just said what was on his mind. Had he been ready to tell her that he thought of her as more than a friend? Oh, how could she have been so blind? How could they both have been so blind?

The creak of leather as the men climbed into their saddles brought Brianne out of her stupor. She rushed down the steps and grabbed Griffin's hand, pulling him down to her for one last kiss.

"You come back to me," she choked through hot tears tightening her throat. "Do you hear me? You come back to me."

A questioning flicker flashed in his eyes before he seared her with a deadly serious gaze.

"I will always come back to you, sweetheart." He leaned in to claim her mouth for one more reassuring kiss. "I will always come back."

•   •   •

Griffin had taken command of the *Sea Gypsy* while Alec captained the *Rising Star.* The *Gypsy* drew near enough to the other ship now that Griffin could see Alec stagger to the rail of the helm and lose his last meal over the side. That made three times that day. Griffin couldn't help but laugh. A sorry affliction for someone with his and Alec's occasional occupation. But the stubborn fool sailed, granted with a sickly shade of green tinting his skin, but he sailed nonetheless. And each time, Alec swore it would be the last.

Until he heard about the next shipload of slaves.

"Now that you are a father," Griffin shouted across the waters, "perhaps you'll become legend as the Puking Papa!" He and Alec had a long-standing joke as to what they should call themselves when out on a . . . liberating run.

Alec's head slowly raised from the side of the rail.

"You are brave with your insults, Griffin Elliott," he shouted back. "Keep it up and your bride will know you as the Grimacing Groom."

Griffin laughed and turned his attention back to the wheel. No one was as much fun to goad as Alec. Damn, he wished the man lived closer.

"Griffin is David." Shaelyn repeated the phrase like a child trying to understand a Bible verse through rote. "David. The David that made you feel like you were kissing a brother the one and only time you kissed."

Brianne shook her head and flopped into the nearest chair before she wore a threadbare path in the handwoven carpet.

"We were thirteen years old then, Shae. And it *wasn't* our one and only kiss." Bri told her then about that last kiss, about how she'd opened her eyes to find David's hot, brown gaze staring back at her. "He nearly melted my bones and sent steam rising off my skin. Trust me, there was nothing brotherly about that kiss."

Shae drummed her fingers on the Linke table beside the sofa and stared at a point somewhere beyond the ceiling.

"You know, it sort of makes sense." She brought her focus back to Brianne. "You two have always been together, even if you weren't . . . you know . . . *together.* And neither one of you have ever come even close to getting serious over someone else."

"What about Heather? Don't forget he's engaged to the bubblehead." Bri scooted sideways in the chair and draped a cloud of pale blue taffeta-covered legs over the arm. It felt so good to be able to be herself.

"Oh, Heather's more a social climber than a bubblehead. She's smarter than she lets on. Besides, it's purely hormonal on David's part." Shae waved away the engagement as if it were no more than a penciled-in lunch date. "I think there's some kind of chemical reaction that impairs the brain when testosterone mingles in the same air with silicone." She stopped and blinked. "Or are they still using silicone?"

Bri snorted and shook her head. "How would I know? I never had people lining up for the name of my plastic surgeon." She glanced down at her barely adequate bosom to make the point, only to see Amily's slightly more endowed version. She shrugged and swung her feet back to the floor. Remembering whose body she was in brought her mind back to Griffin.

"I want to know what Griffin and Alec are up to." Time had been of the essence, according to the message about the ship, and Griffin had only given her a few sketchy details. "What's this deal with the slaves? When did they get involved with stealing them out from under the captains' noses? Isn't that illegal somehow?"

Shaelyn shrugged and shook her head. "It's illegal for the smugglers to bring slaves into the country to sell to begin with. It has been since 1808. But that hasn't stopped the traffic. So Alec and Griffin, along with a few others, are doing something about it."

Fifteen minutes later, Brianne paced the floor, wringing her hands while Shaelyn rocked a sleepy Christopher.

"So, what you're saying is, Griffin and Alec hear about these ships loaded with slaves, and they go out and take them?" She'd already heard the answer a half dozen times, but she still couldn't quite absorb the reality. She kept picturing some swashbuckling pirate movie in her mind.

Shaelyn nodded, shifting Christopher to her other shoulder. "They send them to Nova Scotia, where they can either remain or return to their homeland."

"And they've been doing this for years. Anonymously."

Shae nodded again. "Ever since they met in Europe on their Grand Tour. You'll have to ask them about that meeting someday." Her smile didn't quite mask the worry in her eyes.

Brianne sank back to the satin brocade chair. Slaves. Ships. Hundreds of people saved from a lifetime of slavery. Of course he had to go. She'd insisted, once she understood what was at stake.

And he'd gone, though reluctantly.

"I still can't believe this." She stared off into the distance, her mind muddled with the thought that she might have been married that evening, that Griffin was off chasing slave ships, that David was her soul mate in the future, that Shaelyn was here with her in the past.

"Shae." She turned her gaze to her friend. "Do you ever get used to it? Really used to it?"

She didn't have to elaborate on her question. They thought too much alike for that.

Shaelyn looked down at Christopher's sleeping face and smiled.

"It hasn't been hard for me, Bri. You know I never felt

like I fit in in the future. This time period seems more like home. But I will tell you a little secret. Alec and I have talked about trying to travel to the future, just so Mom and Dad can meet Chris."

"Travel . . . How could you do that?" Was there hope that Brianne could return to her time? If she went back to David, would it prolong their lives here as Amily and Griffin? Could she give up Griffin? Oh, lord, her head hurt.

"One night, after Chris was born, Alec and I were all cuddled up in bed and I was fiddling with my rings." Shaelyn twisted them, even as she spoke. "I got so used to trying to get the betrothal ring off, it just became a habit for me to twist them. Anyway, I lost so much weight after Chris was born, the rings slipped over my finger before I realized it. I had Alec's arm entwined with mine, and we *both* got that weird, dizzy sensation. The next thing we knew, we were in the future. We were still in bed, but I recognized the room the way it looked in the future when I visited the house then. It scared us to death, knowing that Chris was still in 1830. I slid the ring back on and we went back to our own bed. It scared us, Bri, but at the same time it comforted me, to know that I might be able to take my husband and son to meet Mom and Dad. And you."

Shaelyn smiled and Brianne smiled back, wishing she had the comfort of knowing she could get back to her time if she wanted to.

"Amazingly," Shae went on, "Alec was the one to mention our possibly trying it someday with Christopher in our arms. Ever since then we've talked about it, trying to plan how to go about it. We plan to have modern clothes made, so we'd be dressed for the part when we arrive." She grinned conspiratorially. "Won't that be fun explaining to a seamstress? But we're trying to cover every detail. I don't know if we'll ever get the nerve to try, though."

"Sure you will," Brianne assured her. "If anyone can do it, you can." She stood and wandered to the window, staring out into the distance, seeing nothing. "Shae," she said, finally wanting to voice what had been eating at her mind all day, "what if he doesn't come back from this?" The silence behind her stretched until she turned around and looked at her friend. "What if neither one of them comes back?"

That gray, haunted look returned to Shae's face, but she just shook her head.

"I don't let myself think about it. I'd go crazy if I did. I just tell myself they've been doing this for years. They don't take stupid chances. They've never gotten caught. I just don't think about it." She laid a limp Christopher on the divan, propped pillows around him, then came to put her arm around Brianne and stare out the window with her. "I do know this, though. I would rather have the time I've had with Alec, no matter how brief, than to have never had him at all."

Griffin stared out at the expanse of sea, looking for nothing, feeling as though time stretched on before him forever, just as the ocean did. They had only just set sail the day before, and already he felt as if he'd been away from Amily for weeks.

Amily. Try as he might, he could not think of her as this Brianne, though he no longer denied her story.

At the thought, a sickening knot of worry balled in his stomach. If her impossible story was true, could they somehow outwit fate and escape the death Amily swore would claim them? A riding accident. Each of them on horseback. And possibly a washed-out bridge. If only she knew more details—the date, the circumstances—then they could avoid the situation at all costs.

He shook his head and leaned against the rail, his weight

on his forearms as he stared down at the hull of the ship slic-
ing through the water. If it took never getting on a horse
again in his life, then that was what he would do to insure
their safety.

The sound of dry heaves only inches from his ear effectively pulled his thoughts back to the present.

"Hawthorne," he sighed as he slapped a pale green Alec
on the back, "I thought you jumped ship for a round of gambling, not a round of gagging. You could be heaving on your
own decks." He knew sympathy would only embarrass his
old friend. He took a dramatic step away and pointedly
tested the wind for direction.

Alec sucked in a breath of fresh sea air and looked at the
sky.

"Next time I manage to get something on my stomach,
Elliott," he swallowed hard, then slid a narrowed gaze to
Griffin, "I plan to aim at you when it comes back up."

Griffin snorted and leaned his back against the rail. "Did
Esther's suggestion of egg whites and lemon not help? She
is quite good at remedies."

Alec lowered his head and glared as if he wanted to kill
him.

"Think about it, Grif. Swallowing egg whites and lemon
juice. Hell, no, it didn't help. Neither did the wormwood
tincture or the green tea or eating cayenne pepper or chewing mint and sage. Saint's blood, Elliott, the only cure for
this hellish malady is to remove myself from this godforsaken wasteland of pitching, roiling . . ." He leaned over and
retched again, then dropped to his knees and thumped his
forehead against the smooth, varnished rail. "I hate you."

Griffin pulled a deck of cards from his inside coat pocket.
"So what you are saying is, you've no wish for a game of
chance at the moment?"

• • •

"You let him go to sea the night he would have married you?" Rebecca sat across from Brianne and Shaelyn, her eyebrows nearly to her hairline. "What in the world possessed you to allow him to go to sea? What could possibly be that important?"

Alec and Griffin had already given them a story to tell for anyone who questioned their absence.

"One of Griffin's ships ran aground near Cuba, and they took a ship to transfer the cargo," Brianne lied.

"Why could they not have simply *sent* a ship?"

Brianne shrugged with an innocent smile. "I would assume that the cargo was very valuable."

Rebecca shook her head, a genuine look of disappointment on her face.

"Could you not have wed before he left?"

Brianne threw Shaelyn a wicked grin. "Where would the fun be in that? Besides," she said, "there just wasn't time." Brianne nearly kissed Della when the little maid arrived with a tray of refreshments. Anything to get Rebecca off the subject.

She'd arrived at the house just as Shaelyn and Brianne had finished dressing—an unheard of hour for calling, according to Shaelyn. Rebecca apparently had watched for Amily the day before, hoping to catch her and talk her out of leaving, then when the Elliott carriage never passed her house, she'd come this morning to see if Amily had boarded a riverboat from the Shadow Oaks dock.

Brianne's first thought was that Rebecca had trotted right over to console Griffin, but she had to admit that the woman had seemed happy to see her. Maybe Brianne had misjudged her, or maybe she truly was grateful for Brianne's help during the flu epidemic. Whatever the reason, there was no denying that Rebecca considered herself Amily's friend now, and with that title came the right to give her advice about getting married. Shaelyn, bless her, changed the subject before any more questions could be raised.

"Rebecca, you'll get to meet Alec's mother and sister." Shaelyn poured a cup of tea and handed it to their early morning visitor. "They stayed over in Baton Rouge to order some furniture, but they should arrive today by noon. Why don't you stay and have lunch with us so I can introduce you?"

Brianne would have kicked Shaelyn on the shins for that invitation, but she doubted she'd do much damage through all the layers of skirts. As much as Rebecca had changed, there was still something about her that made her so . . . avoidable. Brianne shook her head slightly. She really did need to get past Rebecca's earlier treatment of her.

"Why, thank you," Rebecca gushed, settling back into the brocade chair. "I would love to. And what a perfect opportunity to plan Amily's wedding."

Griffin put the telescope to his eye and focused on the white dot on the horizon. No doubt about it. This was the *Profiteer.* He picked up the signal flag and waved it. Alec, at the helm of the *Rising Star,* responded in kind. With their plan of attack already laid out, Griffin gave the command to sail straight for her, while Alec's ship veered away to come in from the other side.

"Are all identifiable markings covered, Mr. Starkey?" he verified with his first mate.

"Aye, sir," Starkey answered. On Griffin's cue, the men donned the black silk masks that covered their faces and protected their identities.

They were no more than a day's sail out of Cuba, and as low as she rode in the water, the *Profiteer* still had a hold full of human cargo. The *Rising Star* and the *Sea Gypsy* had lain in wait for the ship, until Griffin wondered if the blasted crew of the slaver would ever end their shore leave. But they were in open waters now. Soon the ship would be theirs and he would be on his way back to Amily. More than two weeks without her. He would never let that happen again.

Griffin and Alec both gained on the ship before they were noticed, but the *Profiteer*'s heavy load kept her from outrunning her pursuers. Even at that, it took them a full five hours to close in for their attack, and they would have to rush to take the ship before nightfall.

"Mr. Starkey, fire a warning shot over her bow," Griffin barked. Within seconds the order was repeated, and the deck lurched with the vibrations of the artillery. An answering shot sailed over the *Profiteer*'s stern from Alec's ship. Immediately, the sails on the slaver started dropping and within minutes the cargo ship wallowed in the water, an easy target for dozens of cannon.

"I'll know your business!" the bearded captain of the slaver bellowed across the waves. Alec maneuvered the *Rising Star* close enough to blow them to kingdom come while Griffin sailed even closer.

"We'll have your cargo!" Griffin answered, his voice only slightly muffled from the black silk covering his face.

"Over my dead body!"

Another blast from the *Rising Star* sent a single cannonball crashing through the aftermast.

"That can be arranged," Griffin warned. "If you force us to fight for the cargo, there will be no quarter given."

The setting sun sent its blinding red-orange rays bouncing across the water, painting elongated shadows across the decks, lighting up the helm of the slave ship with a golden glow. Its captain, lean and tall, squinted into the sun toward the *Sea Gypsy,* obviously weighing his options. Suddenly a familiar form scrambled up the ladder to the helm and shoved his face toward the bearded captain's.

Griffin sighed and checked his cuticles while an argument ensued on the captured ship. He gave them only a couple of minutes, but when the sun began to sink into the ocean, he pulled a pistol from his waistband and fired a shot into the air. When the captain and the other man turned to stare, Griffin handed his gun to Starkey to be reloaded.

"Tilburn, have you not given up the smuggling of slaves yet? Will it take your death? Or merely marooning you on an uncharted island?"

"Damn your soul to Hell!" Tilburn yelled, his voice skimming across the calm sea. "I just purchased this load in Cuba. I'll not hand it over to the likes of you!"

"Hand it over or die. Either way, you lose."

While Tilburn ranted and raved, he failed to notice the captain signal his crew to lay down their arms. Once the men had crowded to one end of the deck, grappling hooks from the *Rising Star* flew through the air and tethered the two ships together. Griffin quietly ordered his men to send hooks from the *Sea Gypsy,* and within moments the three ships bobbed in the water, joined by bridging planks.

Griffin and Alec boarded from their respective sides, and while Alec took charge of freeing the poor devils in the hold, Griffin climbed the ladder to the helm.

All he wanted was to get this interminable trip over with and get back to Amily's arms. The sun sank deeper into the western horizon, turning the sky purple, and instead of already making his way back to the arms of his beloved, he was just boarding this slaver, listening to Tilburn's screeches. He flung himself from the ladder onto the deck, took two steps, then plowed his fist into Tilburn's face.

The world went blessedly silent.

Griffin stepped over the unconscious body and took the sword from the captain's scabbard.

"A wise choice," Griffin stated, looking the rough captain of the *Profiteer* in the eye. "This man isn't worth dying for."

The captain glared his defiance—Griffin had to grudgingly respect him for that—but he remained silent.

"Captain!" Griffin walked to the rail and turned to Alec, who stood at the hold, helping the more feeble of the Africans onto the deck. Alec looked up at Griffin's call. "Will we need the ship for transporting, or do we allow—"

Alec jerked and screamed from behind his mask, "Look out!"

Griffin turned to see the silhouette of Tilburn lunging toward him against the evening sky. He didn't see the knife, but he felt it as the blade scraped bone on its way in, plunging to the hilt. He staggered back under the weight of his attacker, then felt himself go over the rail and fall. Falling forever, until he hit the cool, dark Caribbean water. He struggled to keep his head above the surface, but his arms refused to work. A darkness blacker than the water encroached on his consciousness. He kicked with his legs, but still he could feel the water inching higher up his face, until just his mouth and nose broke the surface.

Amily. Dear God, was she right? Would they die before their time? Would he die here, now, and leave his spirit to haunt the generations to come until he found her again? *I love you Amily. I've always loved you.* He sank deeper, struggling to breathe. He sucked in water. *Wait for me, sweetheart. I'll find you. I promise, I'll find you.*

Chapter 16

ALEC'S SISTER, MOLLY, and his mother, Jane, were as
excited about the upcoming wedding as Rebecca. In the
weeks since Jane and Molly's arrival, the three of them
took over, like drill sergeants, and planned the most elaborate "small" wedding Brianne would allow. She would
have preferred a quiet ceremony and a mad dash to the
honeymoon suite, but everyone, including Shaelyn, insisted she would regret not making the day special. They
had everything prepared, right down to making the finishing touches on the wedding gown, just waiting for Griffin
and Alec's return.

Jane had thought it odd, upon arriving one short day after
Shaelyn and Alec, that the men had left on a business trip,
but she hadn't been hard to convince that the trip had been
necessary.

Molly, on the other hand, hadn't believed a word. The
moment she'd found Shaelyn and Brianne alone, she'd cor-
nered them, hands on her hips.

"They've gone off liberating slaves again, haven't they?"

Brianne looked at Shaelyn, who just sighed and shrugged.

The nineteen-year-old female version of Alec had stunned Brianne again when she flopped into a chair and said, "It's that . . . what did you call it, Shae? That testosterone thing."

Brianne had slid her gaze to Shaelyn and whispered, "She knows?"

Shae nodded and smiled at her sister-in-law, who continued to fume. "She was the only one to believe me for a while."

Molly was on that same tirade, weeks later, with the well-meaning edge of impatience known only to the young and inexperienced.

"Their luck is going to run out someday. You mark my words."

Brianne ignored the shiver that crept up her spine.

"This is why I plan to never marry. I would much rather be off having the adventures than waiting, with my hands folded, at home. How can the two of you stand it? Knowing that they sail, armed to the teeth, and with good reason. One of these days they'll not—"

"Molly," Shae interrupted, that worried, gray cast back in her face, "do you remember me telling you about my good friend in the future?"

Molly blinked and looked at Shaelyn.

"Yes. Brianne. You talk of her all the time, but what has that to do with—"

"Amily is Brianne."

That got her attention. And effectively got her mind off predicting doom and gloom for the men, which was no doubt Shaelyn's intention.

"Amily is Brianne," Molly repeated, her blank look turning to one of curious excitement. "Truly? You are Brianne?" She scooted to the edge of her seat. "How did you get here? Did you find a ring, as well?"

Once all the facts were given, Molly pelted Brianne with

more questions than a five-year-old. How did it feel to be struck by lightning? Had there been any new modes of transportation invented during Shaelyn's two-year absence? Did she want to go back to her own time? Did she think falling in love with Alec's best friend was Fate or coincidence?

Brianne answered every question and had to marvel at how well Molly took the answers. She wasn't sure she herself could take it in such stride if someone from the twenty-second century dropped in and started telling her about life and technology in that time. Of course, she reminded herself, Molly had had two years to get used to the idea with Shaelyn.

"Look! It's finished! Come try it on." Rebecca stood in the doorway of the parlor, a mountain of creamy silk, satin and lace in her arms. Molly appeared behind her, along with Mrs. Rosemont, the dressmaker from Baton Rouge Rebecca had insisted they use. Thirty minutes later, Brianne stood in front of the cheval glass and looked at her reflection—at Amily's reflection—dressed in a waterfall of satin the color of clotted cream.

All the women—even Molly, the confirmed bachelorette—got that dreamy look a woman gets when she sees someone in a wedding gown.

"Now, all we need is the groom," Molly declared with a sigh.

Yes, Brianne thought as her eyes automatically met the worried reflection of Shaelyn's, except the groom and his best friend should have been back a week ago, and they hadn't heard a word from either of them.

The dress hung on the armoire, a shimmering reminder each morning when she woke and each night when she went to bed that Griffin and Alec were still out there, and that no word had come from them.

She rolled over and hugged her pillow to her chest, then closed her eyes against the morning sun and tried to connect with Griffin's spirit. They had to be alive. She refused to contemplate otherwise. One thing was certain, though. If he didn't have a darned good reason for taking so long and not sending word, she would kill him herself, with her bare hands.

She kicked off the sheets sticky with humidity and flung away the pillow to rise. The wedding gown mocked her again. Without stopping to think, she pulled the gown from its wooden hanger, crammed the yards of satin and lace into the armoire, then slammed the door on it.

There. Now maybe she could have a moment's peace.

A quiet knock drew her attention, then Shaelyn slipped through the door with a breakfast tray.

"I sneaked this from Ruth on the way up. Want some company?"

Brianne poured tepid water from the china pitcher into the matching bowl.

"Just you. Can you chase away a few demons?"

Shae sat cross-legged in her dressing gown on the bed and picked up a sugared biscuit.

"They're coming back, Bri."

Though Shaelyn would have convinced anyone else in the world that she was calm, Brianne heard the almost subliminal note of fear in her voice. They looked at each other and made an unspoken agreement not to talk about it.

While Shae pretended to eat the biscuit, Brianne wrung out a washcloth and dragged it over skin already damp from the heat. What she wouldn't give for a cool shower and one day in an air-conditioned room. Just the thought of putting on all those layers of clothes made her sweat.

"How do you stand it, Shae?" She flopped into a slipper chair next to an open jib window and fanned herself with the washcloth.

"Stand what?" Shae set aside the half-eaten biscuit and focused her attention on Brianne.

"This." Brianne spread her arms wide. "The heat, the lack of conveniences, the general . . . archaicness of everything. It takes forever to get anything done, or to go anywhere. And it's so quiet. So mind-numbingly quiet. There are times when I actually miss the sound of a car alarm going off, or even the maddening whine of a leaf blower. And how do you stand all the unwritten rules of society? If it wasn't for the Amily side of me, I would have been kicked out of polite society ages ago." In fact, the Amily side of her was so much a part of her now, she rarely noticed the moments of help.

Shaelyn put the bottoms of her feet together and did some yoga stretches.

"You'll get used to it, Bri. You haven't been here that long."

"I've been here for months!" And it seemed like years. "How long did it take you to adapt? How long am I going to crave a long shower? When am I going to get over the urge to pick up the phone and call Mom and Dad? And David?"

Her voice broke at the thought of him. What would happen to David if Griffin died now? Would he be affected?

She rubbed the back of her neck where a dull throb had developed.

"How long did it take you, Shae?"

Shaelyn stopped stretching and gave Brianne a helpless look.

"Not this long. But I told you before, this felt like home right away. Sometimes I think I should have been born in this time."

Brianne only nodded. She'd yet to feel like she belonged here. What if this whole thing had been a fluke? What if she wasn't really there to achieve some purpose? What if she should have died in the future? What if. What if. *What if!*

Shaelyn no longer made a pretense of acting calm, and when she gave up the act, the terror really struck Brianne.

It'd been six weeks. A month and a half since Griffin and Alec had ridden off to free a shipload of slaves. No one tried to deny their fear now. Jane and Molly walked around like ghosts, worry creasing their faces. Even Rebecca stopped her incessant talk about the wedding. A gloom hung over the house, so stiflingly like mourning, all that was needed was a black wreath on the door and black crepe over the mirrors. Only Christopher remained oblivious to the heavy mood. And only Christopher could pull any cheer at all from the members of the household.

Though they continued with their story to Rebecca of a business trip, Shaelyn had finally told Jane the truth about where Alec and Griffin had gone. Jane might have been passive, but she was not a fool, and she'd suspected from the start that she hadn't been told everything.

"Can we not send Lucas or Daniel to the docks," Jane broke the silence of the parlor, "to try and glean some information? To try and track—"

Shaelyn shook her head. "They never leave a trail to follow. That's one of the reasons they've been so successful. Nobody recognizes the ships. Nobody recognizes the crew."

Brianne closed her eyes and offered up a prayer for a miracle. She would stop complaining about being in the past. She would stop thinking about showers and microwaves and cars. And if Griffin walked back into her life that very minute and never offered one excuse, she wouldn't want to kill him. Please, God, believe her. She wouldn't want to kill him.

Chapter 17

SATAN STOOD OVER him with something glowing red in his hand.

Strange, Griffin had never thought he would actually go to Hell when he died. He had done his share of sinning, then again he had also done his share of good works. But he most certainly had died, and if this wasn't Hell, he didn't want to find out what was.

The constant pain in his chest burned like fire, and he prayed for the black depths of oblivion to overtake him again.

Would prayer work in Hell?

Apparently not, since he remained torturously awake.

Satan leaned over him now, his dark face and the red-hot glowing pike no more than a blur in the haze of pain.

"Hold him down," Satan ordered. Strong hands gripped him at his shoulders, then the devil laid the tip of his pitch-fork against Griffin's chest.

Fiery, white-hot agony seared him to his very fingertips, and the smell of burning flesh filled his nostrils. He screamed, fought against the hands holding him down, gagged at the smell of his own skin burning. He bucked against the pain with every ounce of his strength, but not until Satan stood and removed the glowing pitchfork did the hands release their hold.

"Hold on, Grif," Alec whispered in his ear. "I won't let you give up."

"Saint's blood, Alec," Griffin croaked, his throat sore from screaming. "You went to Hell, too?"

A blinding light on the other side of his lids pulled Griffin from the deep, welcome pit in which he'd been floating. He didn't want to open his eyes to see what Beelzebub had in store for him and Alec now.

Alec! Griffin had no sooner realized that Alec was there in Hell with him, had held him down while Satan tortured him, than he'd felt the firm grasp of unconsciousness pulling at him. Now he allowed the light to bring him fully awake. He opened his eyes to the sight of a white sun glaring through the leaded window of his cabin.

His cabin? Then he wasn't dead!

He struggled to rise, but his left arm refused to work. He rolled to his side and shoved with his right arm, then fell back to the bunk when pain ripped across his chest.

"Grif, damn it, if you don't lay still, I'm going to cuff you one!"

Alec's face swam in a distorted blur in front of Griffin's eyes. He stopped struggling and focused on his friend, then realized his vision wasn't as distorted as he'd thought.

"You look like hell, Hawthorne," he rasped. "Who gave you the shiner?" When Alec simply glared at him, he added, "I hope he's at least in worse shape than you are."

Alec snorted. "He is. *You* gave it to me, you lucky bastard, and if you continue to thrash around, now that you're awake, I am going to take great pleasure in giving you a matched set."

Griffin lay still for a moment and stared at his friend. He wore several days growth of beard, and had a dark circle of fatigue under the eye that wasn't swollen in a puffy rainbow of red, blue, purple, and pink.

He tried to sit up again, but just as the pain hit his chest, just as panic seized him when his arm refused to work, Alec shoved him back to the mattress and yelled at him.

"Lie still, damn you! Or do you want that wound cauterized again?"

Cauterized? Was that the glowing pitchfork Satan had laid on his chest?

"Alec, what happened? Where are we? Why can't I move my arm?" He jerked and felt for his left arm.

Nothing was there!

"Alec!" He fought to rise.

The fist slammed into his jaw like the kick of a mule. His head bounced back onto the pillow while pinpricks of light swam in his vision.

"You still have your arm, damn it, at least until you open the wound again, in which case I plan to throw you overboard and be done with you." Alec flopped back into the chair, stretched his legs out in front of him, rubbed his eyes, then winced at touching the swollen flesh on the left side. "Your arm is bandaged as tight as we could get it against your body," he sighed, testing and wincing each time he touched his eye. "The knife wound was so jagged, you kept pulling the stitches. Tilburn, the blackguard, must have held on all the way to the water. If the blade hadn't hit a rib on the way in, I'd be talking to a corpse right now." Alec flexed the fingers of the fist he'd just plowed into Griffin's face, then turned his attention back to his eye. "When the wound showed signs of becoming septic, the doctor we . . . appropriated from his bed in the middle of the night, said it needed to be cauterized. Personally, I think he took a certain amount of pleasure in the procedure."

Griffin moaned at the memory. If the doctor's degree of enjoyment could be measured in the amount of pain he'd inflicted, then the man had had a veritable orgy.

"Where are we? What about the cargo? Where's Tilburn? I hope you killed the son of a bitch."

Alec stopped prodding at his eye and let his hands fall to the armrests of the chair.

"We're a couple days out of Cuba. We had to sail there to find you a doctor. The cargo is on its way north. And, as I said, Tilburn went over the rail with you. We searched the water for him, but it was dark. We were lucky to find your sorry carcass. Needless to say, we searched for you first. You were so close to dead it wasn't funny, Grif. He had to have drowned."

Griffin nodded. The world was a better place.

"And what of the ship? Did you allow the captain to keep it?"

Alec shook his head, a look of wonder on his face.

"I doubt we could have gotten the entire cargo on both our ships. The *Profiteer* had false walls in her hold. She was built with a bulging hull beneath the waterline, where customs can't see the added space. There were as many Africans packed in the extra space as was in the official hold. No, I sent the *Profiteer* north, along with the *Rising Star,* and I set the captain and crew adrift. No doubt they'll soon make Cuba."

Griffin closed his eyes and worked the jaw Alec had abused. He was on his way back to Amily. He had other questions for Alec, but the important thing was that he was on his way back to his beloved. God willing, in less than two weeks he would have her back in his arms, and then noth-

ing, he swore to himself, nothing would ever separate them
again.

Brianne spent her days pacing. She couldn't sit still; she
couldn't eat; she couldn't sleep. She had the beginnings of
an award-winning ulcer. She certainly couldn't sit and do
needlepoint, as Jane kept insisting she do. She didn't *want*
to get her mind off him. She knew that as soon as she let her
guard down, as soon as she stopped worrying for even a moment, someone would trot up that drive and tell them
Griffin and Alec were dead.

Shaelyn at least had Christopher to occupy her time,
which was a blessing. Considering that she'd nearly lost
Alec once before, this latest ordeal had her almost paralyzed
with fear.

Brianne slipped from her room after dressing, then went
down the back steps of the veranda. She had to get out and
be alone, and if the others saw her leave, someone would insist on going with her. Especially Shaelyn, who hovered
over her every moment. Why was it that when you needed
to be alone the most, no one gave you a moment's peace?

A thick layer of clouds blocked out any sign of the sun
and made the stifling heat and humidity of the day almost
suffocating. Yet even with all that heat, her heart stayed
frozen. Frozen with worry and fear.

She struck out in a direction where she would least likely
be seen by someone from one of the windows, then turned
toward the river to walk among the trees lining its banks. A
rumble of thunder rolled across the sky from the distance.

What would she do if Griffin never returned? How could
she stay in this godforsaken time without him? The thunder
rolled again, an ominous answer to her musings.

Maybe she should just go find herself a rip-roaring lightning storm and send a kite up in the middle of it. If she knew

it wouldn't kill her, that it would send her back to David, she just might consider it. Had she screwed up David's future by altering Griffin's past? Would their spirit even come looking for her now?

A chill skittered along her spine and up her neck at the thought of David being Griffin, her soul mate. It made such perfect sense now, she felt like a fool for not seeing him in that light before. But then, they had rushed things. They had gotten curious and kissed at an age when they could only be embarrassed by it, and that awkward moment had set the tone for a friendship rather than a romance.

She wandered on as the thunder drew closer. If she kept walking, walked right into the storm, and just allowed Fate to take over from there . . .

"Shae tells me you plan to kill me with your bare hands."

Her heart skipped a beat and lodged in her throat as blood roared in her ears. She stopped dead in her tracks, her body shaking. When she finally managed to turn, there he stood, not ten feet away, the most beautiful sight in the world. His gaze embraced her, wrapped around her. She offered up thanks for her answered prayers.

"Griffin." The word was a whispered sob. And then she ran to him, not slowing until their bodies connected, until she had him wrapped in her arms, trying to pull him right into her, until his mouth came down on hers, equally desperate. His kiss exploded millions of hot, tingling stars and sent them pinwheeling through her, heating her body, thawing her heart, melting her spine, and buckling her knees. The sky rumbled above them, as if underscoring what she felt.

When her legs gave out, instead of holding her up, Griffin sank to his knees with her, his lips never leaving hers. They knelt there together, among the trees on the banks of the river, and once the desperation lifted, her hands wandered, caressing rough cheeks, the muscled expanse of his back, the length of his neck. Her fingers sifted through his hair, shiny and dark and curling softly from the humidity. Their reassuring touches turned needy, desperate once again, but desperate now for something more. He groaned, deep and low in his throat, and pulled her down onto a bed of leaves and moss. His lips left hers only to trail searing kisses along her neck. He whispered, "Amily. My sweet Amily," and his warm breath bathed her skin with those precious words. No longer did she feel like two people sharing the same body, but one person, one soul, in love with the man who was David and Griffin, one man, one soul. It no longer mattered to her where she was or what name she used. All that mattered was that this man, this one man she would love throughout time, was with her.

He lifted his head finally and gazed down at her, his blue eyes smoky with want.

"When Shaelyn said you were going to kill me with your bare hands, this was not exactly what I expected."

Those words, and his voice, his precious, precious voice, did things to her insides that defied description. She stared at him, held his gaze, then let her hands wander further. He sucked in his breath.

"If I'd known this was what she meant . . ." He closed his eyes and moaned.

Brianne tugged at his shirt, ran her hands across the ridges and plains of his body.

"I'm not through with you yet," she murmured.

He groaned, swallowed hard, then growled, "Good," against her lips.

At first she thought someone had thrown a bucket of icy water on their fevered bodies, until she realized the skies had opened up and dumped a wall of rain on them.

She cursed under her breath and Griffin rolled off of her onto his back, moaning as if he'd been shot.

"This is not at all humorous!" he yelled at the Heavens. The heavens didn't seem to care.

They looked at each other then, and a giggle worked its way up her throat. When Griffin's lips twitched, her laughter bubbled forth. She rolled over and nestled her head against his chest. He stiffened a bit, and she realized what she nuzzled beneath his wet shirt was not hard muscle but a taut bandage.

"What the . . ." She scrambled to her knees and ripped open his shirt, sending buttons flying. Strips of gauze held a bandage in place just beneath his shoulder and just left of his heart.

The dread that had plagued her for weeks came back to haunt her and that queasy sickness roiled in her stomach. What had he been through? What had kept him from returning to her? What had happened that caused an injury so close to his heart?

She glared at him through the driving rain. He gave her an innocent shrug and a little boy smile.

She wanted to choke him.

"Well, it looks like I might not have had to kill you with my bare hands, after all," she said, allowing a little threat to creep into her words. "It looks like someone else tried to save me the trouble."

She pulled herself to her feet and shook out skirts growing heavier by the minute in the pouring rain.

"We're going back to the house to get you into some dry clothes, and on the way you have some explaining to do."

Miraculously, the rain suddenly stopped and the sun came out when he rose to tower over her. He took one limping step and she noticed he was favoring his left side a bit.

"Now, Amily, sweetheart—"

"And you'd better not leave anything out, because, I warn you, what you don't tell, Shaelyn will get out of Alec."

• • •

The celebration was in full swing by the time they got back to the house. Brianne's mind spun, reeling from all Griffin had told her on the walk back, giddy with relief that his life had been spared.

They stepped through the front door, leaving puddles of water in their wake. She caught a glimpse of herself in the mirrored hall tree. Her limp, sodden gown stuck to her body like tissue paper. Dark, wavy tendrils of hair clung to her face and neck like vines clinging to a tree. She looked like hell, but a light lit her eyes from within.

Griffin, on the other hand, looked magnificent. Exhausted, but magnificent. Wet, dry, or even injured, he could make her heart stop with just one look.

"They're back!" Molly announced, and the little crowd spilled from the parlor and converged on them in the entry hall. Shaelyn dragged Alec with her, obviously not about to let go of him for a moment. Rebecca had arrived during Brianne's walk. Molly and Jane offered their hugs, and Christopher added a wet, noisy kiss. Every one of the house servants came in to welcome Griffin home. They'd been as worried, as gloomily silent, as Brianne and Shaelyn.

"I must say, Grif," Alec slapped him on the shoulder, exploding droplets of water from the fabric, "you don't look the worse for wear from the abuse threatened against you."

Brianne's cheeks heated when Griffin slid a hot gaze at her and said, "Appearances can be deceiving, Hawthorne."

Shaelyn elbowed her way into the center, tossed an evil grin at Brianne, and said, "I don't know about the rest of you, but I vote we get these two married today. The sooner the better, before some other disaster befalls them."

Brianne caught her pointed look. She didn't need the meaning spelled out. Get married now and change Amily and Griffin's fate.

The little crowd buzzed in agreement. She turned to Griffin, the two of them all but forgotten while the other's planned their life for them.

"Are you up to this?" Brianne asked, gently touching the still-dripping jacket over his wound. "I mean, just two weeks ago you were close to death."

Griffin smiled down at her, sent her heart fluttering when he cupped her face and ran his thumb across her cheek, then turned her knees to honey when he bent over and whispered in her ear, "Well, then, you shall have to love me back to life tonight, won't you?"

The mental image of that kicked her already thrumming heart into double time and robbed her of the shallow breath she'd been struggling for. A tidal wave of lust, hot and urgent and blinding, crashed over her.

She had never wanted anything so badly, so desperately, as to love this man back to life.

"We shouldn't have let him go on horseback, Shae. What were we thinking?"

Brianne squirmed on the vanity stool as Shaelyn applied an antique curling iron to her hair.

"He didn't die on the voyage without you, and he's not going to die on horseback now. We're going to get you two married and change your . . . er . . . Amily and Griffin's destiny. Stop fidgeting or I'm going to burn you."

Brianne forced herself to sit still, but she couldn't keep her mind off Griffin, who had left again once the storm had passed, to ask an old friend, Judge Falston, to marry them and waive the legalities.

"Look, here they come now." Shaelyn hauled Bri up off the stool and pushed her toward the window. Sure enough, Alec, Griffin, and a portly stranger in a black suit trotted up the drive. "See? Safe and sound. Now sit still so I can finish with your hair."

A huge load of worry lifted from Brianne's shoulders and she settled back onto the vanity stool so Shaelyn could torture her hair some more.

"How did you get so good with that thing?" She watched Shaelyn hold the metal curling rod over the flame of an oil lamp, then wrap a black tendril around it like a pro. "I would have burned the house down, or needed a trauma center to take care of the third degree burns I inflicted on myself."

Shaelyn wiggled her eyebrows at Bri's reflection.

"I'm a woman of many talents. You'd be amazed at what I can do." She dropped that curl and swirled up another. "You know, this time isn't quite as backward as you'd think. Almost every convenience we have in the future, they have here, only not quite so sophisticated. They even have cappuccino machines. Primitive, but workable."

"No." Shae had to be teasing.

"Yes. We have one in Cape Helm. I'll fix you some when you and Griffin come to Maine."

This time couldn't be all bad if they had cappuccino. Maybe she could learn to live in it, after all.

A quiet knock sounded on the door, then Molly peeked in from the hallway.

"Mind if Rebecca and I help?" she asked, then came in without waiting for an answer. Rebecca brought up the rear, carrying a gorgeous bouquet of pale pink roses trimmed with dozens of flowing white satin ribbons.

"We sent runners out with notes to invite the neighbors," Molly all but chirped. For someone who swore she planned never to marry, she got awfully excited about someone else's wedding. Brianne couldn't help but smile. "We already have several acceptances."

"And we cut these for you," Rebecca said as she laid the roses on the vanity.

"Oh, they're beautiful!"

Brianne leaned forward and sniffed, pulling Shaelyn and the curling iron with her.

"Griffin said he'd be ready as soon as he washed the smell of horse off him, but I told him to take his time. It'll be at least an hour before you're ready and the neighbors start to show up."

Brianne took a deep breath and concentrated on relaxing the knots in her shoulders while she exhaled. Married in an hour. This time yesterday she was frantic with worry, fearing he was dead, and today she would be married to Griffin before the sun sank below the tops of the live oaks.

Her stomach fluttered as though a flock of doves were taking flight in there, but she wasn't sure how much of that was excitement and how much was fear. She couldn't forget that Amily and Griffin had died before they had an opportunity to marry. Had that been Fate, or Chance? If it was Fate, would something happen even now? Would the house catch on fire? A tree fall into the parlor? Lightning strike them both?

She glanced out at the cloudless, deep blue sky.

"Molly," she said, deciding to do what she could to prevent disaster, "I think I'd like for the ceremony to be in the gardens. In the center, next to the reflecting pond, where there aren't any trees."

Molly stopped fluffing the tiers of lace on the wedding gown and turned to look at Brianne.

"Very well, Amily," she said, looking a little puzzled. "I'll tell Gaston to have the chairs and decorations moved to the garden." Molly still called her Amily, even though she knew the truth. Only Shae called her Brianne, and then only in private.

Rebecca smoothed the gossamer veil attached to a ringlet of satin rosebuds studded with seed pearls, then hung it next to the wedding gown on the carved oak armoire.

"I'll help," she said after one final smoothing. "We want everything to be perfect."

Bri looked at Shaelyn's reflection after the door closed behind Rebecca. She didn't have to say anything. Her best friend had read her mind again.

"Nothing's going to happen, Bri." Shaelyn shoved a final hairpin into the intricate mass of braids and curls. "You're going to be married today, we're going to change Fate, and there's nothing that's going to stop us."

Griffin fumbled with his cravat, tied it in a lopsided knot, then yanked the knot free with a muttered curse and started over for the fifth time. Alec sprawled, straight-legged, in a chair and viewed the scene with a brotherly smirk.

"Watching you, one might believe this was your first time, in more than just marriage."

Griffin glared at Alec's perfectly knotted tie.

"Dare I remind you who tied your cravat, and very nearly had to button your morning coat, when you wed Shaelyn . . . the second time?"

Alec stared at the ceiling in all innocence, then a private, decadent grin curved his lips.

"Ah, yes. I was merely conserving my strength for the night that followed."

The night that followed. Just the thought of the night to come caused Griffin's blood to pump harder through his veins. He tried not to think about it. It wouldn't do to have to limp down the aisle.

"Damnation!" He jerked the strip of black silk from his neck, wadded it into a tight ball, flung it to the floor, then whipped another one from the drawer. "Lucas!" he roared toward the interior of the house.

His manservant appeared within moments carrying Griffin's freshly pressed coat. He took one look at the wadded cravat on the floor, then laid the coat on the bed and moved to knot the new tie around his employer's collar. He did in ten seconds what Griffin couldn't do in ten minutes.

"I don't recollect you bein' this nervous when you and Miz Florence jumped the broom, Mistah Grif. You sho you ain't makin' a mistake?" A huge white grin split Lucas's dark face. He winked at Alec, but not before Griffin caught the gesture.

"I believe you're right, Lucas," Alec agreed. "Perhaps Griffin should reconsider. It's not too late to postpone—"

"The wit abounding in this room is enough to gag a person," Griffin said with a long-suffering sigh. "But, being un-accountably fond of the two of you, I shall refrain from imitating Alec on the high seas."

"Here now!" Alec straightened his body in the chair and pretended to be offended. "No sense in hitting below the belt."

A knock on the door stopped any more bantering, then Shaelyn's head popped into the room, her hand over her eyes.

"Everybody decent?" She splayed her fingers and peeked, then slipped into the room and gave her husband a quick peck on the cheek. Alec's hand came up to cup her head and bring her lips to his. After a lingering kiss, she pulled away and gave him a sultry smile.

"Mmm. Where was I?" she asked, her gaze heavy and full of promise. Then her eyes focused on Griffin. "Oh! The wedding. Bri . . . I mean Amily's ready. The neighbors who can come have arrived, so we're just waiting for the groom."

Griffin slid into the coat Lucas held for him and tried to calm the army of ants marching around his insides. Alec was right. He felt like an untried youth, not a grown man walking down the aisle for the second time.

"The groom's ready," he managed to say through a mouth suddenly gone dry. His heart raced as his mind leapt ahead to the night and the years to come. Amily as his wife.

At last.

The four of them filed out of the room. Shaelyn dashed into Amily's bedchamber while Griffin, Alec, and Lucas clattered down the stairs, only to be brought up short at the sight of an empty parlor. Molly rushed in from the back gallery at that moment, stopping long enough to glance in a mirror and tuck a stray curl back into place.

"Where is everyone, pest?" Alec asked, using his favorite name for his beloved sister.

"Amily wanted a garden wedding at the last moment, so we've moved everything beside the reflecting pond."

Griffin shuddered at why his bride had suddenly craved an outdoor wedding. No doubt the reason stemmed from the bizarre story he couldn't help but believe. But he wouldn't dwell on that now. He had a wedding to go to.

The hum of the small crowd quieted when he and Alec approached. Judge Falston separated from a group of men and walked with them to the alter of flowers next to the glassy pond while Rebecca seated herself at the harp brought down from the music room. When Molly emerged from the house and gave an excited nod, Rebecca began to play a piece by Handel.

He hadn't remembered Rebecca being so gifted. The music filled the garden, drifted on the breeze, mingled with the scent of the flowers perfuming the air. The group of twenty or so friends and neighbors stood, turning toward the house, waiting to catch the first glimpse of the bride.

Shaelyn appeared first, dazzling in an airy gown of emerald green and white. She slowly walked up the center aisle between the seats, her eyes locked on Alec, the smile on her face of a woman in love.

Griffin's heartbeat pounded in his ears. He resisted the urge to wipe his cold, clammy hands on his trousers. His breath, shallow at best, rushed from his lungs when his bride stepped into view.

She was so beautiful, it hurt his eyes to look at her. As she drew ever nearer, the breeze lifted and fluttered the tiers of white lace on her skirts, ruffled the sheer, wispy veil against her face, sent the ribbons dancing on her bouquet. Traces of her scent found their way to him to tease his senses.

He could see her smile, see the look of love in her eyes. If he was dreaming, he never wanted to awaken.

Alec escorted her the last few feet, then took her hand and placed it in Griffin's. Their gazes locked, and the world receded, leaving just the two of them, standing there, giving themselves to the other. Judge Falston's deep voice droned in the background, and Griffin had to struggle to listen for his vows.

"Repeat after me," the judge finally said, his voice breaking through the haze in Griffin's mind, "I, Griffin Hailor Elliott, take thee, Amily Elizabeth Tannen, to be my lawfully wedded wife."

Griffin hesitated when Amily's gaze flickered with . . . uncertainty? She glanced at the judge, then looked back at Griffin with a smile tinged with sadness. He studied her face, looked deep into her eyes for any trace of regret at this marriage. And then he saw what he had never expected. The hazel in Amily's eyes melted into a clear, pale blue, and he knew with a certainty that he was staring into the eyes of Brianne. He squeezed her hand, their souls so connected he could almost read her mind.

"I, Griffin Hailor Elliott, take thee . . ." he smiled down at her and amended the vows, "Amily *Brianne* Tannen, to be my lawfully wedded wife."

Her smile lit up the world, wiped away any doubt in her face, wrapped around his heart and warmed it with its glow. He finished his vows, then listened as Amily promised to take Griffin *David* Elliott as her lawfully wedded husband. The name sounded strange to his ears, yet somehow perfect. The judge faltered each time at the changes in the ceremony, then cleared his throat and droned on.

Griffin felt her heartbeat through his fingertips, racing as fast as his own, then doubling when the judge declared in a ringing voice, "I now pronounce you man and wife. What God hath joined together, let no man put asunder."

Let no man, Griffin echoed the words in prayer, *or Fate put asunder.* Then he lifted her veil, ever so gently, and brought his lips to hers for the first time as her husband.

Chapter 18

"ALEC AND I have a surprise for you." Shaelyn pulled Brianne and Griffin away from some of their guests, an excited twinkle lighting her eyes. "But you have to leave your reception to take advantage of it."

Brianne and Griffin looked at each other, then at the satisfied grins on their friends' faces.

"I've sent Lucas to signal the *River Queen* when she passes on the New Orleans run," Alec offered. "You'll spend your wedding night in a suite on the riverboat."

"What a great idea!" Brianne could have kissed these two for setting her mind at ease. She'd worried that the memory of Florence might come between her and Griffin on the wedding night. Though she didn't feel that Florence would disapprove of their marriage, Bri simply wanted Griffin all to herself on this very special night.

"We've had Lucas and Ruth pack clothes for a few days, but you might want to pack a small bag yourselves."

As if on cue, the distant blast of the riverboat whistle interrupted the conversation.

"It's rounding the bend now," Griffin said, his head cocked toward the sound. "We'll have to hurry to keep from holding them up."

Brianne hugged Shaelyn, giving thanks for such a special friend. "You're the best, you know that?" she whispered.

"Get out of here before you miss your honeymoon," Shae whispered back, then gave Bri a gentle shove toward the door.

Griffin gave Shaelyn a hug and kiss, then he and Alec shared the all male hug of clasped hands and two firm slaps on the back. He turned to Brianne and smiled.

"Shall we, Mrs. Elliott?" he asked, his look sending her heart into a double gainer.

"By all means, Mr. Elliott."

He took Brianne's hand, and like two excited children, they raced each other up the stairs.

At her bedroom door they stopped long enough for a lingering kiss. Long enough for his kiss to send waves of pleasure rippling through her blood, like a pebble sending ever-widening circles in the reflecting pond. When he finally raised his head, the shocking blue of his eyes telegraphed that this was only an appetizer for the evening to come. He set her away from him with a theatrical sigh.

"Temptress. Get thee to thy packing, e'er the wedding night comes whilst our guests await us in the parlor."

She smiled up at him, letting her hands wander free for a moment, then danced out of his grip and into the bedroom when he groaned and tried to pull her back to him. From behind the closed door she called, "I'll beat you downstairs!"

He sent a delicious shiver up her spine when he growled, "I'll make you pay!"

She stood in the middle of the room for a moment, giddy with anticipation, not quite sure where to start. It wasn't like she could fill up a tote bag with makeup and shampoo and blow dryer. First things first, she supposed, would be to get out of her wedding gown and put on some traveling clothes. She pulled off her veil, draped it across the back of a chair, then was just about to ring for Ruth when someone knocked on the door.

"No sense sending people to slow me down, Griffin," she yelled toward his bedroom, "I'm going to beat you downstairs fair and square!"

Rebecca must have taken her teasing as an invitation to come in, because she pushed the door open and slipped into the room.

"I thought you might need some help."

"Oh, good," Brianne said. "You can help get me out of this dress." She presented her back to Rebecca. "I could have asked Griffin, but then we'd never make it to the riverboat on time."

Rebecca giggled as she started to work at unfastening the tiny buttons.

"You're so funny, Brianne. I wish I—"

She must have realized the slip the same moment Brianne did.

Hot chills shimmied over Brianne's skin, denials and excuses jumping to her tongue. She bit back the denials and slowly turned her head to Rebecca, plastering a puzzled look on her face.

"What did you call me?"

Rebecca's cheeks flamed and then paled. She gave Brianne an innocent look and shook her head.

"I don't know what you mean."

Brianne turned fully around to face her.

"You called me Brianne." She tried to keep her smile questioning.

Rebecca shook her head again, but she couldn't hide the truth from her expression. "No, you must have misunderstood."

Every hair on Bri's neck stood out. Her heart rose in her throat, almost choking her. Something was very, very wrong here. How did Rebecca know she was Brianne? Why didn't she admit it? If she'd overheard someone call her by that name, she would have asked questions, pestered them for an explanation. But she hadn't. It was as if she'd already known.

"No, I didn't misunderstand. You called me Brianne. Why?" She dropped the puzzled façade.

Rebecca stared at her for a moment, all wide-eyed innocence. When Brianne made it clear she wasn't buying the act, the innocence drained from her eyes, replaced with challenge.

"Well, that's your name, isn't it? At least one of them. Brianne Davis."

The chills turned to ice and froze the breath in her chest.

"Where did you hear that name?" she asked, forcing calm into her voice, clinching her hands into fists at her sides to hide the trembling.

Rebecca snorted. "Where did I hear it? Where *didn't* I hear it! 'Brianne this! Brianne that!'" She paced across the rug, then swirled and faced her. "From our very first date I got a steady dose of Brianne Davis. Even in his letters from Russia, he wanted to know if I'd seen you, what you were doing."

"Letters from Russia . . ." The woman wasn't making sense. Brianne's mind hummed with questions that had impossible answers. She stared at Rebecca, who stared back at her with defiance. "Whose letters from Russia?"

Rebecca rolled her eyes in disgust. "Whose do you think? David's!"

Brianne shook her head, as if that would help clarify this bizarre conversation. It wasn't possible. Yet when she looked into Rebecca's eyes, she saw the answer staring back at her. An odd violet hue in what should have been pale gray eyes.

"Heather?" The word came out barely audible.

A haughty smirk curved the other woman's lips.

"Did you think you were the only person to ever transcend the barriers of time? Let me clue you in, Brianne, dear. Dayus managed to send me back, and it didn't take a lightning bolt to do it." She picked at the sleeves of her gown as though it were a shroud. "Pity, though, that in this life I couldn't have found a better body to inhabit. Of course, the plus side is, Dayus knows how to bring me back home."

Head still shaking, all Brianne could manage was, "Why?"

A knock on the door jarred her back to reality.

"You aren't making this contest very challenging, sweetheart," Griffin called happily from behind the door.

"I'll . . ." She cleared her throat and raised her head. "I'll be right there!" When she heard his footsteps fade away, she turned back to Rebecca. Heather. Whoever the hell she was.

"Why are you here?" Bri took one step toward the woman and gave her a no-nonsense stare.

"I came to make sure you got married."

Of all the answers Bri expected to hear, that was not one of them.

"Of course, I hadn't realized that *you* were here at the time," she went on. "I thought I was dealing with Amily. It wasn't until I saw Shaelyn, in the flesh, that I started to wonder." She paced some more and smoothed her already perfect hair. "Imagine my shock to see Shaelyn here, in her own body. I was hard-pressed not to show my surprise." She turned and looked at Brianne with one of Heather's plastic, coy looks, tracing her lower lip with her index finger. "And you really must find more private places to talk if you don't want your conversations . . . overheard."

Brianne couldn't believe her ears. Heather. Here. Purposely. Only one word rang in her mind.

"Why?"

"Why? Because I want David all to myself. I'm sick of sharing him with his 'purely platonic' friend. And then just when I had him ready to set a date, he gets"—she shook her head and threw her arms wide—"possessed . . . by this Griffin person. How do you think I felt when I walked in and found the two of you kissing?" Before Bri could form an answer, Heather surged on. "Dayus and I had already talked about how to keep Griffin's spirit from David. The only way seemed to be to change history. Get him and his precious Amily married so he wouldn't come looking for you in another life. Dayus had been working on perfecting past-life regression to the point of passing through time. Obviously," she gestured at her body, "he's good at what he does. And fortunately, in this life, Rebecca nearly died in the flu epidemic, which weakened her enough to allow me to come in and take over." She raised a brow. "She's been a wealth of information, even if she didn't like sharing her body. But what we hadn't counted on was you being here, unwittingly helping our cause." She gave Brianne a self-satisfied smile. "All I had to do was have a little talk with Bradley and tell him how you'd begged me to speak to him about his unwanted attentions. He really is a very accommodating gentleman. Disappointed, but accommodating."

Brianne pinched the bridge of her nose, closed her eyes, concentrated on absorbing the words battering at her brain.

"You let Dayus regress you to this stage, just to get David away from me." She opened her eyes and looked at Heather. "You love him that much?"

"Yes."

The answer came to quickly. Too flat. There was no passion

behind that one uttered word, and that lack of emotion spoke the truth more clearly than a thousand affirmations.

"You want his money. You want to marry David to get at his money."

Her hesitation answered the question. Brianne didn't wait for the denial.

"Admit it! For once in your life, show your true self!"

"Fine. You're right," Heather admitted with a shrug that showed absolutely no conscience. "People marry every day for less of a reason than that. He's loaded with old money, and he's making it hand over fist himself. Dayus and I could be very happy with what David can provide."

"Dayus!" Good heavens, did the woman not have one decent bone in her body? "You don't have any feelings at all for David, do you? You don't love him!"

Heather looked at her as if she'd lost her mind.

"Me? Love someone who's in love with you?" She actually laughed. "Get real."

Brianne closed her eyes, fought the urge to strangle this woman. She took several deep breaths, then looked up and speared the conniving little bitch with a threatening glare.

"You will never get a dime of David's money," she promised. "If it's the last thing I do, with the last breath I take, I'll warn him about you. You can take *that* to the bank. Or back to your precious Dayus."

For the first time, Heather's air of confidence faltered.

"You've not changed your mind, have you, sweetheart?" Griffin's voice, not quite so teasing, held a trace of concern from the other side of the door. "No second thoughts?"

Brianne glared at Heather. "Don't you ever come near me or Griffin again, or I swear, you will live to regret it," she warned in a voice only loud enough for Heather's ears. She pushed the little bitch through the open jib window onto the gallery, then snatched up the empty valise on the bed, blindly stuffed a handful of clothing from the nearest drawer, then threw the door wide and forced a teasing smile to her lips.

"Second thoughts?" She reached up on tiptoe and gave him a long, lingering kiss. "Oh, yes," she whispered against his mouth. "I have thoughts of you every second." She trailed her lips around to tease his earlobe, explored the hard plains of his body with her hands, molded herself to him until he made a choked noise in his throat. That little noise sent her stomach into somersaults. "And my thoughts this second are to get to that bridal suite before I make love to you right here in the floor of the hallway."

He swallowed hard and she felt his body stiffen . . . everywhere.

"By all means," he rasped, "let's get to the river while I can still walk."

A festive crowd escorted the newlyweds to the Shadow Oaks landing. No one seemed to notice Rebecca's absence, but Shaelyn had immediately seen Brianne's concern.

"What's happened?" Shaelyn asked the moment Griffin turned to speak to Alec. "Why didn't you change clothes? Why are your top buttons undone?" She spun Bri around and fastened the two tiny buttons, then lifted her eyebrows, waiting for an answer. "You're not having second thoughts are you? Because if you are, let me assure you—"

Brianne had to smile at Shaelyn's choice of words.

"No. Heavens, no! It's just that—"

"Ready, sweetheart?" Griffin slid his hand around her arm with a soft caress.

She looked up at him, then glanced back at Shaelyn and gave her a hug.

"Don't worry," she said in her ear. "I'll explain everything when we get back. Just a small thing I need to take care of."

Shae studied her for a moment, clearly unconvinced, but Brianne smiled and squeezed her hand. "Really. It's no big deal." *Or at least it won't be,* she told herself, *once I figure out how to get a message to David.*

The gangplank swung into place and Griffin all but dragged her toward it. She laughed aloud, forcing all thoughts of Rebecca/Heather to the farthest reaches of her mind. This was her wedding day, and she was married to her soul mate. Nothing, absolutely nothing, was going to ruin this day . . . or this night for them.

They raced up the gangplank holding hands, the white lace of her skirts billowing around their legs like a cloud. When they stepped onto the deck of the gingerbread boat, she turned and blew a kiss to Shaelyn and Alec.

"See you in a few days!" she called. "I love you!"

Chapter 19

GRIFFIN STOOD IN the center of their cabin, watching his bride wax poetic about all the luxuries, wondering if she had the slightest hint as to how irresistible she looked with her eyes shining, her gown gently swaying against her legs, tendrils of black silk escaping from her hair to curl along her neck. He swallowed around the constriction in his throat and dragged his icy hand down his face, fighting a losing battle for control.

How should he go about this? Should he leave her alone to prepare for bed? Call in a maid to help her undress? Florence had needed some time alone to ready herself.

No. He wouldn't think of Florence this night.

A quiet knock on the cabin door drew their attention. When Griffin opened it, a half dozen servants in starched white jackets marched in, wheeling a cart laden with food, carrying linens and silverware, a champagne bucket with a bottle chilling in its depths.

"Compliments of the cap'n, suh," one of the men offered. "Congratulations."

Almost before Griffin could pass out a handful of coins, the servants disappeared as quickly as they'd come, leaving behind a linen-covered table set with china, silver, fresh flowers, candles, and enough food to last them for days.

He looked at his bride, standing by the window, bathed in the golden orange rays of the dying sun. The table of food held no appeal for him.

"Would you . . ." He had to stop and clear his throat. Damnation! Alec would roll on the floor to know his voice cracked just to speak to his wife. "Would you care for some dinner?" he managed with a degree more authority.

She looked at the table and then at him, taking a few strolling steps in his direction.

"I'm not really hungry," she said, moving closer, mussing the ends of his cravat. "For food," she added, gazing up at him with a smile begging for attention.

The words, their meaning, her look, all slammed into his brain at once and exploded outward, downward, setting his blood afire.

"Well, yes. Of course," he stammered. Saint's blood, what should he do? He didn't want to make the same mistakes he'd made with Florence. He didn't want to rush her into this and leave her hating the very act he would give his life for right now. Time. He would give her time. Let her know he could be a patient man. With more effort than he ever dreamed possible, he swallowed hard, took a deep breath, and stepped away.

"I'll send a maid. Give you some time. Take all the time you—*ooph!*"

His body moved toward the door, but his neck and head stayed put. Amily smiled up at him from her firm grip on the other end of his cravat. Once he stopped his lower body from stumbling, she gave him an innocent smile and slowly, inexorably pulled him to her. The closer he got, the more her expression heated, until she had him nearly nose to nose, her gaze downright torrid.

"I don't want a maid to undress me," she said, her voice so calm and steady and hot, the sound of it skittered across his skin. "And I don't want time. What I want," she pulled again on the cravat until her lips barely touched his, "is you." Her warm breath fanned across his face. Her mouth molded to his, then her tongue traced his lips with a teasing touch.

His breath caught in his lungs as he wrapped her in his arms, settled his mouth on hers and found her tongue with his. She sighed in her throat, and the sound ripped straight to his soul, jarring every inch of his body, heightening his sensitivity until the very air on his skin felt like a lover's caress.

The kiss went on as her hands came up to cup his face, sift through his hair, trail down his back. She pulled the silk tie free, then unfastened the black onyx studs on his shirt while he loosened her hair to the sound of hairpins pattering to the floor. She rained kisses down his neck, moved aside his shirt and gently kissed his healing wound.

"This won't hurt you?" she whispered, one hand tracing the healthy pink of a forming scar, the other wandering farther afield.

His head fell back as he drew in a quick breath.

"Oh, yes," he teased with a ragged voice. "Torture me some more."

She laughed quietly, then complied with his request. He thought he would go mad if he couldn't touch something besides that blasted wedding gown.

He raised his head, drew in a deep, calming breath of air, then spun her around and set to work on the row of minuscule buttons. She reached up and lifted the mass of dark curls which had fallen down her back, leaned against him, reached back and drew his head to her for a languorous kiss from behind.

"Take your time," she whispered. "We've got all night, and then some."

Her words did nothing to still his trembling fingers, and he fumbled with one button after another, seemingly forever, making no visible progress. Saint's blood, if he didn't get this damned dress off her soon, she was going to unman him.

The warmth of her skin radiated up to him as the back of the gown slowly, torturously fell open. He'd undone a good thirty buttons and had as many or more to go. Why in hell did someone not invent something quicker than these damnable buttons?

She leaned into him again, her backside pressing against him in a most excruciating way. Her head tilted back and she grazed his jaw with her lips. She moved on to his mouth, her kiss more urgent, then she turned in his arms, pulled his shirt free from his trousers, ran her warm, soft hands across the planes of his chest and around to his back. When her touch dipped beneath his waistband, he closed his eyes and sucked in his breath.

"Ohhh, Amily," he groaned, still fumbling with the bloody damned buttons, his arms around her now. "Forgive me," he rasped against her mouth. "We'll have it repaired."

With that he jerked the edges of her gown apart, sending dozens of tiny pearl buttons pinging off walls and windows and furniture.

Her eyes widened, then she giggled and whispered against his skin, "I only planned to wear it once, anyway."

He slid the gown over her arms until it hung on her underskirts.

"Damn!" he muttered aloud before he realized it. He had sorry little experience undressing women. She smiled and stepped away, leaving an emptiness behind, then took her time torturing him as she slowly untied the tapes to her petticoats.

"You are evil incarnate," he growled when she looked up at him through dark lashes. She smiled a wicked, devilish smile and let the layers of skirts drop to a billowing mass at her feet. Stepping over them, she shrugged a strap of her chemise off her shoulder.

"I think you can manage the rest," she murmured, inviting that and more with her eyes.

Want, white hot and scorching, shimmered through his veins. Never in his life had he ever wanted someone as badly as he wanted this woman. And never did he want so badly to give to someone all that he could give.

His hands melted over her, sliding away silky barriers, drawing out bows in ribbons, peeling away the layers of clothing as he added fuel to the flames threatening to engulf them both.

She worked at his trousers and he kicked off his boots even as he continued to relieve her of her multitude of clothing.

Finally, gloriously, the last embroidered garment fell away, and he pulled her to him, desperate to feel her heated flesh against his.

His knees turned to warm candle wax the moment their bodies touched. Before she could devastate him further, he scooped her up and took her to the bed. She clung to him, her mouth as hungry as his, while he removed the last of his clothing, then he pulled her against the length of him, dizzy from the sheer ecstasy.

He nuzzled her silky hair in wonder, let his hands roam free upon the willing body of his wife as she nestled against him, fitting her body to his, exploring her new husband as no one else had ever done.

He took a deep breath and drew her closer, wondering, as he had before, if she could do this to him with a mere touch, would he survive this night, or would he die a death that could only be called exquisite.

Brianne laid her head against Griffin's chest and waited for her heart to slow to something less than a hum. She still floated somewhere above the clouds, where he had taken her, and she didn't care if she ever came down. She sighed and he tightened his arms around her.

"Have I died and gone to Heaven?" he asked, his breath warm against her hair.

She kissed his chest and ran a lazy hand across his stomach.

"You took me to Heaven, dear husband, but I can assure you, you most certainly are not dead."

He gave an exhausted laugh, the sound curling around her heart like a warm summer breeze.

"If I had been a lesser man," he said with a long, drowsy sigh, "you would have put me in my grave."

"If you had been a lesser man," she countered, tracing the outline of his mouth, "I would not be in bed with you now."

His lips curved up in a soul-stirring smile. "Thank Heaven, then, that I am such an exemplary example of masculinity."

She lay in boneless relaxation, her body entwined with his. They were married. Well and truly married, and they were still alive. Life just didn't get any better than this.

She looked around the luxurious cabin illuminated only by the dinner candles guttering in their wax. Various garments littered every available surface. Lingerie dripped from the furniture, one of his boots lay on its side by the slipper chair, the other had landed upright across the room.

Her giggle broke the contented silence, and Griffin dipped his chin to look at her.

"It looks like a clothing store exploded in here," she said.

"Mmm," he hummed, in something that resembled agreement. "But was the detonation not fun?"

Her heart swelled and she giggled, snuggling closer, tracing the outline of his abdominal muscles while he dropped soft kisses on her hair. The kisses took on more interest as he turned to face her. His hands glided over her skin, leaving a trail of heat in their wake, stirring her blood, sending her back up among the clouds. He pulled her across him, seducing her with a thousand sensations, rolling with her until he lay atop her.

She let her head fall back and reveled in the feel of his lips skimming across her flesh, his hands worshipping her with his touch.

She sighed and dug her fingers into her husband's back. If there was a law against knowing how to make love, Griffin would get the death penalty for what he knew how to do.

Brianne had never seen New Orleans the way Griffin showed it to her, never realized the drastic changes a hundred and seventy years would bring. One thing didn't change though. They ate their way through the city, like children at a circus, only this circus offered gourmet food that could make a strong man weep. At times she would have given a year off her life for a pair of Reeboks and jogging shorts, and the opportunity to work off the million-calorie meals, but she had to let the walking suffice. The walking and, of course, the lovemaking. Lord, she burned calories just looking at Griffin.

The town, magical, strange, and exotic as it was, took on a luster with Griffin at her side. They walked the streets hand in hand, browsed through shops and vendors' stalls, bought mementos to celebrate their marriage. They ate beignets and drank café au lait, strolled along the river, stretched out in the grass and watched the sun set. They scandalized more than a few passersby by having a teasing peck on the lips grow into a long, lazy kiss, and then they would race to their rooms, laughing and ignoring the pointed stares, to finish what they'd started.

When they boarded the riverboat for their return trip home, Brianne did so with mixed emotions. She hated to leave behind the fairy-tale world in which they'd lived during the past few days, but she looked forward to starting her life with Griffin, settling in, having a family, trying to put her past . . . or rather her future behind her.

And she needed to warn David.

She'd given the problem lots of thought during the early hours of the morning, while Griffin slept beside her. She hadn't told him yet that Rebecca was Heather, but she would. She just wanted a plan in place when she did.

The simplest, surest way came to her from a movie plot. She would write David a letter, then put the letter in the care of an established law firm, with the instructions to have the letter delivered to David at her apartment at eight-thirty on the evening she was struck by lightning. And she would set up a trust to ensure the law office was well paid for following instructions, or passing the letter on to another firm, should they ever close their doors.

Eight-thirty would be just minutes after the lightning struck, so David would be there, albeit most probably with a 911 crew, but he would be there. She'd decided against sending it any earlier, for fear the arrival would interrupt the chain of events. She had to assume the lightning had killed her, and if so, the message from her might put David's mind at rest, or help him through his grief. At least he wouldn't have the added burden of marrying a scheming little gold digger.

She'd given thought to sending the message to herself, before the disaster with the lightning, warning herself to stay away from the French doors, revealing that David was the man she searched for, that Heather was after David's money. But two things stopped her. She had already tampered with changing the events of the past and future, and she feared what disaster more meddling might cause. But mostly, when she looked at Griffin, his face so peaceful in sleep, his arms so lovingly, possessively around her, her heart ached with love and she couldn't bear the thought of leaving him. Perhaps, if he and his Amily lived a long and happy life together in this time, then she and David would not be so blind to their love in the future.

She looked across their small, intimate table in the boat's dining room to the heart-wrenching face of her husband. She couldn't help but reach out and smooth her fingers along the finely carved line of his jaw. He leaned into her hand, then turned his head to kiss her palm.

"I love you, Mrs. Elliott," he murmured against her skin.

"The feeling is mutual, Mr. Elliott," she whispered back, and then he pulled her from her chair and guided her to their cabin.

Griffin strolled along the deserted deck with his wife in the wee hours of the morning. Rather than exhaust them, their lovemaking had filled them with restless energy, so they'd slipped onto the decks to enjoy the waning moon. An occasional die-hard gambler straggled past them on his way from the men's salon to his cabin. Griffin and Amily had made a game of seeing how intimate they could be without being discovered by the late night passengers.

"Perhaps we should do a little gambling ourselves," she said, slipping her hand beneath the shirt she had surreptitiously unbuttoned.

He leaned her against the rail and pressed his body into hers.

"And what game of chance do you have in mind, Madame Temptress?"

"Do you know poker?" she asked with a little moan, her nails raking along his skin.

His eyes widened. His bride never ceased to amaze him. "Yes. I know *poque*. The English call it brag." Most women of his acquaintance would be unfamiliar with the game, but then again, she most definitely was not most women. "You want to play a round of poker?" he asked, thinking he could find a more entertaining game.

"*Strip* poker," she clarified, dragging his loosely knotted tie from his neck and twining it about her own. "I mean, we're on a riverboat on the Mississippi River. We should gamble at something more daring than just getting caught making out."

He didn't need a definition for "making out." A complete dolt could figure out that one. But she'd most certainly piqued his curiosity with her game.

"And what are the rules of this variation?" he asked, then dipped his head and trailed a row of kisses down the column of her neck.

She let her head fall back, making room for more kisses, then opened her eyes to sultry, heated slits.

"Very simple." Her voice took on a husky quality. "Whoever loses the hand loses an article of clothing."

Fire leapt to his core at the every thought.

"Hmm," he said, "so if you lose, *you* take off something, and if *I* lose, *I* take off something." He laughed aloud. "The way I see it, either way, I win."

"You thieving bastard!" a man's voice growled almost in his ear. Before Griffin could turn to face their intruder, a fist slammed into the side of his head. He heard Amily yelp as he fought to clear the pinpricks of light swimming through his vision.

"What the—" He shook off his shock to see Carlton Tilburn standing with a knife to Amily's throat.

"Tilburn!" Griffin took a step forward but Tilburn jerked Amily up and moved the knife closer, backing away down the deck.

"Oh, yes, you've never had a problem recognizing me, have you, you thieving son of a bitch. And I'd know your voice anywhere, even when it isn't muffled by the mask you and your band of pirates hide behind."

Amily struggled in the blackguard's grip. He brought the knife around and laid the blade against her neck.

"Stay still, sweetheart," Griffin said as his mind raced. "He's not going to harm you." Damn, he had no weapon on him at all.

"Oh, that's where you're wrong, Elliott." Griffin jerked at the sound of his name. "Yes. I know who you are. And I plan to take your most precious possession just as you took my fortune." The gleam of unadulterated hate shone in Tilburn's eyes. "Perhaps I'll let you watch while I force myself on your lovely bride."

Amily seemed to relax in Tilburn's grip. She rolled her head around and actually smiled at the man. "You're not in good enough shape to force yourself on me."

He jerked her up higher, moved the knife long enough to grab a handful of hair as he dragged her along the rail.

"Shut up, bitch. I plan to show you what a real man is like!"

"But wouldn't you actually have to be one," she asked through clenched teeth, "in order to do that?"

Griffin barely saw her hand move when she reached back and grabbed Tilburn's crotch, twisting when he shrieked and holding on even when he let go of his grip on her. Griffin ran toward them. Tilburn drew back his fist and backhanded her.

Oh, God, he couldn't get to her in time. He watched, even as he ran, as Amily tumbled over the rail, disappearing into the inky, churning waters of the Mississippi.

"Amily!" He wasted not a second, climbing to the rail and hurtling himself after her. He no sooner hit the water than another body landed on top of him. Tilburn thrashed at him with the knife, blindingly striking at anything he could hit. Griffin managed to stay his hand, then wrenched the knife from Tilburn's grip and felt the blade cut through the bastard's throat like a hot knife through butter. The man went limp. Even in the rushing water, Griffin could smell the metallic scent of blood.

"Amily!" he screamed, shoving Tilburn's lifeless body away and searching the black surface for any sign of her. He spit out a mouthful of water and turned full circle. The lights of the riverboat faded into the night. "Amily!"

He took a breath and dove, feeling his way in the Stygian waters. He searched until his lungs burned for breath, then came up for another gulp of air and dove again.

His hand encountered long, silky tendrils floating with the current. He found her! Thank God, he found her! He took her hands and pulled to bring her to the surface, but her body wouldn't budge. She clung to him frantically. He pulled again, lungs starting to burn, then followed the length of her body to find her leg and gown tangled in what felt like the limbs of a fallen tree. He surfaced once more to gasp for breath, then dove and ripped at the clinging fabric made stronger in the water, yanked at her leg, caring not if he hurt her, just desperate to free her before she drowned. Her hands clawed at him, panicked, and he swore to himself he wouldn't leave her until she was free. He felt her strength start to ebb and he ripped that much harder. His lungs burned and he knew hers were surely on fire.

When her hands stopped clinging to him, he sobbed, grabbed her face and blew what air he had into her mouth. A lethargy stole into his limbs, a peacefulness, tugging at him to give up and breathe in the waters of the river. He fought against the sensations, fought the murky fog muddling his thoughts. He wouldn't give up until he had her free. He wouldn't lose her, by God. Nothing would ever separate them again.

Chapter 20

B RIANNE CAME TO, shivering from cold, drenching wet, fighting her way up from a blackness that threatened still to overtake her. She coughed, brought up a shaky hand to drag away dripping chunks of hair clinging to her face.

"Sweetheart. Thank God. I thought I'd lost you again."

Strong, masculine arms tightened around her as she lay there, gasping for air, each breath a searing pain in her chest.

She turned her head, brought her hand up to caress the face so close to hers, opened her eyes to assure him she was all right.

And stared straight into the face of David.

"David!" Her voice croaked, rusty and painful as her chest lurched, seared with pain.

"Yes, sweetheart, I'm here." He pulled her to him, lifted her onto his lap, kissed her damp hair and rocked her in his arms as the storm outside battered over them through the shattered French doors.

"David," she whispered, seeing her apartment around her, everything familiar and modern. "David."

"It's okay, sweetheart. Everything's okay. I've called 911. We're going to get you to the hospital and get you checked out, but everything's going to be all right."

"Heather," she managed to rasp, but he put his finger to her lips.

"Shhh. Forget about Heather." He kissed her forehead, holding her as if he'd never let her go. "It's you I love. I've loved you all my life. I just wouldn't let myself face it. Thanks to Griffin," he smiled at her, his warm, brown eyes gazing down at her just as Griffin's had, "I finally found what I've been searching for."

"Griffin," she whispered, searching his eyes for any trace of blue.

"He's with Amily now, as he should be," he told her softly. "They're happy, in the life they were meant to have. And you are here with me, as it should be." He took her hand and placed it on his chest as he settled his palm over her heart. "And they live in here." He brushed a kiss across her lips. "Always. In this life and forever after."

"But how . . . how could you know?"

He smiled down at her, his eyes so full of love she wanted to cry. "Just as you were there in Amily, I was there in Griffin. I was there with you, sweetheart, but you needed to find me for yourself, just as I needed to find you."

She curled her arms around his neck, a peace settling around her more enveloping than the peace that had surrounded her in the river.

"I love you," she whispered, her mouth pressed to his.

He smiled against her lips. "I love you, too," he said, then raised his head and grinned at her with that little boy look that always got her in trouble. "Will you marry me, Amily Brianne? One more time?"

Epilogue

BRIANNE GAZED UP at David through the gauzy white of her veil. David. Griffin. One and the same. Her soul mate for eternity. Her husband from the past. He smiled down at her, his eyes hot and promising, setting free that flock of doves that seemed to live in her stomach.

"If any person here knows just cause why these two should not be joined in holy matrimony, let him speak now or forever hold his peace."

"I have just cause!" a female voice called from the back of the sanctuary.

A rumble grew in the congregation as the minister jerked his head up and squinted toward the back of the church. Brianne spun around with a gasp as David gripped her arm.

"These two aren't getting married today," the woman said, "without their best friends to witness it."

Shaelyn and Alec, dressed in the height of modern fashion, marched up the aisle, with Molly, yanking on the hem of a miniskirt, leading Christopher behind them.

"Shae!" Brianne flew to her friend's arms as David and Alec clasped hands. Alec eyed David and then Brianne, meeting Griffin and Amily's alter egos for the first time. "You're here! You're here! How? When?" Brianne squealed, hardly able to believe her eyes.

"I'll tell you how later. As for when . . . just a few hours ago. I called your apartment and got the answering machine, telling when and where the wedding was. You know, Bri, half this congregation could be telemarketers who just happened to call your house today. And I shudder to think who's in your place right now, pilfering the wedding gifts. Don't you know—"

Brianne hugged Shae again, wondering if this day could get any better.

"Correct me if I'm wrong, Ellio . . . er . . . Marks," Alec interrupted, "but were you not in the act of marrying this woman before my wife made her somewhat dramatic entrance?"

David slapped Alec on the back with a classic Griffin gesture. "Right you are, Hawthorne. Shall we finish what we started?" He took Brianne's hand and brought it to his lips. "I think I've waited long enough for this woman."

Brianne and David cuddled together on the couch in their new apartment, with Shaelyn tucked under Alec's arm on the opposite love seat. While the newlyweds had spent a week in the Mediterranean on their honeymoon, Shaelyn had introduced Alec, Molly, and Christopher to the world in which she had grown up. Molly had taken most things amazingly in stride, having picked Shae's brain about the future for two years. Alec had taken longer to adjust, but once he had, he'd settled in like a native, his favorite toy being the TV remote control.

"And you left a lasting impression on Amily," Shaelyn went on with her story with a huge smile. "She's on a one-woman campaign to outlaw corsets. Then there's the curious fact that she's suddenly taken up exercising and announced that she wants no more fried foods served at Shadow Oaks. Esther had a conniption fit. Griffin mourned the loss of his fried chicken, but he's so happy to have Amily, I think he would have given up eating."

Brianne smiled and cuddled closer to David. "I can't believe they survived. We were certain they'd died in the river and released us to come back to our time." She looked up at the heart-melting face of her brand new husband. "But I guess we were meant to live *here,* just as they were meant to live there. You know, I think I brought part of her back with me, though. I can almost *feel* how happy she is." She cast David a private, mischievous grin. "And Griffin definitely left his mark on Davie." He wiggled his eyebrows at her and squeezed her closer.

"What's this Alec told me about Rebecca . . . er . . . Heather? She tried to steal the ring from your finger?" David asked Shae while he nuzzled the top of Brianne's head.

Shaelyn nodded, reaching up to touch the emerald and diamond ring that now hung on a gold chain around her neck. It would remain there until the Hawthorne family decided to return to 1832.

"Heather is stuck there, in Rebecca's body. She came to me after you and Griffin left, begging for help when she didn't progress to this time. I told her I didn't know what to do for her since my ring was what brought me to the past. Before I knew what was happening, she had ahold of my hand, yanking on the ring. I guess she thought if it could send me to the past, it could take her to the future."

Bri shook her head. "But why is she stuck there?"

Shae jumped up and pulled a handful of newspaper clippings from her purse. "The papers are full of the story. Apparently Dayus wasn't all fake. Through Heather's regression, he realized he'd been Carlton Tilburn in the past. He had always believed that events in a past life were what caused him to be such a failure in this life, and when he discovered how Griffin had played a part in Tilburn's losing his fortune, he regressed himself so that he could have his revenge. Obviously he never expected to die back there, and I'm sure Heather . . . er . . . Rebecca . . . *whoever,* never expected him to go back, too, and leave her there with no one to bring her back to the present! Heaven only knows where Dayus's spirit is now, mooching off someone else. After he and Heather were found in his apartment in comas, the police found tapes Dayus had made, recording his notes on Heather's regression, as well as recording his own regression. All of this was on the tapes. Even his fight with Griffin."

Brianne looked up at David, stunned, the handful of clippings in her hand forgotten. David pulled her ever closer and dropped a kiss on her forehead.

"They went through all that for the sake of money," he said with a note of pity, "and what they never realized was, if I lost every penny I had today, I'd still be the richest man in the world. I'm holding life's greatest treasure right here in my arms." He looked down at Bri, all the love he'd denied for so long shining in his eyes. "I love you, Amily Brianne," he said, a hint of awe still in his voice.

"I love *you,* Griffin David," she whispered against his lips. "And I'll love you with the last breath I take. Every one of them."

About the Author

Jenny lives in west Tennessee with her husband, two teenagers, and the family baby, an eleven-year-old Samoyed "puppy." She loves hearing from her readers at P.O. Box 382132, Germantown, TN 38183-2132.

TIME PASSAGES

___CRYSTAL MEMORIES *Ginny Aiken*   0-515-12159-2

___ECHOES OF TOMORROW *Jenny Lykins*   0-515-12079-0

___LOST YESTERDAY *Jenny Lykins*   0-515-12013-8

___MY LADY IN TIME *Angie Ray*   0-515-12227-0

___NICK OF TIME *Casey Claybourne*   0-515-12189-4

___REMEMBER LOVE *Susan Plunkett*   0-515-11980-6

___SILVER TOMORROWS *Susan Plunkett*   0-515-12047-2

___THIS TIME TOGETHER *Susan Leslie Liepitz*

                                                                               0-515-11981-4

___WAITING FOR YESTERDAY *Jenny Lykins*

                                                                               0-515-12129-0

___HEAVEN'S TIME *Susan Plunkett*   0-515-12287-4

___THE LAST HIGHLANDER *Claire Cross*   0-515-12337-4

___A TIME FOR US *Christine Holden*   0-515-12375-7

All books $5.99
Prices slightly higher in Canada

Payable in U.S. funds only No cash/COD accepted. Postage & handling: U S./CAN $2.75 for
one book, $1.00 for each additional, not to exceed $6 75; Int'l $5.00 for one book, $1.00 each
additional We accept Visa, Amex, MC ($10.00 min.), checks ($15.00 fee for returned checks)
and money orders. Call 800-788-6262 or 201-933-9292, fax 201-896-8569; refer to ad # 680 (4/99)

Penguin Putnam Inc.	Bill my: ☐Visa ☐MasterCard ☐Amex_____(expires)
P.O. Box 12289, Dept. B	Card#_____
Newark, NJ 07101-5289	
Please allow 4-6 weeks for delivery.	Signature_____

Foreign and Canadian delivery 6-8 weeks

Bill to:
Name_____

Address_____City_____

State/ZIP_____

Daytime Phone #_____

Ship to:

Name_____	Book Total	$_____
Address_____	Applicable Sales Tax	$_____
City_____	Postage & Handling	$_____
State/ZIP_____	Total Amount Due	$_____

This offer subject to change without notice.